"Not that your opinion about my love life matters, but for the record, I know exactly what to do with a 'real' woman."

Cassie laughed. "Hit a nerve, didn't I? Poor Alex, relying on all those little college girls to—"

He moved so fast, she didn't even finish her sentence before his mouth closed over hers.

His warm body felt lean and hard against hers, strong and vital.

"Don't hold back," he murmured. "I'm counting on you to show me how a real woman kisses. Don't disappoint me."

Low and seductive, it was a blatant challenge—and Cassie *never* refused a challenge.

**One Way Out**

**is also available as an eBook.**

# MICHELE ALBERT

# ONE WAY OUT

POCKET BOOKS

New York   London   Toronto   Sydney

POCKET BOOKS, a division of Simon & Schuster, Inc.
1230 Avenue of the Americas, New York, NY 10020

This book is a work of fiction. Names, characters, places, and incidents are products of the author's imagination or are used fictitiously. Any resemblance to actual events or locales or persons, living or dead, is entirely coincidental.

ISBN: 0-7434-8502-5

First Pocket Books paperback edition March 2005

10  9  8  7  6  5  4  3  2

POCKET BOOKS and colophon are registered trademarks of Simon & Schuster, Inc.

Manufactured in the United States of America

For information regarding special discounts for bulk purchases, please contact Simon & Schuster Special Sales at 1-800-456-6798 or business@simonandschuster.com.

# One

CASSIE ASHTON SHADED HER EYES WITH HER HAND and squinted up at a man dangling halfway down the face of a bluff, twenty feet off the ground. The guy in the climbing harness wore jeans, heavy boots, a long-sleeved blue shirt with the sleeves rolled up, and a very familiar battered white Resistol hat.

She'd finally run her quarry to ground.

Grinning, she tipped her head back and watched as he braced one gloved hand on the rock and worked the ropes with the other. She waited until he'd secured his footing, then cupped her hands around her mouth and yelled: "Hey, Martinelli!"

The white hat dipped as he looked down, and even though he was too far up for her to hear it, his lips formed a coarse word she easily recognized. "What the hell do you want?" he shouted back.

"Gotta talk to you!"

"In case it's escaped your notice, Ashton, I'm kind of tied up at the moment."

She'd noticed, all right. The leather straps and ropes nicely framed the best, and the most arrogant, ass in all Wyoming.

"Whatever's in that rock has been there for over sixty million years, and it's not going anywhere now. What I have to talk to you about is important."

"Christ, couldn't you once call ahead for an appointment?" He twirled above her as he repositioned himself, muscles pulling at his cotton shirt, straining its seams. "You can't expect me to come running every time you snap your fingers."

As the voices of the crowd gathering behind her grew louder, she affected a look of bored amusement and made a show of gazing around the rocky, scrub-brush terrain of dinosaur-rich Como Bluff. "An appointment? What do you think you are, Martinelli? A dentist lounging around some posh office?"

"This *is* my office. Now go away, call my department, and leave me a message."

*Which he wouldn't return.* Cassie grinned. "I don't think so. Get your ass down here, Professor Martinelli, because I'm not going anywhere until we talk. And you know I mean it."

"Don, what the hell is she doing here? Why didn't someone stop her before she got this far?" he demanded.

"Sorry, Alex. The new kids on the crew don't know

her," answered a familiar gravelly voice. "And I was busy working on that hadrosaur leg we found yesterday. I guess she slipped right past me. . . . You want me to throw her in the creek? I'd really enjoy that."

"You're welcome to try it, Igor." Still smiling, Cassie didn't bother turning around to face Don Cleary, the wiry old man she'd teasingly nicknamed Igor because he was Martinelli's second banana.

Above her, Martinelli called, "That's a pleasure I'm reserving for myself, Don."

Before Cassie could retort, a young man's voice from behind her yelled cheerfully, "Hey, hey, everybody, look who's here . . . it's showtime!"

Fine; if they wanted entertainment, she'd give them something to remember. Something to match that night eight months ago in Medicine Bow when Martinelli had humiliated her in a bar full of people. And last year, and that October three years earlier . . . and it wasn't like she'd ever live down the acrimonious showdown that had started their feud five long years ago, either.

By now, their clashes were nearly legendary.

Smile widening into a grin, Cassie pretended not to hear the increasing catcalls, acting as if it didn't matter that her kind would never be welcome here.

"Come on, Martinelli. Are you just going to dangle up there, safely out of my reach, or come down here and face me like the big ol' manly man you are?"

She couldn't resist the "manly man" bit. With his half-supported stance against the rock emphasizing his lean, strong build, he looked like a poster boy for a wilderness outfitter advertisement.

For a moment Cassie thought Martinelli would refuse the challenge, but after another mouthed curse he began lowering himself, working the lines and pulleys with an expertise that came from years of climbing mountains and cliffs the world over, hunting fossils, looking for that elusive "big find" that would put his name in the history books.

Too bad for him that she'd just beat him to the finish line.

As he descended, Cassie couldn't help focusing once more on how the harness cradled his rear and groin over the worn denim of his jeans, revealing a most impressive package, front and back.

Mortal enemies they might be, but she could still appreciate what he had to offer a woman. It just wouldn't ever be her, not in a million years.

"Mmm-hmm, he is one hot bitch, all right," said a female voice in a soft, near-purring tone.

Cassie turned to see a woman who fit Martinelli's usual type—mid-twenties, blond, leggy, and striking in an athletic, wholesome sort of way.

The woman smiled faintly when she met Cassie's eyes. "You have to admit he has a great ass."

*Heck yeah.* "I wouldn't know, as I don't have

hands-on experience—thank God. You do, I take it?"

The woman's smile elongated into a smirk. "And working on keeping it exclusively mine."

Ah . . . staking out territory. Another starry-eyed grad student, fallen to Martinelli's dark, dubious charms.

"It shouldn't take too much work." Cassie glanced upward. Damn; the harness really emphasized things that weren't meant to be emphasized in decent company. "He screws anything female that moves."

As if on cue, Martinelli unclipped the harness and hit the ground, puffs of dust rising from beneath the thick soles of his boots. "Not quite anything." He sent a pointed look at Cassie. "Even man-whores like me have standards."

Someone in the crowd made crowing noises, and another young man said in faux sportscaster voice: "Martinelli scores a point for the home team, and the crowd goes wild!" Scattered laughter followed.

Cassie smiled, since some perverse part of her actually enjoyed these little sparring matches with Martinelli.

She glanced at the dusty card table she was leaning against in her best nonchalant pose. It held a number of soil samples, fragmentary fossils, and what looked like ordinary rocks to the untrained eye. But she knew fossilized dinosaur dung when she saw it. In fact, just last week she'd sold a nice specimen to a sweet old lady from Coral Gables.

She counterattacked with the ammunition at hand. "This is some real nice shit you have here, Dr. Martinelli. Some of the finest I've ever seen. Congratulations on a job well done."

A woman laughed somewhere to Cassie's right, then added, "And the opposition bounces back to make a brutal hit. Ouch!"

Martinelli advanced, moving with the confidence of a man who looked good and knew it. He pulled off his Resistol, slapping it against his thigh to knock off the dust before he wiped the sweat from his face with his forearm, then quickly unbuttoned his sun-faded chambray shirt and stripped it off. Without looking away from Cassie, he grabbed a large bottle of water from the cooler by the table, twisted off the cap, then dumped the entire contents on his face and chest.

He had a lean, spare build, the sinews and tendons neatly outlined beneath sun-browned skin, and the water made tracks in the grit on his face, flattened the dusting of dark hair on his chest, and gleamed wetly along the hard lines of his chest, ribs, and belly.

Cassie almost laughed, knowing this show was all for her benefit, but the leggy blonde beside her mewled: "Oh. My. God."

"Please. Have some self-respect." She eyed the woman. "It's just a chest. A pretty ordinary chest."

The blonde raised a brow. "You can't be serious."

Cassie shrugged. "Take it from one who knows. I've been married, given birth . . . At this point, men and sex hold no mysteries or surprises."

"And isn't that just . . . sad." Martinelli pulled his shirt back on—not that it made any real difference, since both skin and shirt were damp—and locked his gaze with hers. "You're too young to be so cynical about men, Ashton."

"Not all men. Only players and posers."

"Ashton?" The blonde gasped, taking a step back as her eyes widened with sudden understanding—and maybe awe as well. Or so Cassie liked to imagine. "Ohhhh . . . *you're* that commercial collector Alex told us about."

"Nothing flattering, I bet," Cassie said wryly, turning her attention back to Martinelli. "Was it?"

He flashed the grin that had probably broken legions of coed hearts and mucked up the academic careers of a few earnest graduate students as well. Then he settled his hat back on his dark hair, pushed his sunglasses up his nose to hide his eyes, and strode toward her, arms outstretched as if they were two old buddies about to embrace. "Cassie, Cassie."

Feeling the kick of her heartbeat, she raised her arms as well and ambled forward to meet him, smiling. "Alex, Alex."

"The players get into position," yelled a curly-haired grad student with a mustache. "And the crowd holds its breath in anticipation! Who will win this round of the Dinosaur Wars?"

Cassie allowed Alex to take her by the arms and position her at a safe distance from him. The palms of his hands were dry, rough, and warm against her bare skin.

"And how," he asked as he released her, "are you going to make my life hell today?"

Cassie shoved her hands into her back pockets. "You sure know how to make a girl feel special, Martinelli."

He gave her an unsubtle once-over, his gaze lingering on her breasts beneath her camouflage-print T-shirt. "What's with the G.I. Jane look? Going for a sneak attack? Didn't work, but it's a good look for you. Kind of cute."

To her eternal annoyance, she was doomed to be cute until she grew old and wrinkled—and even then she might not escape it.

"Martinelli, I'm cute like a rattler is cute."

"And match point to the little lady in the tight camouflage shirt and even tighter jeans."

Cassie glanced over her shoulder at the bearded, bespectacled young man who'd spoken. He was covered in dust and dirt, good-looking, and grinning, his gaze frankly appreciative. She arched a brow at him, then patted her behind. "Kiss this, honey."

"Can I?" Spectacles eagerly moved forward, only to be brought short by Cleary's hand on his shoulder.

"Don't," Cleary intoned. "You'll catch something."

"Lame, Igor." Cassie grinned. The older man always tried to draw blood, but he really didn't have it in him to do so.

Ordinarily she'd have played out the game a little longer, but she was impatient to deliver her news and see the look on Martinelli's face. "It's been fun, as always, but showtime is over, kids."

She seized Martinelli's belt buckle—a calculated familiarity to piss him off and give the blonde fits—and hauled him a short distance away. "I have news . . . and it stays between you and me. I mean it. I don't want even a single word of what I'm about to say shared with anybody else."

Martinelli knocked her hand aside, then shifted to put the sun behind him—so it shone directly in her eyes and obscured his face. The bastard wasn't above a low trick or two.

"It's something big," he said.

At the guarded, tired tone of his voice, a faint discomfort prickled over her, but she shook it off. "Oh, yeah. *Hugely* big, and I want you to see it. You were my first choice to verify it, Martinelli. As always."

"Because that way you can twist the knife just that much more." He stepped closer, then leaned down until they were almost face-to-face. He smelled like wind and earth and wholly male. "Not interested."

Cassie smiled, unperturbed by the crackling intensity of his hostility. "You might want to wait until you hear what I've found." She inched closer until she could feel the heat radiating off his body, glanced around to make sure no one else was within hearing distance, then lowered her voice. "I had a tour group digging at a private ranch up toward Thermopolis, at what used to be an old riverbed. We found an infant rex, Martinelli. I think it's nearly intact . . . and you damn well know what this means."

His face went slack in shock. A second later his jaw tightened, muscles working beneath the dark beard stubble, and she could imagine the emotions in the eyes behind those sunglasses: anger, envy, regret, longing.

After a moment, she said quietly, "You want to talk about this or not?"

He gave a short, taut nod.

"I thought so. No way would you pass up a chance to study this animal and write it up. It's what you live for, isn't it?" He didn't respond, and after a moment she added, "I'll meet you at the Dip Bar tonight. Eight o'clock. I'd come earlier, but my ex is picking up my kid for a visit and I need to be there."

"I bet he's looking forward to another round of emasculation by Ashton."

His flat, unflattering comment stung, but Cassie

flashed him her sweetest smile. "No doubt. So you'll be at Dip's, right?"

"I'll be there."

"Alone and sober?"

"Not if I can help it," he said with feeling.

"Either way, I'm sure we'll find common negotiating grounds. Bye, Dr. Martinelli. Have a nice day . . . and I hope you find something interesting up there in that old slab of rock."

Flushed with triumph, she walked away, aware of his furious stare boring a hole in her back—and an almost physical tendril of dislike followed her as she passed his crew, curling around her as she headed back to her truck.

Once she was a safe distance away, Cassie stopped and glanced back at the familiar, ragged line of Como Bluff, sloping up toward a blue, cloudless sky. She could clearly see Martinelli's excavation tucked within a weathered ravine, and listened to the familiar sounds of pickaxes on rock, shovels slicing into hard earth, voices and laughter, and the low rumble of an engine. His crew had returned to business as usual, ducking beneath protective tarps or hunkering to the ground under the harsh sun, sweat gleaming on muscles and skin as they dug and crawled amid the rocks and dirt.

The sight filled her with equal senses of longing and regret. They were always like that, these mixed feelings that followed her clashes with Martinelli. Why, she couldn't say.

But when she inserted her key in the ignition, her hands were shaking so bad that it took her three tries to get it right.

# Two

❖

"BE CAREFUL," CASSIE PANTED. "IF YOU DROP HER now, I swear I'll shoot you . . . Wyatt! Could you possibly pay attention to what you're doing?"

After meeting with Martinelli, Cassie had returned to her Hell Creek lab—which was more of a glorified shed—and was now hefting her precious find from its protective crate to a worktable. All her staff plus a few ranch hands had gathered to watch the momentous event, and the two dozen bodies crammed into the small building made maneuvering that much more difficult.

"Ow! Goddammit. Cassie, you just dropped the fu—"

"Wyatt, children present."

"Mom. Please. Like I haven't heard worse."

Cassie glanced over her shoulder, breathing hard from the physical exertion, her fingers cramped from the strain of holding on to the solid rock. A baby rex might be small, but baby and rock and plaster combined were heavy as hell. "Not from Uncle Wyatt, I'm sure."

Her fifteen-year-old son, Travis, looked suspiciously innocent—a look helped along by the fact he'd inherited his father's fine blond hair and thickly lashed gray eyes.

"Nope," Travis said brightly. "Not at all."

*"Goddammit!"* The low, sharp curse brought Cassie's attention back to her younger brother, whose temper was as frayed as his work clothes—and whose expression was as dark as his eyes and hair.

A frequent look for him these days.

"Wyatt, I *am* trying to raise a civilized child here. It may be just another of my pipe dreams, but I'd appreciate it if you'd tone down the cursing when Travis is around."

"Raisin' the kid to be a pussy, you mean." He glowered. "And do you think I can put this thing down here or not?"

God, she hated that word. With an effort, she reined in her own temper and repeated, "Yes, but carefully. This is worth a small fortune, if it's what I think it is and as well-preserved as I hope it is. Mae . . . grab that side and help Wyatt, would you?"

Her lab manager, the epitome of mousy geek girl, was only too happy to rush to Wyatt's side. Cassie had long suspected Mae had a thing for Wyatt, since she had a habit of materializing out of thin air whenever he was around. Cassie occasionally considered pointing out that while her brother might look like a man, he had the emotional maturity of a three-year-old. But Mae was an adult, smart, and capable of making her own decisions and screwups.

"Okay, just a little more to the left and we're set," Cassie said, her voice tight with strain as she lifted her side.

A moment later, with Wyatt's and Mae's help, the precious burden of rock and plaster was settled safely on Cassie's worktable.

"Hey," Travis said from behind her shoulder. "If she died while she was just a baby, then her mom sucked at being a mom."

Giving a sigh of relief, Cassie stepped back from the table and turned to her son. "I wouldn't say that to her mom."

"Like I'd diss a *T. rex*. Even if I could." A gleam lit Travis's eyes. "But you're a good mom."

"Flattery will get you many places—but not to the mall to buy an Xbox."

"Mom, you said—"

"What I said and what you're rewriting in your head are not the same thing," Cassie said. "And I'm not arguing about this again, Travis. I have a lot of work to do with this specimen. I don't have time."

"So what's new," he muttered under his breath, loudly enough for her to hear.

Even though she knew he was up to his usual trick of "guilt out Mom," it worked. Which only made her more annoyed.

"Travis, you know I love you, and you're too old to pull this guilt shit!"

"Language," murmured Wyatt from the other side of the worktable. "Tsk-tsk."

She briefly closed her eyes, wondering if she was the only woman in the world who struggled with such overpowering urges to bury her family in a hole. A very deep hole.

"Playing poor little abused child will not get you an Xbox. It will not change the fact that I have work to do." Travis backed down, but his jaw was still thrust outward in a familiar, mutinous angle.

Cassie turned and faced everyone gathered in the spartan, well-used lab. "And let me take a moment here to remind all of you once again that no one is to speak of this fossil to anybody without my express permission. No exceptions."

She made a point of meeting each and every pair of eyes: Wyatt, Travis, Mae, her mother, Ellen, the lab's computer guru, Amy Gupta, all her diggers and the ranch's hired hands, and the new part-timer who'd been the one to unearth the fossil.

"Don't look at me like that. I promise my lips are

sealed," said her newest employee. Russ Noble was a slender, black-haired man with a mixed white and Cheyenne heritage who also freelanced for a wilderness travel outfit. "But I don't know about Vern. The old guy's really the one who found her."

Despite her stern orders, Cassie knew better than to expect her discovery to stay under wraps for more than a week or two, which if all went well, would be more than enough time. "I don't want this news leaking out until I get all my ducks in a row. Which is why I have to leave in a couple hours to pay a visit to a certain somebody and make a few arrangements."

"Oh, great," Wyatt muttered, and Cassie didn't miss the look of commiseration that passed between her brother and her son. "And we all know who that somebody is, just like we know those visits always leave you in a shitty mood."

"Can't be helped, but this time I have the last word to end all last words." With a smile, she turned to the table where the lump of rock and plaster lay, all its secrets safely hidden within. A little tingle of excitement shot through her, an excitement of the kind she'd almost forgotten.

"I have the first intact specimen of an infant *Tyrannosaurus rex*. It's the find of the century. He'll never top that, and he'll know it. I don't expect him to give me any trouble at all."

Beyond the little stuff, anyway.

"Excuse me, but who the hell are you talking about?" Russ asked and immediately glanced at Travis, grimacing. "Sorry. I'm not used to having kids around."

"I'm not a kid! I'm—" Travis began hotly, but Cassie quickly interrupted him.

"Yes, you are. The law says so. More important, I say so." She turned back to Russ. "I keep forgetting you're new and don't know about Alex Martinelli."

"Boo, hiss," said Amy Gupta, with a wide grin. She was a lushly built woman whose New Delhian ancestors had given her shiny black hair, black eyes, and a toffee-colored complexion that worked wonderfully with the bright orange shirt and pink and lime striped capri pants she wore. Her wrists were smothered in bracelets that tinkled and clacked, rings adorned every finger, and a diamond stud pierced her nose. If Mae had the mousy geek look down pat, then Amy had colorful eccentric covered.

Come to think of it, her lab was a little heavy on the estrogen.

"He's our enemy," Travis added helpfully, drawing Cassie's attention back. "He and Mom have been in a feud for years."

"A rat bastard," Wyatt elaborated, winking at his nephew.

"And I'm still way confused," Russ said flatly.

Cassie folded her arms across her chest, smiling. "Let's just say he has something I need."

"And it starts with a *P*," explained Mae. She glanced at Wyatt and turned pink.

Russ eyed Mae—and her blush—and his face split with a grin. "Ah, a penis, huh? What's the big deal? Because, hey, I've got one of those, and you wouldn't have to go to any trouble for that."

"Ack! Child present!" Despite his shout of mock horror, Travis was grinning.

Sex talk and the fifteen-year-old male of the species—the combination was so predictable, although in a very entertaining way. Cassie couldn't keep her smile from turning into a grin. "And I'm sure it's a very nice one, Russ, but one which will have to remain an eternal mystery to me."

"That's *so* gross," Travis added, nose wrinkling.

Ignoring her son's dramatics, Cassie added for Russ's benefit, "And the *P* is for Ph.D. It's a nuisance, but all my scientifically significant finds have to be verified by a real paleontologist."

"And you're not a real one?" Russ looked surprised. "You seem real enough to me."

Silence filled the lab.

"Remember he's new." Mae brushed a tendril of brown hair away from her thin face, her Bambi eyes wide. "Please don't eviscerate him."

"I'm not 'real' in that sense," Cassie said curtly. "I do all the things a degreed paleontologist does, and probably better than most of them, but because I don't have those three little letters after my name I don't get to play with the big boys."

"Oh." Russ looked embarrassed. "Sorry."

"Don't worry about it. But that's why I need it verified. And since I have to be the maid of honor at my best friend's wedding in a few weeks, I'm also short on time. And that, Travis, is why your dad is coming by in an hour or so to pick you up to spend the rest of the month in Laramie with him."

A look of disappointment crossed her son's face, since he truly enjoyed helping out around the lab, but when the disappointment faded, she suspected he was already calculating how he could talk his father into buying him an Xbox. And Josh probably would, because Josh spoiled the boy something awful whenever he had him.

But that was a small price to pay for a few weeks of around-the-clock, interruption-free work time.

"Travis, why don't you and I go pack for your stay with your dad," said Ellen Parker, and her frowning glance at Cassie broadcast disapproval of her daughter's maternal skills.

Ah, well. Nothing new in that. She and her mother came from different generations; they'd never see eye-to-eye on certain matters.

"Will you call and tell me how it's going with the baby?" Travis asked.

Even knowing he'd hate it, Cassie affectionately ruffled her son's hair. "You know I'll call."

"What are you going to name her?" he asked, ducking away from her hand.

"We're not sure it's a girl, and I haven't given it much thought." She hesitated, sensing that he wanted to name the find but for some reason was too self-conscious to ask. "Would you like to name her?"

He brightened. "Can I?"

"Yes, but don't go overboard," Cassie cautioned. "Think posterity. It has to look respectable in the history books."

"Trixie," Travis immediately stated with finality.

Baffled, Cassie stared at him. Wyatt repeated, "Trixie? Where the hell did you come up with a name like that?"

"It's a pun. You know, a play on words," Travis said, defensively. "She's a *T. rex*, so Trixie sounds a little like *T. rexie*. Get it?"

Cassie laughed. Sometimes she forgot how smart he could be. There were days she missed the little boy who thought his mother was the center of the world, but mostly she was enjoying the young man who'd taken that little boy's place.

Even when he was being a total pain in the ass. Or when he still looked young and vulnerable and hopeful, and made her worry that she wasn't paying as much attention to him as she should.

"You know, I really like that name. Trixie it is."

"Yes!" Travis crowed, raising both arms in a show of victory. "I win!"

"It sounds like something you'd name a dog," Wyatt said.

"Wyatt, zip it and put those muscles you're so proud of to good use. I want her turned with that bumpy part facing up. I have a feeling that's where we'll find the rest of the skull, if it's still there, and where I want to start working."

Her brother put his impressive musculature to good use, as ordered. Mae watched in admiration, but all Cassie could wonder was why she couldn't seem to exchange a civil word with Wyatt these days.

They'd always had a fractious relationship, but when had it devolved into something so tense and . . . bitter?

"Now what do we do?" Mae asked.

"We get back to business as usual and nobody comes near Trixie but me. Then later, I have to go lock horns with Martinelli." She sighed. "Twice in one day. What a lucky woman I am."

# Three

❖

"THAT LUCKY BITCH." DON CLEARY SAT DOWN heavily on the nearest boulder, and Alex joined him.

For a long moment, Alex said nothing, listening to the buzzing of flies, the low rumble of voices, the *chk-chk* of metal tools meeting rock. Then he rubbed his hand over his face and said darkly, "Tell me about it. How the hell can one woman be in the right place so many times in a row?"

It occurred to him that skill was likely involved, but he was in an ugly mood and didn't feel like acknowledging it to himself, much less to Cleary.

"An intact infant rex. Just think what finding one of those would do for our funding." Cleary slumped over, staring at his boots. "Instead it's Ashton who hits the big one, and you know she'll probably sell it to whoever pays her enough. Like she did with that old triceratops with the battle scars I wanted to study. Now it's somewhere in freakin' France."

"By the way, don't say anything about this yet to anybody. I wasn't supposed to tell you, but if I'm going to take Ashton up on her proposition to prep and study the specimen, that'll leave you here alone on the dig. The least I can do is tell you why I'm dumping all this work on you."

"Alex, I was digging up bones before you were even an embryonic gleam in your daddy's eye," Cleary said mildly, picking away the ever-present dirt caking his dry, gnarled hands, the knuckles swollen by arthritis and years of harsh weather and physical labor. "I think I can limp along on my own for a few days while you're off glory hunting."

Alex turned, his already raw temper further chafing at Cleary's comment. "Why the hell do you always say that? Lately I'm getting the sense you resent the hell out of me."

"It's not resentment, exactly." The older man had gone still, his expression a mix of wary surprise and guilt. "Look, there's an ebb and a flow to all things in life. I had my day in the sun, now it's your turn. I can't say I was happy when some controversial young Turk from California hit the department like a whirlwind, but—" Cleary grinned as he slapped Alex on the back—and it wasn't exactly a gentle tap. "Then I decided that if my glory days were done for, I wanted to be working with one of the top guns in the field. And that happens to be you."

Cleary's answer took Alex by surprise. He'd never considered how he must appear in the older man's eyes, and he couldn't blame Cleary for viewing him as a usurper.

An ebb and a flow summed it up very well, and someday he'd find himself ebbing, too.

"If it helps, I want you to know I have every intention of bringing that fossil back with me to the department, no matter what I have to do to get it. Then it'll benefit everybody, not just the glory hounds like me."

Cleary laughed, but Alex didn't miss the sudden flash of longing in the man's pale eyes. "It would be something, to get a chance to look at an animal like that . . . one nobody's ever seen so young."

Alex couldn't help grinning. "Then I guess whatever I have to do will be worth the hassle."

"You've never had to work with Ashton on a professional basis before. Do you think you can manage it?"

"I have issues with her ethics, but from all accounts she does decent work. A few guys I know and respect speak well of her."

"If those few guys are the ones I'm thinking of, they're more than a little controversial themselves."

"Birds of a feather and all that." Alex pushed to his feet, then massaged the aching muscles in his back.

"You okay?" Cleary asked.

"There are days I feel every year of my age, and today is one of them. That exposed vertebra we found up there this afternoon is one stubborn bitch. I was turning myself into a pretzel trying to clear it enough to identify it."

"Did you? In all the excitement, I forgot to ask."

"The vertebra is honeycombed, so it's a tyrannosaur. But I didn't see anything else near it."

"Just another discarded Jurassic snack, then."

"Yeah, I doubt it'll pan out to be more than a few scattered bones. Nothing to get excited about."

"Not compared to what just fell into your lap, anyway."

"Can't argue with that," Alex admitted, but despite his aching muscles and the weariness dragging at him, a lingering charge from his confrontation with Cassie Ashton sizzled hot inside him. He couldn't wait for a rematch, even one he had no chance of winning.

The woman always riled him to a point where rational thought simply ceased and his primal instincts took over. After every confrontation, it took him hours to cool his temper down to nonlethal levels.

"Here comes your little Melissa."

As Cleary's wry tone broke into his dark thoughts, Alex looked up. A familiar blonde was headed his way, and his gaze lingered on the swing of her hips, the bounce of her breasts—and the part of him not totally preoccupied with the coming clash with Ashton acknowledged that Mel was a fine-looking woman. Fast on the heels of that thought, though, came a prickling of guilt: she didn't rouse any emotion stronger than appreciation for something warm and pretty, and God knew, she deserved better.

"You've kept her around longer than I'd expected," Cleary said, as if reading Alex's mind. "Could it be you've finally met the right one?"

"The look on your face says you don't approve."

"Only because there's rumors that she's been hanging around Billy Landry more."

Alex wasn't angry or jealous, just resigned—and curious. He tried to place the name but drew a blank. "Landry?"

"New guy. You've got him working with Lee."

"Oh, yeah . . . nice kid. Stutters when he gets excited."

"That's him. I think he has an eye on your Miss Melissa."

Miss Melissa was almost upon them, and Alex swung his shoulders from side to side until his back cracked. There; that felt better. "He's more her type anyway. If she has half the brain I know she does, she'll figure that out before long."

Behind him, Cleary sighed. "Sometimes I worry about you."

"Don't." Alex glanced down, grinning at his colleague's mother-hen expression. "I'm not worth the trouble."

Then he walked forward to greet Melissa and allowed himself to enjoy her soft warmth as she hugged his arm against her breasts. Until she woke up and smelled the coffee, he might as well enjoy the perks.

# Four

❖

"So . . . how'd Martinelli react when you told him?" Amy demanded. "Spill all the gory details. Now."

Cassie flopped down on a relatively debris-free chair, allowing herself to relax now that she was back in comfortable territory. She needed the downtime to prepare herself before heading to Medicine Bow. "About as I expected. He loathes me, I despise him, but we have this strange relationship where we sometimes need each other. Or at least I need him," she amended sourly. "I think this is the first time in the five years we've known each other that he really needs me."

"Must be a nice change?" Mae looked uncertain, her brown eyes concerned.

"It's certainly different." Cassie swiveled on the chair; it was a nervous habit that annoyed most everybody in the lab, but she couldn't help it. "I'm meeting him at the bar tonight because I figure he'll be less aggressive after a few beers."

"Idiot," said Amy, nearly nose-to-nose with her massive computer monitor, and sucking on a carrot stick she'd eventually eat, her ever-present water bottle close at hand. "Have you forgotten the dozen or so epic battles you two have waged while *in* a bar?"

Cassie scowled. "Not likely. The last time, he humiliated me in front of his entire team. He actually had the nerve to tell me that I deserved all the criticism coming my way. He was really pissed when I sold the old triceratops. I still don't get why. It's not like triceratops are all that rare, even elderly, beat-up ones."

"And you think he'll behave better *this* time? Honestly, Cassie, sometimes I wonder what goes through that brain of yours," Amy said, then crunched loudly on the carrot.

"He'll behave because he doesn't have a choice." Cassie shifted so that she could see the rock-and-plaster bundle on its table. It had seemed so big when they were trying to move it. Now it looked so small. The poor little thing hadn't had much of a chance to live before she'd met her end. "And because I'm asking him not only to verify it for me but also to help me prep the fossil, study it, and write it up. He'd practically kill for this opportunity, and I'm giving it to him, no strings attached."

Wyatt, carrying a bag of shovels and pickaxes in need of repair, walked into the lab at that moment. "Are you crazy?" he demanded, with his usual bluntness. "He's been trying to put you—and all of us—out of business for years."

"This time it's different."

Wyatt narrowed his eyes. "Why? Because you think you'll finally get the respect you've always wanted from him?"

For a moment, Cassie was too startled to respond. "How do you come up with these half-baked ideas? I don't give a damn one way or another if I ever have that man's respect. Why should I?"

"Keep telling yourself that."

With an effort, she maintained her temper. "It's different, Wyatt, because this is a rare infant fossil from a pristine bed of sediment, which means there's a very good chance parts of her soft tissue or other fragile remains have been preserved. And as good as I am at this, I'm not taking any chances. I need to get somebody in here who's an expert in the field, someone whose skills I respect, and that would be Martinelli."

Everybody stared at her.

As the startled silence stretched on, she added, a little embarrassed, "Not that I'd ever tell him that."

Wyatt eased his burden down to the floor. "And if you do all this, Martinelli will figure he deserves the fossil. He's gonna want it."

"Everybody's gonna want it, m'boy," Amy said and crunched aggressively on her carrot stick. "No surprise there."

Wyatt didn't take his gaze from Cassie. "And what's the chance of you thinking you should do the right thing, for the sake of science and all that shit, and handing the fossil over to him for next to nothing?"

"I haven't given any thought to what I'll do with her, beyond getting her cleaned up."

"I know you too well, Cassie, and like hell am I gonna let you hand this fossil over to that bastard. You'll sell it to the highest bidder, we'll make a nice profit—and *everybody*'ll get a big, fat Christmas bonus this year. For once we have a chance to make some serious money. Don't fuck it up."

"Look," she snapped. "I make the decisions. Period. And in case you've forgotten, I'm the one who sacrificed—"

"—your whole life, yes, we've heard this before." Wyatt glared back. "Give it up, Cass. Nobody asked you to leave college and come back here after Dad died. Nobody asked you to take over running the ranch or the shop. Nobody asked you to stay. Nobody asked you to get yourself knocked up or married or divorced. So don't give me that shit. The guilt worked when I was a kid, but I'm not a kid anymore."

"If you don't like how I run things, then leave!"

"And that's supposed to be an answer? Sounds like a dodge to me."

She took a long, deep breath to calm herself, beating down the prickling of guilt—and very real hurt at his accusation. "No, nobody asked me to come back and give up all my plans and dreams. I know that. But what did people expect me to do? I couldn't let everything our family worked so hard to create over so many years just disappear. Our parents give us life and raise us, and it's right to give something back to them when the situation requires it."

"It's wrong when you keep using it as an excuse to do everything your way because you're a selfish control freak." Along with the anger coloring his face, Cassie saw hurt and frustration in her brother's dark eyes a split second before he dropped his gaze. "I see your point of view more than you think. But you laid a guilt trip on us for years to force us to do everything your way, and now—"

"No one else was doing anything at all! You and Tom were too young, and Tom never had any interest in the ranch anyway. After Dad died, *somebody* had to step in to keep everything from falling apart, and you know Mom never had a head for business. Staying here cost me a lot, Wyatt," she finished quietly. "All I ask is that you remember that."

"Like I can forget, with you telling me at least once a day," her brother said bitterly. "Saint Cassie, savior of the Parker Ranch and Hell Creek Rock Shop. And God forbid that I dare disagree with any of your almighty decisions."

He grabbed his bag of tools and stalked off, clanking with each forceful stride, and leaving her with a sudden awareness of Mae and Amy, sitting in a frozen silence of embarrassment. Amy had been at Hell Creek long enough to grow accustomed to the occasional blowups between Cassie and Wyatt, but Mae had joined them only some eight months ago, and she always looked like she wanted to cry following these shouting matches.

"Sorry about that," Cassie told Mae. "Wyatt and I don't see eye-to-eye on a lot of things. He's also getting to the point where he doesn't want to work for his big sister; he wants to run the show."

Mae tried smiling, which made Cassie want to give her a reassuring hug. Mae always brought out her protective streak; it had to be those Bambi eyes. She seemed so unworldly, Cassie sometimes wondered if the woman had lived her life in some kind of bubble. How could any woman be that naïve in this day and age?

"It's okay," Mae said softly. "You're both so much alike, really, and I wish you'd get along better. It must be hard for him."

*And what about me?* Why did everyone assume she had it easy just because she was in charge?

"Hey, Mom," Travis called, poking his head through the door that led from the shop to the lab. "Why's Uncle Wyatt all pissed off again?"

"Pick your flavor of gripe of the day."

"Ooookay. Forget I asked." He walked in and edged closer to the table. "So how do you think Trixie died?"

"It's too early to say." Cassie stood and absently removed a bit of loose plaster, revealing paler bone. So slender and fragile; hard to believe she would've grown into a massive killing machine. "We found her in what used to be an old riverbed, so it's a pretty safe bet that she drowned in a flash flood before being quickly covered by mud. That's why she's in such good shape."

Touching a tiny bone gently, Cassie felt her gaze blur as she imagined the infant rex's fate.

### 67 Million Years Ago . . .

*The flying thing had drawn her away from her safe place. She'd followed, curious, trying to catch it as it buzzed from one leaf to another. Soon, her chase had taken her far away, to a place where everything looked and smelled strange.*

*Before long, water had fallen from the sky. Scared and alone, the creature had cried out for her mother. Then, trying to hide, she'd fallen into a cold, watery dark.*

*Despite her efforts, she couldn't climb back up the slip-*

pery incline. Light flashed above, blinding her. Even young as she was, fear registered clearly. She understood her mother, her body both a comfort and safety, was not near. The water tickled against her belly as more fell from the black sky with its burst of lights.

Over and over, she tried with all her strength to climb out of the rising water. She smelled mud, but not the refuge of the place where she belonged. Fear pulled her down as surely as the strong currents of the water.

The torrential rains had turned the dry riverbed into a brown, churning maelstrom. Ripped from her precarious hold on the shore's edge, she was tumbled and pushed forward by the current, dragging her under the water.

She cried louder for her mother, never stopping until the water pulled her under for the last time. Weak, too weary to fight, she let the darkness take her to a peaceful place.

For a long while she bobbed and swirled to the whims of the wind-whipped river, until finally the rains eased, the winds died down, and the current turned sluggish once again. Her small body drifted toward the muddy shallows and sank into the softness, where it was soon covered by layers of fine silt that washed down from the hills and mountains. Tiny hands curled inward, her head arched back, the mud swiftly entombed her.

Once the rains receded, the sun emerged, and long, hot days followed, baking the mud hard as rock and sealing the little one within a cradle of dark earth.

• • •

"She's really worth a lot of money, isn't she?"

Travis's voice pulled Cassie back to the present, to her own vulnerable child.

"Sweetie, she's priceless."

Seeing his wistful expression, she added quickly, "But as incredible as she is, she's not as important to me as certain people in my life. I think you know who I'm talking about."

"I know." He heaved a sigh. "I didn't mean what I said earlier."

She nodded, understanding why he'd trailed back into the lab just now. Her son didn't have a mean bone in his body; he couldn't hold a grudge even if he wanted to. He was a good-natured kid, and the fact that she could still say that during adolescence had to be a miracle.

"Trav?" Ellen Parker called through the lab door. "Your dad's here, and he brought Trina and the kids."

Travis groaned. "Oh, great. They'll be crawling all over me. I *hate* that."

Being a teenager with two half sisters half his age didn't do much for his dignity, especially since their way of showing how much they idolized him was to torment him. Mercilessly.

"You'll survive." Cassie turned as her ex-husband walked in, laughing at something Ellen had said. He was still tall, still thin, still blond and gray-eyed, and still cute in that grown-up-little-boy way that had been her utter undoing so many years ago.

Now there were times she looked at him and wondered what the hell she'd been thinking. Not that she regretted it; how could she, with the fantastic kid she'd been blessed with?

"Hey, Cass," Josh said lazily. "You're lookin' good. The old bone business must be doing right by you."

"It's a living," she answered, as she always did. He'd never shared her fascination for geology, much less dinosauria, so no one had been too surprised, herself included, when their marriage had gone sour pretty much from the start. Still, he was an okay guy, as was his wife. Cassie returned Trina's smile. She wouldn't consider Trina a friend, but she liked her well enough—and it helped that Trina was truly fond of Travis.

"You ready to go, buddy?" Josh asked his son, grinning from ear to ear. Their marriage may have been a disaster, but she'd never once doubted that Josh loved his son.

"All packed. My suitcase is out by the garage." Travis nodded at Trina and gave a wave at his two half sisters, who were clinging shyly to their mother. Somewhere by the lab's back door, Wyatt laughed loudly, and the little girls moved even closer to their mother. Cassie couldn't blame them; Wyatt had an overwhelming effect on a lot of people. Especially female people.

Cassie gave her son a quick, firm hug, wishing she could hold him close or kiss his cheek like she'd done so often when he was small. But she knew better than to embarrass him. Instead, she said cheerfully to Josh, "Here you go, then: one prime specimen of *Pesticus bratticus*. Please return the creature to me in the same condition as you received it."

Travis groaned. "That is so lame."

"I know. Can't help it."

Still grinning, Josh asked, "Is there anything I need to know? Any rules or orders?"

"I'd tell you not to spoil him rotten, but I'd be wasting my breath."

"Okay, Trav, let's go. You can give your mother a call when we get back to Laramie."

Everybody said good-bye and Cassie waved until she could no longer see the trail of dust down the long driveway.

Strange how the place always seemed so quiet once Travis left. At moments like this, she wondered how she'd deal with the empty nest thing. It wouldn't be long before he'd hit eighteen, and then he'd be impatient to head out into the big, bad world all on his own.

And of course he should; that was the way it worked. Kids grew up and left home. Mothers suddenly had to find something else to fill up the hours they'd once spent chasing after kids.

"God," she mumbled to herself. "Am I in a mood or what?"

As Cassie passed through the shop, she automatically checked the shelves and stock. Housed in a log shed built by the first Parker settler in 1910, it had been modernized and expanded as the business grew but still possessed a quaint charm. She'd loved playing in the shop when she was little, and it was still her favorite part of the business, even if it made the least profit.

For pint-size rock hounds, the shop had barrels of quartz, pyrite, geodes, and other showy rocks and minerals, as well as fossils too fragmentary or damaged to be of value, or too common to be worth cataloging, like the fossil shark teeth that sold so well. Shark teeth and kids went together like Hershey's syrup and French vanilla ice cream.

But once she'd taken over the business, she'd started catering to the serious collectors in addition to the casual tourists who wanted a pretty rock or two to take home as a souvenir.

The nicer specimens were shelved in display boxes, and the big-ticket items were up front by the cash register. And some of those big-ticket items were just plain big, like Opie the juvenile triceratops—or the front quarter of him, anyway—who would stand on display near the front door until somebody came up with the money to take him home.

Her mother stood at the cash register, chatting on the phone while she priced little sand buckets full of plastic dinosaurs and colorful shovels. As Cassie approached, Ellen finished up the conversation and hung up.

"It was nice of Josh and Trina to take Travis on such a short notice," she said.

"It's only a week earlier than we'd arranged. He always spends time with his dad before school starts. It's not that big a deal."

"Still, it was nice," Ellen repeated. "You're expecting to be really busy with that thing, huh?"

"Yeah, it will take a marathon of cleaning. How's it going today? Looks like we've been busy."

"Just the typical end of summer rush, last-minute vacations before school starts. We've had a lot of families with kids today. Oh! And that reminds me, I took a call from that nice gentleman in Dallas who's looking for eggs. Anything you've got, he said he'd take."

"Hmmm." Cassie leaned back against the counter, watching a family with three small boys who were pawing excitedly through the barrels of polished rocks, all oohs! and aahs! and excited whisperings. "I'm not sure we have much in stock. I'll have to check with Mae. Did he leave a number?"

Her mother handed it over. "He said to leave a message if he wasn't there."

Cassie slipped the paper into her back pocket.

"So what's next with that thing?"

It didn't require a genius IQ to deduce that her mother didn't much care for Hell Creek Fossil Company's newest prize. "Mom, you could be a little more excited about it. We're going to be able to sell this one for major money."

"I know, but I'm not looking forward to all the stress. I remember what it was like when Wyatt and his people found that partial rex last year, and that elderly triceratops that caused your last big fight with Mr. Martinelli. Lately I find myself missing the times when we just ran the rock shop. I hate disruptions."

"Then you'd better brace yourself, because when word gets out on this one, the phones will be ringing off the hook."

"I'm sorry, honey. I know this means a lot to you. And I know it's important." Ellen sighed. "But I'm dreading the long hours and the arguments. You and Wyatt haven't exactly been getting along these past few months."

"Leave Wyatt to me. He'll get over it."

"So what are you going to do now?"

"I'm going to check on Trixie, then get ready to head into Medicine Bow to negotiate terms with Martinelli."

"Cassie, I hope you know what you're doing. He's never been very nice to you. In fact, he very nearly—"

"Martinelli and I have a basic understanding,"

Cassie interrupted before her mother could start in on the laundry list of Martinelli's Crimes Against the Parkers. "He won't try to get me arrested this time. I promise." She pushed open the lab door. "I don't know when I'll be back, so don't wait up for me."

Once back in the lab, she asked Mae to check on their fossil egg stock, told Amy to run numbers to get an idea of what this fossil was going to cost in terms of work hours and supplies, cautioned the whole crew once again to keep their mouths shut about Trixie, then headed to the main house to change into something more appropriate for "negotiations."

The ranch house had started out small, and over the years various Parkers had added on to it as needed, so it was an odd mix of styles. But it was home, and that made all the difference. Sometimes Cassie longed to move away to her own place; at other times she found the familiarity, the memories, and the connection with family long since gone to be comforting.

It was a good place to raise a kid, although there were days when she wished it had more than one bathroom with a shower. With four people in the house—though technically Wyatt was living in the apartment above the garage—bathroom time was a precious commodity.

Right now, though, she was the only person in the house and the shower was all hers for as long as she wanted.

After leisurely washing away the day's sweat and grime, she toweled dry, powdered and perfumed herself, then rummaged through her closet until she found what she wanted.

It qualified as a dress, even if there was barely enough of it to do any qualifying. She'd bought it a few years back on a shopping trip in L.A. with her best friends, Diana and Fiona. She couldn't remember why she'd bought it; it wasn't like she had many opportunities to dress up out here in the middle of Nowhere, Wyoming. The skin-colored crochet lace sheath, lined in a matching knit that created the illusion of nothing beneath, hugged her curves and bared a lot of leg and cleavage.

Not a dress for the faint of heart or the modest of soul, neither of which had ever been an issue for her.

Cassie eyed herself in her dresser mirror and laughed softly. "All's fair in love and war and dinosaur hunting."

Curious to see the reaction to her newly created man-eater persona, she traipsed back to the lab in high heels. The second she walked through the door, silence fell over the room. Russ, talking with Wyatt, nearly let his jaw hit the floor; Wyatt just grinned.

"Jesus," Russ said in awe. "What the hell is that?"

"My war gear. History has shown that the best way to deal with Martinelli is to distract him with boobage."

"You know, I almost feel sorry for the guy." Russ

hadn't stopped staring. "Poor bastard doesn't stand a chance."

"That's the whole point." Cassie pirouetted, thoroughly enjoying her rare plunge into femaleness. "You like?"

"What's not to like?" Russ's focus dropped to her backside. "Very nice."

"I do have a pretty decent ass, don't I?" Cassie peered at her bottom, clearly outlined beneath the tight dress.

"The magnificence of which nearly matches your ego, yes," Russ replied with a grin.

"Hey, none of it's *my* doing. The good Lord giveth." She slapped her hands on her rear, then over her breasts as she added mournfully, "And the good Lord also taketh away."

"Hey, none of that." Russ eyed her breasts with a lazy appreciation. "You have great boobage. And you're so damn cute."

"Uh-oh." Amy gave him a look of mock alarm. "The newbie just used the c word. Now you're in for it, Russ."

Cassie laughed. "Lucky for you, Russ, I'm in a good mood. But for the record, calling me 'cute' won't win you any points."

"Sorry." He didn't look in the least contrite. "But I call 'em like I see 'em, and you're as cute as cute can be."

Amy said, "It comes from being barely five foot

tall and all perky and bouncy. Disgusting, isn't she? But damn, if I weren't straight, I'd do her."

Everybody laughed, and Russ said, "I *am* straight, and I'd do her, too." As Cassie sent him a quelling glare, he added, "Martinelli's never gonna know what hit him."

"Excellent. Just what I wanted to hear. Okay, kids, I'm off to the bar to pick up slutty paleontologists. Play nice while the lab mommy's away, and remember—nobody plays with the baby *or* talks about her."

With a pert finger wave, she spun on her high heels and sashayed out to the garage, carefully making her way over the gravel. Stepping up into the pickup in her tight skirt took a little ingenuity, but she wiggled onto the seat without ripping or snagging anything crucial. And then she was headed toward the nearby town of Medicine Bow.

# Five

CASSIE WAS AWARE OF THE TRUCKERS CHECKING HER out as she passed them, and she enjoyed the attention. Still, it was so unfair.

A man like Martinelli could show up all sexy and attractive just the way he was, while women needed to stuff themselves into skinny clothes, balance on high heels, fluff their hair, and make up their faces. She enjoyed the sprucing up, though; it had been a long time since she'd had an opportunity to feel like a desirable woman rather than a mom or a boss.

Along with the familiar hum of excitement, jitters staked out their territory in her belly as she approached the bar. Martinelli was bound to retaliate before giving in to her demands, and he was his most dangerous while acting charming or harmless. For that reason alone, she hoped he'd greet her with snarls and jabs rather than

smiles and the charisma that worked its wiles on her far
more than she liked to admit.

A group of skinny, weathered cowboys outside the
bar surveyed her with unabashed appreciation as she
walked their way, and their catcalls and whistles followed her into the dark, smoke-choked bar. In the
heart of Wyoming, sexism and non-PC behavior still
flourished.

Above the sound of a jukebox, the clink of bottles
and glasses, and the hum of conversation, Cassie
heard the solid *thwack* of pool balls hitting one
another, and she spotted Martinelli and his syco-
phants by the back pool table. He'd spruced up a bit
and appeared to be wearing clean jeans, a clean shirt,
and a shiny, twenty-something blonde.

The shiny blonde didn't deter her. While Cassie
might have left her twenties behind some time ago,
she still looked good. More important, she was
sneaky, unscrupulous, stubborn, and thick-skinned.
Sometimes success was nothing more than being the
last one standing.

Martinelli pretended not to see her, although he
couldn't possibly have missed her arrival since the
entire bar fell dead silent. She moved forward, aware
of the male and female gazes following her, assessing
and judging.

"Hey, Martinelli." Cassie leaned her hip against the
pool table. "I see you're well-accessorized, as always."

Lazily, he looked at her over the blonde's head. "You're just jealous."

"Of what?" She grinned as she hitched herself up to sit on the side of the pool table, then deliberately crossed her legs, causing the intensity of the stares directed her way to increase a gazillion-fold. "Your reputation as the biggest slut west of the Mississippi?"

The blonde turned and Cassie recognized her as the grad student working on obtaining exclusive rights to Martinelli. And very attractive rights they were; the dim light of the bar only added to his classic good looks, the patrician nose, firm lips, and hooded eyes that clearly marked his dark, volatile Mediterranean heritage.

"Oh, it's you." The other woman's voice was cool, her expression scornful. No trace of the earlier friendliness; the girl was a quick study on whom to look down upon.

"Yes, it's me, and I have business with your boss. Now be a good girl and go away."

"Don't you give me orders, bitch."

Oh, my. Dramatics! It was like having an angry puppy yapping at her heels.

Cassie smiled gently. "In this little world of ours, I'm the queen bitch and you're nowhere near my league. Truth is, you're just a nuisance. Now go away."

The woman pulled free from Martinelli, who didn't move. A nice man would've jumped to his girl's defense; instead he looked like he was enjoying the skirmish.

"Alex? Are you going to put up with—"

"Mel, why don't you get a beer and keep Cleary company for a few minutes. I'll come for you when I'm done here."

His low, pleasant voice carried a note of authority, and the blonde simply glared at Cassie as she walked past.

God, had she ever been *that* young and emotionally transparent?

"Bye, Mel," she chirped at the woman's stiff, retreating back.

"Pull in the claws, Ashton," Martinelli said, his tone still pleasant. "Your business is with me, not her."

Cassie arched a brow. Admirable of him to defend his date, if rather pointless *after* the woman had left. "But she's so easy to offend."

"And when you scent a weakness, you go for the kill. Nice habit." His voice had an edge to it she hadn't heard in a while.

He was furious. Ice-cold, raging, blindly furious— and there wasn't a damn thing he could do about the reason for it.

"The laws of survival, my friend," Cassie said easily. "Something we should be well aware of in our line of business."

"My line of business and your line of business

aren't alike." He turned toward the pool table and picked up the cue. "Despite your fantasies to the contrary."

At what point had the other men at the table faded away to leave them alone? Absolutely alone, in the center of the room, with the neon gleam of the Budweiser sign on the wall casting his face in a cool, blue light.

Cassie slid off the table and picked up a cue. She wasn't much of a pool player, and letting Martinelli win might help ease the brittle tension. Twirling the cue, she ambled to the other side of the table.

"Like it or not, this time our business is mutual. Play a round?"

Wordlessly, he bent, aimed, and sent balls smacking across the table. The number six dropped into a corner pocket. "Take your best shot."

"I always do, Martinelli. You should know that."

She did her best but managed only to send a few balls wobbling over the worn green felt. She glanced up, and caught him eyeing her cleavage.

Yup; distraction techniques in place and working fine.

"If that was your best shot, I'd pay money to see your worst." Martinelli looked up, not the least embarrassed at being caught ogling her boobs.

"We can't all be brilliant at everything. So, have you thought over my little proposition?"

"Drop the nice act, Ashton. I like you better bitchy."

She smiled, reveling a tiny bit in her victory over him. "I just thought you might have a few questions."

"You're getting off on this, aren't you?"

Cassie leaned back against the table and did her best to look bored. Again his gaze lowered to her breasts; the look almost as physical as a touch. Her entire body warmed in a way that was pleasant but most definitely unwelcome.

"Why not?" she answered. "Serves you right for being such a bastard to me for all these years."

He merely stared at her, his mouth thin. "You're sure it's an infant rex?"

"Keep your voice down," she ordered, after glancing around to make sure no one was in earshot. "And, yes, I'm certain."

"So you can prove it?"

"Oh, Martinelli, you're just making this harder on yourself."

He turned away, and more pool balls cracked against one another before thudding into the pockets. "You're such a nice girl."

"Been there, done that. When I played nicely, by the rules, it got me a big fat nothing. You've got so many rules to play by, it must really chap your ass that I can go where I want and do what I want without departmental bullshit and grant committee red tape tripping up my every move."

"At least I have respect."

A direct hit, and he knew it. With another smile, though this one took a bit more of an effort, Cassie sent a few balls skittering across the table. Again, she could feel his gaze on her, heated and physical as a touch.

"It wasn't your turn, Ashton."

"I'm not much for waiting. I've already won what really matters, haven't I? So here's the rundown, even though your ego won't allow you to ask for it: The remains are in very good condition, and from what I've already cleared, I'm pretty confident the skull's intact. We did find one of her arms and a portion of a foot washed downstream, but we've excavated that area as well. If any other small bones drifted away, we should recover most, if not all, of them. And if we're lucky, some of the soft tissue might have been preserved and we'll get skin impressions. Maybe more."

"You can tell it's female?"

"Nope." At his raised brows, she elaborated. "I'm going on instinct. When it comes to bones, anyway, my instincts rarely fail me."

"So what exactly do you want from me?"

"For starters, the usual—I need you to verify it's what I already know it is."

"Yeah, the validation behind those three letters is something you can't claim, no matter how much you lie, cheat, and manipulate situations to your advantage."

Old words, old accusations. There was no real heat or conviction in his voice.

"Seems to me that precious little bundle back in my lab is all the validation I'll ever need for the rest of my life." She smiled at him and watched his expression darken. "Now, what I'm about to say may come as something of a shock, but I'm completely serious."

She walked around the table until she faced him. It annoyed her that she had to look up, and she wished yet again that she hadn't been born with an overabundance of "cute and tiny" genes. Her looks had a few advantages, but most of the time they made for a struggle to be taken seriously.

"Despite what you and most of your colleagues believe, I run a damn good business and I know my work. But because this is an important find, and because half the members of the Society of Vertebrate Paleontology will be out to discredit me, I want somebody with credentials working at my side. You may have a certain notoriety within your circle of peers, Martinelli, but nobody questions your skills or judgment. If you're there to back me up, I won't have to waste so much time defending every minuscule move I make."

"What's in it for me?"

"You need to ask? You get your name attached to the biggest paleontology find of the century, which ought to translate into a whole lot of journal papers and attention for your department. Maybe *National Geographic* will even pick you to be their next cover boy."

"Maybe I don't give a rat's ass about that."

"And maybe I'll wake up tomorrow looking like your tall blonde over there." She leaned into him, close enough to feel his heat and smell the freshly showered scent of him beneath the bar's miasma of stale beer and cigarette smoke. "Best of all, you get to uncover, with your own hands, something nobody else has ever seen. You're not going to turn me down."

"No," he said after a long moment, his expression not in the least friendly. "No, I'm not. But there's one more condition you need to meet before I agree."

Cassie nodded, waiting. She knew what he was going to say even before he opened his mouth.

"I want first crack at acquiring the finished specimen."

"Deal," she said, without hesitation.

Wyatt would have screamed at her for that. Martinelli didn't look as if he believed her.

"You heard right," she said, answering the question in his eyes. "I know what you think about me, that all I ever want is to make a quick buck—"

"And this isn't true?"

"I make no apologies for wanting to earn as much money as I can, although I barely break even most of the time. And even that's hard when unexpected court costs and lawyer fees nearly bankrupt the family business."

Their gazes clashed, and an old, bitter anger washed over her as she added softly, "But a girl can still dream, right?"

For a long moment, Martinelli stood very still, not even blinking. "I told the truth."

"You told *your* version of the truth."

"Because that was the only version I had."

"And it nearly landed me in jail. Not that you cared."

"Why should I?" he asked, his tone so quiet that Cassie heard him only because they stood close together.

Too close together. When had they moved toward each other?

And when had the bar grown so quiet?

She glanced around and saw the room's occupants were watching her and Martinelli as if the two of them were acting out a drama on center stage— except for the stiff-backed blonde at the bar, who stubbornly faced away.

Cassie stepped back, hoping Martinelli didn't notice her retreat. "As I was going to say, even I'm not rapacious enough to sell a fossil this valuable to a businessman with too much disposable cash on his hands. She's not ending up in a bank lobby or somebody's living room. You get first dibs—but that's all I'll promise."

"And you'll price her so high, my department will never have a chance in hell of buying her."

Cassie stared back at him. "You just don't get it, do you? I have bills to pay. Like you, I have employees and overhead and business expenses. It costs me time and a *hell* of a lot of money to dig up fossils, clean them, put them back together again, and get them ready for display. You expect to be paid for *your* work. You don't seriously think I do this out of the generosity of my heart, do you?"

At that, he smiled. "And all this time, everybody's been saying you're heartless. Who knew?"

Beneath the jab, she sensed an easing of the tension between them.

"So do we have a deal, Martinelli?"

"You knew you had me before you walked through that door, Ashton, but I appreciate the fact you dressed up for me, even if it was just a tease. You're a fine-looking woman, and if you didn't make me feel homicidal every time we get within arm's reach of each other, I'd even think we could get along better. Much better."

"I don't want to get along better with you. You are so damn sleazy sometimes." Cassie rolled her eyes, but her heart was racing. "What time can you be at my lab?"

"I'll be there tomorrow morning but can't say exactly when. I'm in the middle of a dig; give me time to put matters in order first. I have to bring Cleary up to date—"

"You don't tell him a thing," she said flatly. "I don't want to be dealing with telephone calls, reporters, or any of your pals stirring up trouble for me. Ideally, I want as much of her cleaned in the next few weeks as possible."

"Deadline?"

"A friend of mine is getting married soon, and I'm in the wedding party."

He still looked resentful, but anticipation had toned his hostility down to a manageable level. "I'll see you tomorrow. Shall I buy you a beer to seal the deal?"

"Your little woman is waiting for you, Martinelli. If you bring me over to the bar, there's no way you're getting laid tonight. See you later, dino boy."

With a wave, Cassie left the bar to the sounds of a few more catcalls from Martinelli's team. But Don Cleary's narrow-eyed, hostile glare almost stopped her. She'd never seen that look on his face before. Exasperation and angry resentment, yes, but nothing that close to . . . hatred.

To be sure no one noticed her reaction, she blew

the old man a kiss before walking out into the cool, clear night air.

She'd won, but for some reason it didn't feel like much of a victory.

# Six

WHEN ALEX WALKED BACK TO THE BAR AND MELISSA, he felt her hostility before he even saw her eyes.

"Having fun?" she asked, her voice brittle.

"More fun than ripping out my own liver," he answered. "Can't wait to do it again."

"You like her."

"Mel, it's late, and maybe we—"

"*We* aren't doing anything."

He sighed. "I'm really not in the mood for this."

She stood and grabbed her backpack, each motion tight, angry—the height of a female snit. "I'm leaving with Billy. Don't bother coming by the trailer."

Billy? Alex turned to see one of his diggers waiting in the shadows by the door, looking guilty and smug at the same time.

Right. The nice guy with the stutter. He'd forgotten.

"I see," he said, understanding what she was

telling him. He'd seen it coming but would've preferred a better time and place to be dumped by his on-again, off-again bed partner.

She stared at him. "You don't care, do you?"

"Yes, I do."

Something like pity flickered across her fresh, pretty face. "No, you don't. That's your whole problem, Alex. There isn't anything you care about. Not even your work, despite the big act you're always putting on. And that's why you fight with that woman, isn't it? So nobody will notice you're just going through the motions."

She hesitated, clearly wanting to say more. It seemed as if she'd spent a lot of time rehearsing this, and he owed it to her to take whatever she threw at him. "And you were just going through the motions with me, too. I tried, Alex, I really did, but you were never really *with* me. I kept telling myself it was because you weren't the emotional type, but then I saw how you acted with that woman and . . . I can't pretend anymore."

Mel's mouth tightened and she looked away, as if she were fighting back tears.

*Please, not tears. Not now, not here.*

But when she looked up again, anger glittered in her eyes. "You know, I thought I'd found the right man for me, and that all those warnings about you being a selfish jerk weren't true. My mistake, for believing I was ever more to you than a warm body and an easy lay."

Alex didn't answer, since nothing he said would be what she wanted to hear. After a long moment her eyes narrowed, then she spun and stalked away. He knew she wanted him to go after her, make some sort of passionate declaration—but he couldn't. She was mostly right.

"Smooth," Cleary said from his spot at the bar. "There goes another one."

Alex dropped down on an empty barstool. "Looks that way."

"Why *do* you do that? I can't figure out why you act like such a bastard sometimes."

Alex ordered a beer before answering. "Because I *am* a bastard."

"I know you too well for that excuse to work."

Sighing, Alex slumped over the bar, feeling every one of his thirty-seven years in his sore muscles and aching joints. In the guilt crowding in on that dark emptiness inside. For once, he didn't feel like dodging Cleary's questions. "She deserves better. They all do. I just make it a little easier for them to see it."

Cleary blinked, then frowned. "You be the bad guy and take the blame, so it's easier for the girls to move on. Is that what you're saying?"

"Something like that."

Cleary mulled that over for a moment. "Why do you get involved with these girls if you don't intend to get serious about it?"

Another damn good question. "I never make any promises, never pretend, and I never cheat on them. She was the one who asked me to sleep with her, and I guess I wasn't in the mood to say no."

"That's not an answer."

His beer arrived, and he took a long drink, wishing Cleary would drop the subject. When a glance at the old man showed him still waiting for an answer, Alex shrugged. "I don't know . . . maybe it's just better than being alone."

Cleary gave a snort of exasperation. "If you feel that way, you should find yourself a wife and have a kid or two."

"Tried that. I was a lousy husband and an even lousier father."

"Don't you think you're being too hard on yourself? What more do you think you can do when your ex moves your kid halfway across the country?"

"My daughter is like a stranger to me. She's in high school, and I don't—" Alex broke off. "Forget it."

"You think you're the only man who ever got the short end of a divorce deal? You call your kid, right?"

"Yeah."

"Send her birthday cards and gifts? Visit her?"

Alex nodded, cupping his hand around the bottle,

feeling the cold condensation against his skin. "It's not enough."

"Maybe, but aside from packing up and moving next door to your ex, what more can you do?" Cleary nudged him. "Hey. One bad marriage shouldn't put you off the whole deal. Marriage is good for a man. It's been good for me."

"Because you're a marrying kind of guy. I don't think I'm one."

"So how long will you keep playing these stupid games?"

"I prefer to think of it as saving some nice girl from years of misery by keeping things casual until she moves on to someone better."

"It's still a shitty thing to do, any way you look at it."

Alex didn't argue the point, since it was true. "What they don't know can't hurt them, and it's not like they don't bounce right back. Women like Melissa will always find a nice young guy eager to make them feel like queens again. Though she stuck with me longer than I expected—and I'm still not sure why she got so pissed off tonight."

"You serious?"

"Don, I am so damn tired . . . if you have something to say, say it."

"When you're with that Ashton woman, there's a huge arc of energy between you, so strong everybody notices. So strong the two of you don't see or hear anything or anybody else."

Alex looked down, absently tracing the worn lines of a heart somebody had carved into the bar long ago. "If I don't look at anyone but Ashton, it's because I don't trust her enough to take my eyes off her. The second I did, she'd kick me in the balls."

"I think Melissa had a different take on it."

This was a line of conversation Alex didn't intend to follow. "Mel was seeing what she wanted to see, and all you saw was five years' worth of frustration busting out. So, yeah . . . I'd say there were sparks flying, but not for the reason you're thinking."

"Damn fool." Cleary shook his head, then guzzled down the rest of his beer.

Alex pretended not to hear the "damn fool" part, but tonight not even his well-honed avoidance skills shook off his growing unease. Maybe it was the tiredness, stress, and frustration, or maybe it was simply the embarrassment of being dumped in a bar in front of half his crew, but Melissa's angry accusation continued to gnaw at him. Finally, he swiveled the stool around to face Cleary.

"Can I ask you a question?"

Cleary rubbed his chin, his whiskers rasping. "Guess so."

"Do you think it's true what she said? That I don't care about my work?"

"It doesn't matter what I think. Do *you* think it's true?"

Alex stared down at his beer. "Sometimes I wonder if I put in as many hours as I do to keep myself from noticing I don't have a life. Then I think I'm an idiot for even wondering such things."

"Dunno. It's your life. But it's been a while since I've seen a fire in your eyes like I saw it tonight."

"Yeah, well, Ashton always was real good at pissing me off."

"Looked more to me like a fire of excitement than a fire of anger."

"I can't say I'm not looking forward to examining that infant rex," Alex admitted, and for a long while they nursed their beers, deep in thought.

By now, most of his crew had left the bar, since they'd only come to see the showdown between him and Cassie. For a moment, Alex almost regretted not going after Melissa and soothing her ruffled feathers. At the very least, he could've gotten some mind-numbing sex out of this rotten day.

Instead, Billy the Nice Guy would get to pass the night with Mel's warm, responsive body and not have to think until the morning.

"It's a smart move, though," Cleary said suddenly. "Get close to Ashton, make nice . . . and once you're on her good side, you figure out how to keep the fossil for yourself."

"That's the general idea. She understands the scientific value of this find and is being cautious, I'll give her that, and I told her I'd help her out only if I get first crack at acquiring it for the department."

"And she agreed?"

"Yup."

"Somehow, I don't think it'll be as easy as that."

Alex laughed quietly. "If it were easy, it wouldn't be half as much fun."

"I gotta hand it to you, Alex, you have more patience with her attitude than I ever would. I'd have popped her one years ago."

It was a strange comment, and his surprise must've shown, because Cleary chuckled.

"Yeah, I know. I'd never hit a woman, but she's the kind that riles you up so bad, you can't decide if you want to screw her or deck her. Lately, I've been leaning toward the decking part."

"I never knew you thought that way about her."

"Alex, I may not be anybody's idea of a stud, and I may be happily married, but that doesn't mean I don't have eyes. She's not the kind of girl you can ignore. She's right there, in your face, every second she's around. And I have to tell you, I find her scary as hell."

*Scary* neatly summed up Cassie Parker Ashton. "She's so tiny. And cute. Even knowing what she's like, her toughness always catches me off guard. It's all wrong, like having a killer poodle or something."

"I always thought you could've saved yourself a lot of trouble, and the rest of us a lot of stress, if you'd hauled her off to some motel and screwed her brains out."

Alex tightened his fingers around his bottle. "Where the hell did that come from?"

"You know you want to . . . you've wanted to for years."

"Never considered it." Alex hunkered further over the bar. "I prefer to enjoy sex. And survive it."

Cleary grinned and Alex added, "Man, she'd argue about *everything*. How to do it, where to do it, when to do it. She'd probably want to always be in charge and tell me what to do—"

Cleary gave a snort of laughter. "I thought you said you never considered it? Sounds to me like you've considered it plenty."

Annoyed, Alex swiveled back toward the bar. "She flaunts her assets every chance she gets, and since I'm only human *and* a selfish bastard, the possibilities have crossed my mind. That doesn't mean I want to give her access to any body parts I highly value."

Cleary made a *brawk-brawk* chicken sound.

"So, you do her. Maybe she'd like you better."

"At my age, she'd kill me. Plus I already told you, she scares the shit out of me. Nope, it's all up to you. You're our last hope, Obi-Wan Martinelli."

"You're drunk," Alex retorted, but with a note of fondness for the crazy old coot.

"So are you."

"I must be." He wasn't but still grinned. "It's the only way I'd ever talk about having sex with Miz Cassie Parker Ashton, that's for sure. How the hell am I going to get through the next few weeks without losing my temper a hundred times a day? Goddammit." He sighed. "She really does have all the luck."

"Yup."

"Why? Why her and not me? I'm good at what I do. I work hard. I play by the rules—" God; he sounded like he was six years old. What the hell was wrong with him tonight?

"That's the problem right there," Cleary said, his tone flat. "You have to beg money from the department and from grant agencies, she doesn't. She can go wherever she wants whenever she wants because she doesn't have to answer to a board of directors, teach classes, or write enough papers to keep the money rolling in. She can move faster than we can because she has less bullshit to plow through."

Hardly news to Alex, and it didn't make him feel any better. "I can already hear the jokes in the office, at the conferences: 'Martinelli loses out to Ashton. Again. What's the count by now, Professor? A dozen times? More?'" He stared morosely down at nothing.

"And the jabs at my lack of competency aren't going to be toothless. One of these days, somebody's going to decide their grants will be better spent by a paleontologist who actually finds dinosaurs. And there I'll be, just like—"

*You.*

Alex stopped himself before a word slipped out that he couldn't call back, a word that would be unforgivable and cruel. He couldn't believe he'd thought it, much less almost said it out loud, no matter how bad his mood, and he quickly glanced at the older man to see if Cleary had caught the meaning behind his unfinished sentence.

Cleary was watching him, his pale eyes steady and direct, but with no anger or shock, fortunately. "It's not that bad, Alex."

Brow raised, Alex asked, "Then why am I feeling that being a Ph.D. ain't all it's cracked up to be?"

"Look on the bright side. At least you get respect . . . most of the time," Cleary amended, with a grin that had an uncharacteristically nasty edge.

Since he'd deserved that one, Alex let the comment slide. After finishing off his beer, he decided against ordering another since he was already acting like an idiot. "I can live without respect. What I want are the good discoveries—and there are days I wonder if I'd have been happier doing things her way."

"You're doing it the *right* way, and that's what matters."

Not so long ago, Alex would've agreed without a moment's hesitation. Now, he wasn't so sure.

"I hate that woman," he muttered. "I really do."

"Too bad you can't call Melissa. I bet she could've taken your mind off things."

Christ, the old guy was in a mood himself. "Hey, thanks. I feel so much better, now that you've reminded me what a complete failure I am as a man *and* a paleontologist."

"You need to learn how to look at the positive side of adversity. Listen to me, I'm old. I know things." Cleary grinned. "And sometimes I even remember them."

Alex grinned back. "You think there's a positive side to all this?"

"Sure. At least now you don't have to feel guilty if you hit on Ashton."

"I'm *not* hitting on Ashton!"

Although he couldn't help wondering what sex would be like with the mouthy brunette, with her curly hair and sparking eyes and more attitude stuffed into that tiny frame than seemed humanly possible. But sleeping with the enemy was the last thing Alex could afford.

He slid off the stool and tossed a twenty-dollar bill on the bar. "I'm outta here. I'll see you tomorrow at the dig to make sure everything's covered. Then I'll head over to the Hell Creek lab and sell my soul for the glory of the University of Wyoming."

Cleary waved him off. "Get some sleep. Looks like you need it."

"You're staying?"

"For a while longer. I have some things to think through before I head back to camp."

Alex made his way to his truck, trying to forget Cassie Ashton in her tight dress and how alive she made him feel whenever they clashed. Cleary was right; there was a thin line between love and hate. Or, in this case, lust and hate.

And as much as he hated to admit it, Melissa was right, too. When it came to his work, the spark was gone. It had faded out a long while ago, even though he did a pretty good job keeping up pretenses and telling himself it didn't matter all that much as long as he was pulling in a paycheck.

For some reason, though, the wrongness of that had started to matter to him tonight. For the first time in a long while, he found himself missing the old fire.

As Alex drove back to camp in the thick darkness, he wondered if he could ever find that spark again. Was it even possible, after all this time, to light a fire when it felt as if all he had left inside were ashes?

The longer he thought on it, the clearer it was

that the answer to that question had come to him tonight, sashaying through the door in a skintight dress and high heels. Over the past few years, she'd been the only thing in his life that had made him feel any heat at all. And if he dared to strike a bigger spark off her now, he only hoped it wouldn't leave his pride, and his career, in a heap of smoking ruins.

# Seven

❖

CASSIE TOOK THE DRIVE BACK HOME SLOWER THAN usual, needing the darkness, the peaceful quiet of the truck and nearly empty road to clear her head so she could do a little strategizing—and to calm her jitters.

She wasn't blind to the many risks in dealing with Martinelli. He couldn't be trusted, not with his history of taking the smallest opportunity and turning it against her. He always came away looking good, because technically he never did anything wrong.

But he wasn't the one who had to lay off workers or tell the ones remaining there'd be no holiday bonus. He wasn't the one to run his credit cards too far into the red so that Travis could have a decent Christmas, or—

Why dwell on it? The past was past, and resentment never solved anything.

In a way, though, she couldn't blame him. Martinelli was only doing what he could to survive, same as she was. In the end, only one of them could come out on top, and she was determined that would be her and Hell Creek Fossil Company.

Wrapped up in her grim thoughts, she didn't pay much attention to the headlights reflected in her rearview mirror. It wasn't until the glare became near blinding that she glanced back at the dark truck coming up fast behind her.

"So pass me," she muttered, irritated because the road ahead was wide open.

Probably some tanked-up cowboy on his way home from the bar and feeling like a game of bumper tag.

When the big pickup didn't pass her, Cassie swore under her breath and hit the gas, pushing her old Silverado to its limit to put as much distance as possible between her and the other truck.

The headlights were now pinpricks, which meant the driver must've understood her message.

Then, to her stunned disbelief, the headlights suddenly closed the distance with a frightening speed, and the pinpricks became brilliant circles in her mirror.

What the hell?

A chill skittered up her spine, and the long, open stretch of night highway no longer looked so soothing or peaceful.

Then a sudden jolt snapped her forward with

enough force that her seat belt locked and yanked her back against the seat.

The pickup had rammed her back bumper!

Before she'd barely registered what had happened, the truck plowed into her once more, this time hard enough that the back of her truck fishtailed and she began skidding.

Her heart seemed to stop. She didn't breathe. All she could do was hold on to the steering wheel and struggle to maintain control of her truck. She pumped the brakes, steering to correct the skid, but a heavy old pickup going seventy miles an hour didn't stop on a dime.

She swerved toward the shoulder, praying the gravel would slow her down. Jolts and bumps jarred her to the bone as the wheels left the smooth blacktop, and the steering wheel jerked and jumped in her hands. She fought to hold on to it, frantically trying to steer away from the ditch.

Finally, she brought her truck to a sliding halt, half off the highway. An engine gunned loudly, and the dark truck sped past her. Still frozen in shock, weak with relief, she watched as the truck's red taillights rapidly faded into the distance.

It all couldn't have lasted more than a few seconds, but it had felt like an eternity.

Dear God. Somebody had deliberately tried to run her off the road!

Hands shaking violently, Cassie dropped her head onto the steering wheel, her eyes squeezed shut as she sucked in even, steady breaths. She already felt light-headed, and her heartbeat pounded with sickening thuds in her ears.

She sat there, shivering and gasping, until the roar and rattle of a passing semi snapped her out of her daze. Slowly, she straightened; her hands were still shaking, but not so badly that she couldn't drive. She put the truck in gear and pulled back onto the highway—and tensed at every gleam of headlights in her rearview mirror.

As the miles passed and her nerves settled, Cassie tried to remember any details about the truck. She knew it was a big, dark pickup, and fairly new, but there were nearly as many big, dark Fords, Chevys, and Dodges in Wyoming as there were people.

She considered reporting what had happened to the police, but she had nothing substantial to tell them. What could they do, anyway? Calmer now, she admitted that it was far more likely that a drunk had harassed her out of an alcohol haze of aggression or mischief than that someone had deliberately tried to hurt her.

Who would want to run her off the road?

Alex Martinelli's dark, angry face sprang to mind but she immediately pushed the suspicion away. Martinelli was a lot of unpleasant things, but she couldn't believe he'd take their rivalry to such dangerous extremes.

She hadn't forgotten about that look of undisguised hatred on Don Cleary's face but couldn't believe him capable of such a thing, either. The old man didn't like her, but he'd always been fair with her.

No, it had to be some random asshole. There were plenty of those around, after all.

By the time she pulled into her driveway, she was feeling back to normal, her fear replaced by anger. Her mother had already gone to bed but had left the porch light on for Cassie—and Wyatt as well, since it didn't look like he was home. A glance at the shop showed only dark windows, and she hadn't seen any cars or trucks parked by the lab's back door. Everything looked empty and securely locked for the night.

The night's combined excitements left her with a need to check on her baby rex before calling it a day. She let herself into the shop, turning on only the lights in the display cases. A quick glance showed nothing in need of straightening or restocking, and by the cash register she found a small pile of messages, including one from Travis.

Cassie checked her watch; it wasn't too late, and he'd worry if she didn't call him back. For all his attitude and budding machismo, he could be such a little mother hen. She dialed, and smiled when he picked up on only the second ring.

"Trav, it's me. I just got back and saw your message."

"Hey, Mom. Thanks for calling."

"I see you arrived safe and sound in Laramie. Did you have a nice trip?"

"No. The girls were a pain in the ass."

Correcting his language was a losing battle, and she was too damn tired to play Super Mom tonight. "Remember that they're a lot younger than you, and they're only showing off for their big brother, especially since they don't see you that often."

"I know. It's just really annoying."

She smiled at the exasperation in his voice. "You'll live."

"How'd it go with Professor Martinelli?"

Unlike the other members of her family, Travis seemed to think Martinelli was an okay guy. God knew how he'd come to that conclusion, considering the colorful commentaries on Martinelli's character he must've overheard. "He's coming by tomorrow and we'll start working on the specimen—"

"Trixie. Her name's Trixie, remember? You make her sound like some science experiment instead of a baby."

Her smile widened. "Right. We'll start working on Trixie tomorrow, and I hope we'll get a lot accomplished before I have to head down to New Orleans for Diana's wedding."

"Do you think I can come?"

"Is that what you really want? You'd have to dress up, and there won't be many other kids your age to hang around with."

"But I want beignets."

"I can bring you back some."

"It's not the same, Mom. I know you haven't bought the plane tickets yet, because you always wait to the last minute to save money, so it's no big deal to buy two instead of one. Right?"

It would be an inconvenience to take him, since she was in the wedding party, but it sounded like he really wanted to go, and it wasn't like she'd have to babysit him. "I'll think about it, okay? But if you want to stay an extra week at your dad's, that'd be fine, too."

"Okay. Talk to you later."

Now that he had what he wanted, chat time was over. She smiled again. "Yup. Sleep tight and behave over there."

"Yes, Mother."

She could practically hear him rolling his eyes. "Good night. Love ya."

"Yeah. Me too."

After she hung up the phone, she laughed softly. When had he become such a male? She'd brought him up with open affection, but when boys reached a certain age, saying "I love you" to their mothers was too awkward. And he was undoubtedly getting pointers on guyhood from Wyatt and the ranch hands, none of whom were exactly the sensitive type.

She pulled open the lab door and headed inside, switching on the overhead lights. Even with the lights, it seemed eerily dark and empty, and the narrow heels of her shoes echoed sharply on the concrete floor.

Trixie rested on the workbench where she'd left her, and Cassie touched the cold stone that had blanketed the little body for millions of years, keeping her secrets safely hidden away.

This wasn't luck, this was a miracle: a once-in-a-lifetime miracle.

"Well, little girl, you and I are going to get to know each other very well. I hope you'll behave and tell me your secrets. Every last one of them."

She stood for a while longer, gaze lingering on the plaster-protected bones peeking from the rock, and wondered why she had to swallow back tears when she should be the happiest woman on the planet.

# Eight

❖

WYATT STEPPED OUTSIDE AT DAWN, A MUG OF COFFEE in hand and a bottle of Advil tucked into the back pocket of his jeans, and took a deep breath, smelling the fresh morning air and a faint scent of cattle.

God, he was tired. Too many late nights, too much drinking, and all roads still led back to this: another day feeling like a fifth wheel, another day wondering why, at thirty, he lived at home and took orders from his big sister.

But even when he told himself that he should leave, that Cassie didn't need him at the shop and his mother didn't need his help to run the ranch, he knew it wasn't true. Someday this little ranch would be his, and eventually his sister would realize she couldn't do everything by herself. He'd tried telling her a couple times that working so much on everything but her fossils was making her unhappy, but she'd just yelled at him, he'd lost his temper and yelled back, and as usual, nothing changed.

So he stayed; because his mother worried about him and because every passing year left Cassie looking more worn down.

Why did she keep pushing him away? Every idea for the shop he'd come up with had worked out. He'd suggested adding tours, which were now taking in good money. He basically ran the everyday part of the digging and was a one-man fix-it shop for whatever broke, from truck engines and drills to desk chairs.

By now she should trust him to run the business side of things, so she could get back to doing what she liked best. He'd proved himself. He'd earned it. Hell, he'd stood by her through good times and bad, and he believed in her more than anybody, yet she wouldn't loosen her tightfisted control over everything and let him help—

"Wyatt?"

Startled, he turned a little too quickly, spilling hot coffee down the front of his jeans. He swore under his breath at the stinging burn, barely glancing at the woman in front of him.

He'd recognized that whispery voice, and the last person he wanted to face this morning was Mae.

"Oh, Wyatt! I'm so sorry! I didn't mean . . . here, let me help."

"No, it's okay. Really. I can do it myself and—"

Too late. Mae had already scrambled forward, using the tail of her shirt to wipe at his thighs, working higher as he gritted his teeth and waited for her to realize what she was doing. He didn't have to wait long; when she reached his groin, she stopped abruptly.

Wyatt held back a sigh as she skittered away, blushing pinkly.

"Um, I'm sorry about . . . I didn't think."

"It's okay," he repeated, wanting nothing more than to back away from the painful awkwardness that hovered like a cloud around her. He might not be the smartest guy when it came to women, but he'd have had to be stupid *and* blind not to see she had a thing for him.

"I'm always doing the wrong thing when I'm near you." Mae pushed her glasses up the bridge of her nose, looking so embarrassed that Wyatt was tempted to pat her on the back.

He wasn't heartless; he just didn't feel that way about her—but he at least had the good sense not to touch her. "I never noticed if you did."

She smiled, looking away. "You know that's not true. But it's nice of you to pretend otherwise."

Oh, Christ. He was doomed to live his life surrounded by women who made him feel like an insensitive jerk. "Mae, don't say things like that."

"It's okay. I know I'm not *really* stupid. At least not

about some things, but other things . . ." She trailed off, avoiding his gaze. "Never mind. I'm sorry I bothered you."

As she turned to walk away, he sighed inwardly and said, "Wait. Was there something you needed to ask?"

"It's not important."

Damn, somebody should just shoot him. "C'mon, Mae. You came over here for a reason. Spit it out. I don't bite, I swear it."

She glanced back at him, and he smiled, hoping it looked to her like a "you can talk to me" smile and not an "I wanna stuff you, baby" smile.

Mae squared her shoulders and asked, "Why don't you like me?"

Wyatt froze. Even when wide awake and not hungover, he didn't know how to deal with these things. What the hell was he supposed to say?

"I like you, Mae."

"You're kind to me. That's different. I know I'm not pretty, or funny, or exciting, but I thought . . ."

She trailed off again, and the brave little square of her shoulders rounded, then hunched. Wyatt wanted nothing more than to run like hell, but he couldn't do that. It wouldn't be right. "You thought what?"

Mae gave a soft sigh, then finished in a near whisper: "I thought I'd ask why. I wanted to know. I guess I expected it to make a difference."

Again, he squelched the urge to touch her in any comforting way, knowing it would be the worst thing he could do. "I don't think I can say why. I like you, Mae. I really do; I just don't feel that way about you."

She was bobbing her head up and down before he made it halfway through his stiff reply. "I know, I know. And it wasn't very nice of me to put you on the spot like that. I've never been very good in social situations or making small talk. Forget I said anything about me." She smiled with a false brightness and laughed, but it came out sounding shaky. "You like Amy. I've seen how you look at her."

Wyatt hadn't believed this conversation could get any worse, but it just had. He *did* watch Amy, and liked what he saw, but he would never act on it. First off, his sister would kill him if he had sex with any of her employees. Also, Amy had a tongue on her that could shred the flesh right off a man's bones—and it wasn't like he needed any more of that.

"Yeah, I like Amy. She—she has a lot of energy."

*Energy?* Had he really said something that lame?

"I know. She's pretty and colorful and funny. Everything I'm not. But it's okay," she added quickly. "It's not like I really thought I ever had a chance with you. I just . . . Well, your sister always says that if you want something, you have to go after it."

His sister was stubborn, gutsy, shrewd, and she always landed on her feet. Cassie was everything Mae could never be. And probably shouldn't be. "What works for Cass doesn't work for everybody." He stared down at his coffee mug, wishing it had something far stronger than Folgers instant in it.

Mae smiled a little, and Wyatt realized that she looked softer, even cuter, when she smiled and wasn't all tensed up. "I'm beginning to figure that out, actually. I envy her so much, and I wish I could be like her, but I think she's kind of an original."

"One of Cassie is enough," Wyatt agreed with feeling. Then, shifting so that he came a fraction of an inch closer to her, he added, "Don't be afraid of me, Mae, okay? I like talking with you."

Did that sound bad? Or cruel? He wanted to smooth over the awkwardness but feared he'd only made matters worse.

She was silent for a moment. "Thank you, Wyatt. You really are very kind. Cassie shouldn't fight with you so much."

He smiled ruefully. "Takes two to fight, I guess."

"You're both so much alike. Two alphas fighting for the same territory."

Wyatt wasn't sure he liked being compared to a dog, but he couldn't argue with the logic. "And today we get one more in the mix. Should be fun," he finished glumly. Seeing Mae's confusion, he added, "I'm talking about Martinelli. You've never seen Cassie and Martinelli together, have you?"

Mae shook her head. "Will there be a lot of shouting? I don't like all that . . . conflict."

"Probably. And Cass will be in a bad mood the entire time. Take my advice and steer clear of her unless you don't have any other choice."

"I'll do that. Thanks."

She started to move away, and again he called out to stop her. "Hey. You okay? I don't want you to think . . . I don't want you to feel bad."

"Don't worry. You were honest. That's all that matters."

Wyatt watched her walk back toward the lab, knowing he'd done the right thing as well as he could, but still feeling like shit. What had brought all this on? Why had Mae picked today, of all days, to ambush him?

With another heavy sigh, he headed for the equipment shed. Banging around the innards of an engine was something he could handle, and the closest thing to sanctuary he could hope to find once Martinelli arrived.

Mr. High-and-Mighty had better be damn careful. Cassie couldn't be counted on to see things clearly where that man was concerned, and Wyatt would have to make sure his sister didn't do anything she'd regret. Martinelli always made her crazy.

He glanced back at the lab, but Mae was nowhere in sight.

Hell, there was a lot of crazy going around today.

• • •

Cassie's morning soured the second she walked through the lab door and Mae handed over a phone message, her eyes wider and rounder than usual.

From that alone, Cassie knew it couldn't be good. Still, she had to skim the message slip a second time to be sure she'd read it right. "So . . . Mr. Hayashida would like to buy Trixie and would like me to call back to discuss the matter with his assistant."

"Cassie, I swear nobody—"

"I'm gonna kill him."

Mae paled. "Who?"

"Wyatt, who else?"

"Cassie, I really don't think he—"

"Where is he?"

"He's in the equipment shed with a sick Bobcat," Amy answered. She was wearing red and yellow today, so much silver on her hands that they nearly glowed as she clacked away at the keyboard. "By the way, he's hungover. And cranky."

"What's new?" Cassie retorted tightly, then spun around and marched out the back door, ignoring Mae's anxious calls to calm down.

She headed toward the equipment shed and found her brother exactly where Amy had said he'd be, the top half of him buried in the engine of a Bobcat.

"Hey, Wyatt. Do you happen to know anything

about this? Being stabbed in the back is just the best way to start the day."

He straightened, scowling, his shirt, jeans, face, and hands coated with grease and dust. "What the hell are you talking about?"

Cassie held up the phone message. "After I specifically told *everyone* not to talk about the baby, so I could avoid having to deal with precisely *this*, someone decided that wasn't good business sense and leaked the news." She didn't want to believe it was her brother, but she knew he was itching to run Hell Creek his way, and making her look incompetent would help things along.

He read the note, his face expressionless. "Selling it to a guy like this will bring in a lot more money than letting Martinelli walk away with it for free."

Anger boiled hotly from her head to her toes, leaving her a little light-headed. "I'm not giving it away to Martinelli. If he gets it, he'll have worked and paid for it. You had no right to do this, Wyatt."

"I didn't do it, and it's nice to see you trust me so much that the first person you blame is your own kin."

She wanted to believe him; he was her *brother*. "If you didn't, then who did?"

"Christ, Cassie, it could've been anyone thinking about their bank account and what a big, fat bonus they'd get if you sold that pile of bones in there for what it's worth."

"That so-called pile of bones—"

"Is just a pile of *bones!* That thing's dead. It's been dead a long, long time. But the people who work for you are living, breathing bodies with families to feed and bills to pay. You keep that in mind while you're trying to score points and get into that boys' club you've been chasing after for years."

She stared at him, momentarily speechless with hurt and anger and shock. "I care about my family *and* my employees, Wyatt. But I also care about maintaining the integrity of an important scientific discovery. I'm not doing this just for me, I'm doing it for the sake of future generations."

He burst out laughing. "Integrity, my ass. You wanted to crush Martinelli into dust, and you did, fair and square. But now you're feeling guilty, so instead of doing what's good for you, you want to do what's good for him. Don't bother denying it, Cass. You want his respect, and the respect of those old bastards in their lecture halls and stuffy offices."

"And there's something wrong with earning respect?"

"Why should you give a damn what they think of you? And if that kind of respect is so important to you, why didn't you ever go back to school and get that all-holy Ph.D.?"

"You know why. I had too many responsibilities, and Travis—"

"Excuses don't wash with me. I don't believe anything you've ever done is wrong or not good enough, and I *never* have—but for some reason that makes me the bad guy here."

She stared at her brother, not certain if she wanted to slug him or hug him. Finally, she said softly, "Thank you for that. And I do understand what you're angry about, but that's not the way it is. I admit a little respect would be nice, and so would a lot of money, but that infant rex means more to me than either of those things."

"The hell?"

"It's not something I'd expect you to understand, Wyatt. This was always just work to you, but to me . . ." She trailed off, not sure how to explain to him something she wasn't entirely certain *she* understood. "To me, dinosaurs are more than a job. It goes way, way back to when I was little. When Dad and I—"

Wyatt said gently, "Cassie, he's been dead for over fifteen years. Don't you think it's time you stopped trying to please a man who's no longer around?"

She shook her head before he even finished speaking. "I knew you'd say that. You don't understand how there was this incredible wonder to it back then, when I was a kid, and I want . . ." Again, her words trailed off as she struggled to find the right words. Finally, she sighed. "I suppose I want to find that feeling again, and keep it. Or something like that."

Wyatt looked as if he meant to say something but

instead turned back to the engine. She watched him for a moment longer, then said, "I noticed your truck has a broken headlight."

He didn't look at her. "Somebody took it out the other night when I was parked at Missy's place."

Missy was his current bed partner, a barmaid Ellen highly disapproved of. "You're sure?"

Wyatt turned. "As sure as I can be, since I wasn't there when it happened. I'll get it fixed soon, if that's what you're worried about."

Cassie hesitated, wanting to confide in him about what had happened last night and ask his opinion, but she realized, belatedly, that the way she'd asked about the headlight would make him think she was accusing him. Instead of talking, they'd fight, and she'd end up feeling smothered beneath a ton of guilt again. She'd handled this badly; she was always handling things badly with Wyatt.

Suddenly, he straightened and frowned. "Maybe you ought to ask Martinelli if he spilled your big secret."

"What big secret?"

Startled by the deep, familiar voice behind her, Cassie turned.

Alex Martinelli had arrived earlier than she'd anticipated. He stood in front of her in worn jeans, scuffed hiking boots, and an old navy T-shirt beneath a red cotton shirt, looking lean and vital and rapacious as ever. His hat was pulled low, and he was tall enough and wide-shouldered enough to block out the sun. And she didn't need to see his eyes to read his mood. She could practically feel his dark mood radiating outward, curling around her.

Instinctively, she backed away from him, only to be brought short by Wyatt behind her, filling her with the uncomfortable sensation of being trapped between Wyatt's simmering anger and Martinelli's barely leashed hostility.

Did she bring out the best in people, or what?

"I said, what big secret?" Martinelli repeated.

"Some Japanese businessman called with an offer to buy my baby rex. Somebody blabbed. Was it you?"

"You didn't tell me until yesterday. I'd have had to move pretty damn fast to do that." He tipped back his hat, revealing dark eyes filled with frustration and a wry amusement. "And I would've had to have had a complete personality transplant in the last twelve hours, too. I'm the slut for glory, remember? That baby spells glory in capital letters."

"Point taken." Cassie shot a look at her brother. "I know you've met before, but I don't believe we've ever done the formal introduction thing. Martinelli, this is my brother, Wyatt. He oversees field operations and works tours. Wyatt, this is Alex Martinelli. I think you know what he does."

The two men sized each other up, and Martinelli smiled, despite Wyatt's undisguised dislike. At least neither man was foolish enough to offer the other his hand for a congenial shake.

"Lovely! Now that the niceties are out of the way, let's go to the lab." Cassie turned, trusting Martinelli to follow. She was still angry about the phone call. Not to mention absolutely baffled about who could've been so careless—or malicious—as to disregard her orders.

"So who has the big mouth?"

"I don't know, but I'll find out." She glanced up at him. "You're sure you didn't say anything?"

He didn't answer, and a sinking sense of dread pulled her to an abrupt stop. "Goddammit, Martinelli, you *told!*"

One thing about the man, he held his emotions close to the surface and had all the guile of her fifteen-year-old.

"Just Cleary," he said quickly, barely avoiding crashing into her. "I needed to tell him something about why I had to be here, and he wouldn't talk. He wouldn't have any more reason than I would to try to sell your fossil out from under you, much less to a guy from Japan. Where do you think we'd get contacts like that? And in such a short time? Unlike you, we're not in the retail business."

"Everybody has an excuse, yet somebody said something." She rounded the corner to the back of the lab. "From here on out, you can park here and come in through the back door. I don't want you walking through the shop. The fewer people who know you're here, the better."

"I've always wanted to be somebody's dirty little secret."

"Oh, shut up," Cassie said, irritably. "I'm already having a really bad day and it's hardly eight in the morning. I don't have time to fight with you, or the energy to be clever and witty."

She swung open the heavy door and walked inside. Martinelli followed, keeping his mouth shut for a change. Most of her crew had gathered in the lab, hanging around and talking—and likely preparing for the boss's detonation.

All eyes turned to Martinelli, and she wondered briefly if he suddenly felt like a big ol' *T. rex*, no longer top dog in his territory and facing down a pack of rivals waiting to tear him limb from limb.

God knew it was how she'd felt half the times she'd ventured into *his* territory.

"Most of you already know Dr. Martinelli. For those of you who don't . . . well, now you do." She stood in the middle of the lab, crowded on all sides by specimens in various stages of cleaning, buckets of dirt and rock, plaster dust and casings, tools, the quiet hum of computers and power tools. Over it all, the old Bunn gurgled and spat as it pumped out its zillionth pot of thick, black coffee.

"And as I'm sure most of you have heard by now, I have an offer on the table for Trixie. Which means somebody said something they shouldn't have, and I want to know who."

Asking for a confession was a long shot, and she wasn't surprised when nobody stepped forward. As she glanced around the room, an oppressive sense of despair bore down on her. Any one of those gathered around her *could've* done it—and with good reason.

Still, she doubted Amy, Mae, or Betty, the middle-aged woman who scheduled tours and took care of the daily ranch business, would've said anything. For them, working at the lab was a sweet little deal, and they were the types who wouldn't be happy working a nine-to-five office job. Her equipment operators and fieldworkers had only heard about the find within the last few days and didn't have connections to wealthy overseas businessmen. Russ Noble was her newest employee, but he freelanced for the novelty of it and had nothing to gain.

Then again, he'd been responsible for finding the fossil, and money could be a powerful inducement. He was one of the few who'd known about Trixie long enough to have had time to make contacts. But he didn't strike her as the sneaky type.

Then there was her mother. Ellen Parker had made it clear that she disliked the stressful atmosphere around Hell Creek lately, and that she thought it was time to turn the business over to Wyatt so Cassie could do more important things, like get married and "settle down."

Whatever the hell *that* meant.

If it were her mother, Cassie would find out soon enough. If it were Wyatt . . . well, she'd fire him. It would be hard, but it would have to be done. There was no excusing this kind of behavior, even from family.

And despite Martinelli's reasonable explanations, he wasn't off her list either, especially since he'd admitted to telling one person, right after she'd told him pointedly *not* to talk.

Did everybody think she issued orders just for the hell of it?

The silence had gone on long enough, and she let out a sigh. "All right, if anybody hears anything about this call, I want to know. And if it was somebody here in this room and it was an honest mistake, I'd appreciate it if you'd come clean. The damage has already been done. At this point, we'll just have to prepare for the calls that'll come in and the curious who'll stop by. For now, please get back to whatever you were doing. Martinelli and I will be working on the baby, and prepping this specimen is a top priority for the next few weeks."

There was a murmur of assent, and Cassie turned to Martinelli. He was scrutinizing her lab, his expression flat, not missing a single detail.

"Come this way," she said after a moment. "You want coffee?"

Martinelli shook his head. "Right now, I want to see if you've got what it takes to back up your big words."

Hmmm. Maybe he hadn't been spying, only looking for Trixie. She'd have to put aside her knee-jerk distrust of him if they were going to work together for any length of time.

All the same, she flashed him a smug smile. "Sorry to disappoint you, but I've got everything I need to back up my big words."

She led him to the table, pulled off the protective covering, and stood back to take in his reaction.

He approached the table as if he were approaching a holy relic, each step slow and careful. His chest rose sharply, and then she heard him let out a long breath.

"Beautiful, isn't she?"

Martinelli only nodded.

They'd uncovered a fair amount of the remains while still in the field, and she could see his gaze moving along the curved bones of the ribs, the unmistakable lower jaw, a tiny three-toed claw. Most of the remains were obscured by sedimentary rock, but he could tell that the bones were articulated, which boded well for a nearly intact skeleton inside, just waiting for them to coax it out.

"We excavated her surroundings, of course, and my lab people are processing the results now. From what we can tell so far, she died in early spring and was probably caught in a flash flood. There were remains of shallow-water dwelling animals with her."

"You still think it's a female?" Martinelli was bent over the jaw, examining where bone ended and rock began.

"Still no evidence one way or the other since we haven't uncovered the first tail chevron yet, but because she's so small, everybody settled into calling her a 'her,' even though the female rex was larger than the male. As I said, my instincts tell me Trixie is indeed a girl."

He half-turned toward her. "Can I touch her?"

"Go for it. We're going to be spending a lot of time with her, so you might as well introduce yourself."

He had fine and long fingers, she thought. Rough, but gentle. He carefully examined the remains, seemingly oblivious to those watching him, and Cassie could sense a grudging, wary respect for him because of it.

Nor did she miss Amy frankly checking out his rear as he bent over the worktable. Cassie hardly blamed her; he had a purely physical aura about him, rough and earthy, and she liked the look—more than overly developed muscles that told her a guy spent hours in a gym. Martinelli's lean, edgy good looks came from hard work.

Finally Cassie moved in, as conversation and activity in the lab slowly returned to normal. Keyboards clicked, chair casters clattered on the hard concrete floor, and the high-pitched whine of an air-brade filled the silence.

"So," she said at length. "What do you think?"

"Incredible." Martinelli glanced up, the look in his eyes serious. "I think you're right and she's intact, or very close to it."

Cassie nodded, moving closer. "I'm hoping that we get skin impressions and, if the skull is there, scans of the brain. If these babies were feathered, as some are theorizing, maybe we'll find evidence of that as well."

He straightened, nodding, and looked around. It was hardly the first time he'd been in her lab, but it was the first time he'd had to work in it, and she could tell he was evaluating, weighing. "What resources do you have here?"

She grinned. "Whatever you need. Ask, and you'll get it."

He arched a brow. "Looks like you run a first-class lab."

"And you doubted that I did?"

He surprised her with a rueful smile. "I've never doubted your abilities, Ashton. Just your ethics."

His answer raised little prickles of anger, despite her best efforts to keep calm, but she managed to bite back her usual retort. "My ethics are adequate to the occasion. You haven't answered my question. What do you need?"

"Probably a cup of coffee. And before I do anything, I want to look at your notes. Who found her?"

"That'd be me." It was Russ Noble. He'd been hovering, waiting for the opportunity to enter the conversation. "Or more accurately, it was one of the volunteers on my dig. An eighty-something guy who was there with his grandson. I tell you, that was one excited duo."

"I bet." Martinelli turned to her. "Did the old guy or his grandson know what they discovered?"

"It's hard to hide that kind of information," Cassie said. "Everybody gets excited over the bigger finds."

"So that makes even more people who could've spilled your secret," he pointed out. "And you did cover your ass on this, right?"

An awkward silence followed, and Cassie knew he was remembering the same courtroom drama she was.

"Hell Creek Fossil Company now has its own lawyer, and Allan Folkes is responsible for covering my ass. I don't so much as put a toe on a piece of land until he's cleared it legally, no matter how accommodating or nice the landowners may act. These days, I'm erring on the side of paranoid caution."

Martinelli grunted. "Smart."

"Especially since you can bet people are going to do everything in their power to discredit my findings or meddle just for the hell of it. When something this important is involved, not to mention money, all the greedy and nasty bastards come creeping out of the woodwork."

He had the good sense to keep quiet, well aware she'd classified him in the "nasty bastard" category.

To cover the continued awkwardness, she said, "I'll get you coffee and the notes and plots. Most of it's still rough, but there's a few computer files you can go through, as well. Mae's collecting data on the organic remains found with Trixie, so you can talk to her about that. In case I forgot to introduce you, Mae's the brunette with the lab coat and glasses."

Martinelli waved. Mae turned pink. Cassie frowned and muttered, "And if I catch you trying to pick up any of my employees, you will regret it."

"Contrary to your peculiar beliefs, I *don't* sleep with anything that breathes," he retorted, annoyance plain on his face.

"Forgive me for not trusting you. After all, you have a habit of screwing me over. Now sit," she ordered. "And what do you take?"

His look was innocent. "Anything I can get away with."

"I meant the coffee, and you know it."

"I do?"

Cassie frowned, almost as irritated with herself— and that little, inner flutter of attraction—as she was with him for flirting when they *both* knew he had a girlfriend squirreled away.

"Behave," she ordered peevishly. "If you don't, I can't guarantee you'll walk out of here today in one piece, considering I'm in a really, *really* bad mood."

He only laughed. "Thanks for the warning, but I can handle anything you throw at me, Ashton."

"Hmph. We'll see about that."

Challenge issued. His eyes gleamed with a familiar light, telling her the challenge had been accepted.

So much for a nice little truce.

# Nine

❖

ALEX WATCHED ASHTON WALK AWAY, APPRECIATING the fine curves in her tight denim. He felt a twinge of guilt for eyeing her so soon after having parted ways with Melissa, but only a twinge.

This *was* Ashton, after all, and in his own way he'd had a longer relationship with her than he'd had with any other woman, his ex-wife included.

Crazy, dysfunctional, unhealthy . . . but true.

He turned back to the business at hand, and a pang of longing spread over him. God, this little fossil was the most beautiful thing he'd ever seen. She looked as if she'd simply fallen asleep . . . nearly 70 million years ago. For all that time, she'd lain curled in her cradle of sediment, waiting for someone to find her and bring her to the light again.

The dark-haired man who'd found Trixie moved closer. "You look impressed."

"Hard not to be," Alex answered. "What's your name? Cassie didn't say."

"Russ." The man turned to look at the exposed bones on the table. "I may have found her, but Cassie and Wyatt did most of the hard work to get her here. As soon as Cassie heard the news, she came up and went to work while the rest of us watched." He motioned at the table. "So is this what she said it is?"

"Oh, yeah."

"So she did good, huh?"

Alex didn't pretend to misunderstand. "That woman's got the devil's own luck." He turned back to the worktable. This time, the sense of longing came with a familiar rush of healthy, natural envy. "And a lot of talent."

The main lab line was ringing when Cassie returned with the coffee. Amy picked up, then yelled across the room, "Cassie! It's that Hayashida guy on the phone again. Um . . . actually, it's his assistant, because the other one doesn't speak English. Anyway, he says he won't talk to anybody but you."

"Oh, for God's sake, I don't have the time to—"

"You might as well take it. He's not going to give up," Mae said, looking glum.

If she ever found out who'd tattled about Trixie, forget mercy. Leaving Martinelli alone with the baby, under the watchful eyes of both Mae and Russ,

Cassie walked to the phone at her desk a short distance away and picked it up.

"This is Cassie Ashton. How may I help you?"

The voice on the other end was pleasant and heavily accented, but easy to understand. "Miss Ashton, thank you for taking my call. I am Hanshiro Katayama, assistant to Mr. Hayashida."

It was an effort to remain as polite as her caller, but she did her best. "Yes. I know why you're calling, and I'm sorry to have to tell you that the fossil is not for sale at this time. It's likely I won't offer it for sale at all, considering its importance."

Over the next fifteen minutes, through the unflaggingly polite Mr. Katayama, she learned that Mr. Hayashida was aware of the fossil's importance, and that he was eager to place it with a respectable museum in Tokyo. The man had plenty of cash and wasn't a crackpot. For any other specimen, she'd have gladly done business with the guy, but not this time. For all his respectfulness, Mr. Hayashida's assistant was also distressingly persistent.

By the time she managed to get off the phone, what little was left of her patience was shot. Fortunately, the lab had begun to clear out as everybody went about his or her daily routine. The shop opened, and Russ and Wyatt had taken a group of dinosaur enthusiasts on a two-hour hunting trip for common fish and turtle fossils at the old riverbed on their land. It was one of the easier ways to make a little extra cash, although Cassie had no patience for these excursions. Amazingly, Wyatt did.

"So, where do you want to start?" she asked, as Martinelli sipped his coffee and thumbed through field notes and diagrams, eyes flicking over details.

"Clear the skull," he said without hesitation. "We need to make sure it's all there or your little discovery is going to be a lot less exciting."

"Fine. Once we get going, please deposit all detritus in the labeled buckets over there. Mae will go through them for any organic remains."

He arched a brow. "I do know how this works, you know."

Her face warmed. "Sorry. Sometimes I get a little bossy."

"I never would've guessed."

She opened her mouth to retort, thought better of it, and instead sat down beside him and began working. Before long, she was lost in the painstaking process.

Halfway through the morning, Ellen called Cassie to talk to the first reporter.

Alex watched her go, knowing how frustrated she must be at the interruption. But it would've happened sooner or later, and getting it out of the way sooner was best. Cassie wanted him to keep a low profile, but he wouldn't hide. The more attention he earned by being associated with the fossil from the beginning, the better his chances of getting his hands on it permanently. He hoped.

Cassie returned in an even worse mood, and he watched her work in silence for a while, observing how she exorcised her anger in the process—and noticing she did *good* work. Meticulous, cautious, and with far more patience than he would've expected.

Being this close to her, he also noticed she smelled really nice. On a certain level, he'd always been aware she was pretty, sexy, and desirable, but he'd never really looked at her as just a woman—or for that matter, as the boss of an impressive laboratory facility with an equally impressive staff.

Suddenly aware that he was being watched as well, Alex shifted around to find the surly brother standing a short distance away. Alex remembered this particular Parker, as they'd gotten into a small ruckus a few years back over a supposed insult to Cassie. It looked like the younger man had a temper to rival his sister's, but less willingness to live and let live.

Alex turned back to Cassie. "So what'd the reporter want?"

"He heard we found an intact infant rex and wanted to verify it was true."

"And what did you tell him?"

"I told him it was indeed a juvenile, and there was

a possibility that the specimen was in good shape, but I couldn't say more than that."

"News travels fast."

"This is Wyoming. When not tending the ranch, nobody has anything else to do except gossip and poke their noses in other people's business. Of course news travels fast."

He heard the frustration in her voice. "You said yourself you couldn't keep it a secret for long. It's remarkable you kept it quiet even this long."

Cassie sighed and put down her dental pick. "I know, but I wanted to have her ready for viewing before I sprang her on the scientific community. Sort of a coup d'état, I guess. Once the deed was done and done well, there'd be less shit to deal with."

She was close enough that he could feel her warmth, and remembering what Cleary had said in the bar last night, Alex wondered if it really would've been that easy to end the bad blood between them with a quick tussle in bed. Something told him not. Then again, it might've been fun to try.

He blanked out the burgeoning images of a naked Cassie in his bed and asked, "Where's your kid?"

"With his father. Travis usually spends a few weeks with his dad before school starts, but I thought it best for him to leave a little earlier. With tempers around here shooting off like bottle rockets, he's better off prowling the malls in Laramie and conning his dad out of new toys. Who's babysitting your dig?"

As she talked, he glanced through the data her team had collected. So far, he couldn't find any fault. A few quirks, perhaps, but he couldn't have asked for more from his own team.

"Don Cleary," he replied. "He's been at this so long he can do it in his sleep."

"God, he's practically prehistoric himself. Is he ever going to retire? You'd think after all this time, he'd throw in the trowel, so to speak."

Alex grinned. "Nice quip."

She glanced up, a faintly startled look on her face. "What was that? Did I just hear you say something nice about me?"

"Fishing for compliments, are we?" He gave a short sigh. "You run a top lab, Ashton. You do good work."

She grinned at him. "I always told you I was good, but you were too arrogant to listen."

"All's fair in love, war, and bone hunting."

She blinked. "So it would seem."

Alex wondered why she looked so startled, then shrugged it off as he turned to Trixie. "Shit, I still can't believe she's in such good shape."

"I know. I spent days pinching myself, to make sure it was real. I really lucked out on this one."

When she glanced up, Alex realized that his mouth was only inches from hers—and that she really *was* a fine-looking woman. He liked the scattering of freckles on her tanned face, and the little lines around her eyes that only accentuated their darkness and thick lashes. She had a wide, generous mouth, and a wild mane of corkscrew curls that begged for a man's hands to smooth it away from her face.

Damn Cleary. If he hadn't brought up the possibility of hooking up with Ashton, Alex wouldn't even be thinking like this.

She eased back a bit. "Did you want to do some cleaning?"

"Are you ready for a break?"

"Nah. I could do this for hours, but I'm trying to be nice."

He quickly switched places with her, hoping he didn't come across as too eager, then took the dental pick she'd just abandoned. Very carefully, he started to scratch away the matrix of rock.

"You mean all that hard-ass talk was just an act?"

"Don't worry; your worst suspicions about me are still true." She yawned, stretching back until her small breasts pressed against her red T-shirt—a view he couldn't help but appreciate.

"I can't sit still and watch, though. I'm going to clean the tail vertebrae while you work on the jaw."

Ashton pulled a stool toward her, its legs scraping on the concrete floor, and they worked in a companionable silence for quite a while. It occurred to Alex that even their cleaning styles were similar: neither liked to talk. Frowning at the thought, he broke the silence: "Hey. Ashton."

"Yeah?" She looked up, peering over her safety glasses.

"Thanks."

She looked momentarily confused but quickly recovered and rolled her eyes. "Don't go soft on me, Martinelli. And don't for a minute forget I had my own reasons for asking you here."

"And don't for a minute forget I had my own reasons for agreeing."

Her expression turned wary. "I know, and in the event I ever forget, everybody in my lab will be quick to remind me that you're an untrustworthy bastard who'll take me for everything you can get."

Nothing like having his own words thrown back in his face. "It'd be boring if it were too easy."

She snorted. "I believe excitement is overrated. There's something to be said for predictability and ease; life shouldn't always be a struggle."

He hadn't expected that response. "No, but if it's too easy, we start taking it for granted and forget all the little stuff that makes it worthwhile."

She went still, then returned to work without saying another word.

# Ten

✦

By the time Martinelli had left at a little after six, Cassie had the beginning of a migraine. Why, oh why, had she been born the overly emotional type? Even minor stress took its toll on her.

Their first day together had gone better than she'd expected. There hadn't been any bloodshed, so that had to count for something.

Rubbing absently at the stiff muscles of her shoulder, she walked into the shop as her mother was locking up, the register noisily cashing itself out. Glancing over her shoulder, Ellen asked, "How'd it go with your paleontologist?"

Cassie hitched herself up on the counter, then poked around the register for the bottle of Tylenol; her mother always kept a spare on hand. "It went well, if you don't count the calls from the reporter and the Japanese guy who wants to buy a fossil that nobody was supposed to know about."

She caught her mother's gaze, searching for any sign of guilt, hoping not to find any—and her mother, looking away, answered, "I didn't do it. I know how important that thing is to you."

Cassie held back a sigh. "That's good to know."

"But the fact that you'd suspect your own family is enough to make me cry. Can't you see what this is doing to you? I'm tired of seeing you and Wyatt fight, and I don't like how you send Travis away when you don't have time for him—"

"Mom, don't go there. He would've been leaving at the end of the week anyway, and he's fifteen, not two. He's hardly a neglected child."

"I still don't like how everything has changed. There was a time when this was only a side business bringing in a little extra money. Lately, it seems there's hardly an hour when you're not working, and now we have to watch our every word so we don't say something to the wrong person. I don't think it's good for you anymore. Just give the thing to that Martinelli man and let him deal with all the troubles. It's his job, after all."

Not trusting herself to keep from saying something she'd only regret later, Cassie didn't answer for a long while. She finally said, "And it's my job, too. I know things have been tense around here for a while, but handing over this fossil to somebody else isn't the answer."

Silence fell between them, bringing back memories of years full of conflict and resentment.

Ellen wanted to see Cassie married and with children, and while Cassie sometimes missed having a man around—and not just for the sex—she didn't mind not being married. She'd already had a kid, so she had time to wait for the right guy to come along. Unfortunately, she could never make her mother see her point of view.

It hurt; it always had and always would, that they couldn't connect at such a basic level as understanding what made the other happy. "Look," Cassie said to her mother, "I know you never wanted me to take up this line of work, but I can't be what you want me to be. I'm not going to change, you're not going to change, and going through this again and again solves nothing."

"Cassie, honey, I only want you to be happy. You're a young woman yet, and I see you working so hard but never taking any time for yourself. I'm afraid that one day you'll wake up and realize you're old and alone. And you'll regret it."

The tremor of emotion in Ellen's voice kept Cassie's temper in check, because she sensed her mother was really talking about herself.

"I'm not alone. And neither are you. If you want a break, ask somebody in the lab to take over for you; Tom will drive up here and take you back to Cheyenne or Laramie. And if you're tired of working at the shop, there are plenty of people around here who can take over. Travis is getting old enough that he'll want a job soon. If you want to spend more time with your friends, that's fine."

"Is that supposed to make me feel better? That I'm so easily replaceable?"

Cassie rubbed at the pounding ache between her brows. "You know that's not what I meant. I'm trying to help, but there's only so much I can do."

"Maybe I should take a little time off," her mother said, in one of those lightning-quick changes of mood that always left Cassie off balance—until the exasperation kicked in. "Unless you get rid of that thing, it's only going to get worse. I told you it'd turn into a circus. Look what happened to those folks in South Dakota a few years back: the National Guard, the FBI—"

"Yes, but that won't happen here. The worst we'll have to put up with is a barrage of ringing phones and lines of gawkers wanting to see the lab. Look, Mom, why don't you go back to the house? I'll finish straightening up in here."

"You sure?"

"Yeah. I need some quiet time to unwind."

"What about dinner?"

"Mae brought in pizza. I'm set."

"You're not eating right."

Cassie let an edge slip into her voice. "Mom, I'm thirty-six. I know how to make myself a sandwich if I get hungry. You go on."

With a long-suffering sigh, Ellen handed over the key ring, then left, shutting the door behind her.

"Ah. Blessed silence." Cassie leaned back against the sales counter. Already, it seemed as if her headache had begun to fade. This small room was the heart of the whole business, and when Cassie felt uncertain about herself or where life might be taking her, she always came here to find an answer.

Or at least a little peace, here where nobody asked anything of her. Here was the closest she'd ever come to being a kid again, that magical time when her only worries were school, boys, clothes, and who was dating whom.

She'd spent a lot of time in the shop with her father, and her mother had been fond of saying it was because John Parker was the eternal child, and in Cassie he'd found the perfect partner in crime.

They'd gone rock hunting and scoured for fossils. He'd patiently listened to her spin dreams and ramble about whatever came to her mind, and she'd been a curious kid who asked a lot of questions. When she was with her father, she felt a sense of belonging, a freedom of being herself, and being understood. Too often, with the others, she'd been left feeling like the family freak.

God, she still missed him. His death had changed her whole life. Some of it, she knew, was her own choice, but the rest . . . what else could she have done?

Despite Wyatt's arguments, there hadn't been anyone but her to step into the void. Her mother had been helpless with grief and confusion, and Wyatt and Tom too young to take on adult responsibilities. Not that she'd been much of an adult herself at twenty. She'd left college to put affairs back in order at home, telling herself it would be for only a short while—and sixteen years later, she was still here.

At times like this, when the place was quiet and night was settling in and she had time simply to think, she could admit that more than an unplanned pregnancy and a hurried marriage had put an end to her youthful dreams. More and more over the years, she realized that she'd unconsciously sabotaged her chances of going back to school. After all, who could ever blame her for choosing a baby over school? But what was the point in analyzing why? She couldn't go back and change anything; she could only go on.

Pushing away from the counter, Cassie went around to the back of the display case and started dusting and rearranging. She pulled out a 9-inch allosaurus claw, admiring its cleanly lethal lines. Pure killing perfection.

The work always soothed her, and she hardly noticed the passing time or the gathering darkness outside.

Until she heard a sound from in the lab.

The memory of that dark truck forcing her off the highway flashed across her mind, and for a moment she went still with fear.

Ridiculous. No one was out to get her, she was just tense because it had been an unusually stressful day.

Besides, she'd locked up and checked everything herself. It was possible Wyatt, Mae, or Amy had come back to work, but it had been a long day for them as well, and they'd seemed anxious to call it quits.

Frowning, Cassie cracked open the lab door and called, "Wyatt? Is that you?"

A sense of danger niggled at the back of her mind.

Grabbing the baseball bat her mother always kept behind the counter, she carefully opened the door, ready to slam it shut at the first whiff of trouble.

A plaintive meow sounded, and something small and soft brushed against her leg.

"Damn cat." With a sigh of relief, she looked down at the little calico bundle of fur twining around her ankles. "You must've missed that lecture about curiosity and cats."

"Who on earth are you talking to?"

The voice echoed from the dim interior of the lab. Cassie jumped and screamed, sending the kitten skittering away. An answering shriek came from Mae's workstation.

"Mae?"

"Yes!" The light at Mae's desk suddenly snapped on. "Wow, you scared the crap out of me . . . don't scream like that!"

"You scared me first," Cassie retorted, her heart still thumping a million beats a minute. "What are you doing here?"

"I forgot my cell phone and came back to get it. My mother's sick again, so I need to keep a phone close by in case she calls."

"Oh. Sorry to hear that." Mae's mother was a textbook hypochondriac, and Cassie wondered how Mae had the patience to deal with it. "What is it this time?"

"Knee surgery, probably."

"You should've just come through the shop. I'd already locked up the back door for the night."

"I know, but you looked busy and I didn't want to disturb you, so I let myself in."

"You saw me in the shop? I didn't even hear your car pull in."

Mae laughed. "You were deep in Dino Zone. I was standing right there at the door, but you were staring at that big claw. So I went around back."

Embarrassed at having been caught mooning, Cassie managed a smile. "Dino Zone? Is that what everyone calls it?"

"Travis does, and the rest of us sort of picked up on it."

The embarrassment doubled. "Um . . . am I in the Dino Zone a lot?"

"Yes, but we all know it just means you're dedicated. You were in that zone all day today. Then again, if I had a man who looked like Professor Martinelli at my side, I wouldn't notice the coming of the apocalypse."

Cassie blinked, then made a dismissive sound. "I don't think of Martinelli that way. We were both in our Dino Zones, concentrating."

"While the rest of us were waiting for the maiming to begin. You guys were so polite to each other it was boring."

Cassie smiled. "No show today, huh?"

"Amy said you two can be very entertaining when you go at it," Mae admitted sheepishly.

"The situation was too important for either of us to act like our usual idiot selves." Cassie sighed. At moments like this, she really missed Diana and Fiona. She wanted to girl-talk about Alex Martinelli, but Mae wasn't the girl-talk type. The poor thing didn't seem to have much of a life outside of work.

Though, Cassie thought, the same could probably be said of her lately.

"He really is very good-looking."

"And knows it," Cassie replied. "The man's not just a total slut for glory, he's a slut, period. You should've seen him with this twenty-something blonde last night. Every time I run into him, some female's either draped around him or panting after him. It's kind of irritating."

"Is that why you dress up when you go see him? So he notices you?"

The question took Cassie by surprise. "Maybe. It's part of the whole competition thing. Even though I'm not competing with those girls for that kind of attention," she added hastily. "Martinelli and I have been jabbing at each other for so long, I don't even think about why I do what I do anymore."

"He doesn't seem nearly as bad as everybody said. I thought he was nice." Mae hitched her purse up. "Well, I should go. I'll see you tomorrow."

"Bright and early, as always." Cassie waved her off. Then, to be safe, she did a quick walk-through of the lab, retrieving the spooked kitten from behind a pile of printouts and gently putting her outside. Finally she checked to make sure Trixie was still on her table, tucked away for the night beneath a protective sheet. Then she shut out the lights and headed to the house to collapse in her bed.

# Eleven

SLEEP DIDN'T COME EASILY, AND WHEN IT FINALLY did, Cassie dreamed of being hunted.

In the dream, she ran and ran, but never fast enough or far enough. Clawed hands reached out from everywhere to pull her down. No matter where she tried to hide, the hands kept grabbing, clawing at her hair, covering her mouth until she couldn't breathe.

She woke gulping for air, shaking with lingering terror. Her sleep T-shirt was damp with perspiration, and tears inexplicably gathered at the back of her throat, thick and hot.

It took a long while to fall back asleep, and when her alarm went off she seriously considered smashing it into a million pieces.

Her eyelids feeling swollen and scratchy, she rolled out of bed and plodded toward the shower. Afterward she ran a comb through her wet hair, dabbed on lipstick and concealer for the dark shadows under her eyes, then pulled on jeans, an old denim shirt, and her boots.

She headed to the lab, walking around to the back. To her surprise, the door was already open, and she heard low voices inside. Who was here this early? She was almost always the first person in the lab.

"Hello?" she called. "Who's here?"

"Hey, Cassie!" Amy's cheerful voice answered. "I came in early to get some work done, and Dr. Martinelli was waiting outside when I got here, so I let him in. We're trading California stories. Did you know he's from Berkeley?"

Score another for the Martinelli charm—no easy feat, since Amy wasn't a pushover. But she seemed quite chummy with the man, sitting close to him and drinking coffee.

Martinelli looked disgustingly alert, and Cassie had a sudden, intense urge to pinch the man just because he had no right to look that good so early in the day.

She sighed. "Yes, I know he's from Berkeley. Though at this point he's gone completely native."

There was nothing stereotypically "California" about him. He'd never fit the blond surfer boy image; not with his broody Italian looks. And factoring in the jeans, denim shirt, and battered white Resistol hat, he appeared more ranch hand than Berkeley alum.

Martinelli grinned. "Somebody wake up cranky?"

"I slept like shit," she retorted. "Amy, if you came in here to get work done, it's not going to happen sitting on your ass there."

"Ooookay," Amy said, a shade too brightly. "I can take a hint, especially when it hits me on the head like a brick. I've got payroll, and a bunch of stuff Mae gave me from yesterday to run analyses on. You got anything for me besides that?"

"Whatever Mae gave you is probably what I need, so make that a priority after the payroll. Where's Wyatt?"

"Don't know. Not my turn to babysit him. He's probably on his way to Turtle Creek; I'm pretty sure Betty said he's got a group going out there early this morning."

Meaning it would be quiet in the lab today. Cassie turned to Martinelli. "You look all bright and eager. Guess it wasn't a late night for you, huh?"

"If you're fishing for details, I slept alone last night."

"Like I care who you sleep with," she retorted and headed for Trixie's table, ignoring Martinelli's lazy grin as he followed her.

As she pulled out her stool, a suspicious item on her side of the worktable caught her attention: a styrofoam cup and white bakery bag smelling of fried sugary goodness.

"What do you call *that?*" She pointed at her desk.

Martinelli glanced at the bag, then back at Cassie. "Uh . . . I call it breakfast."

"Mmm-hmm. Looks like a bribe to me. You're not trying to sweeten me up with fresh donuts and decent coffee, are you?"

"Gee, it's not working?"

She sighed. "You thought it would?"

"It works for me. I'm easy."

"Tell me something half the women in Wyoming don't already know."

"Hey." He put his coffee down. "What are you, thirty-something going on three?"

"Oooh, classic male avoidance maneuver. Well done."

"Oh, for Chrissake." He looked annoyed. "Since when did enjoying life become a crime?"

"It's not, providing you don't leave any roadkill behind as you zip along your Happy Highway."

"Ah." He leaned back. "Meaning legions of weeping women."

"It wouldn't be half so bad if they *were* women," Cassie retorted. "But you date little girls."

"I do not date girls." He scowled. "They've all been at least twenty-one."

Cassie burst out laughing. "Like that makes a difference."

"You're just jealous because you're all alone."

Why was he moving so close? "Some call it alone. I call it self-sufficiency."

"And a lot of guys I know would call it something else."

Heat washed over her, but she refused to believe it was anything more than embarrassment or irritation. "Ah, yes—any woman who's not panting after a man must be frigid or a lesbian. Hate to break it to you, but I happen to like men. I just don't necessarily want to own another one."

He laughed, and Cassie was vaguely aware of the table's hard edge bumping against her bottom.

When had she started backing up?

Martinelli smiled, showing a little too much tooth in a predatory way.

"Um, you know, I think I'm going to step outside," Amy announced loudly. "It's a little hard to concentrate on spreadsheets with all the yelling. And since all the yelling is about sex, now I need a smoke."

Cassie, cornered between the table and some 180 pounds of aggressive male with dubious intentions, barely noticed Amy's departure.

"I like women, too. Looks like we've reached common ground."

She wasn't sure what he meant, and didn't intend to find out. No more retreating; this was *her* lab, and *she* was the one calling the shots.

"Martinelli, you wouldn't know what to do with a real woman if one bit you on the ass."

Amusement gleamed in his eyes, and she tensed as he leaned down toward her. "And your definition of a 'real woman' would be you, right?"

He moved even closer, and Cassie had nowhere else to retreat. "Not that your opinion about my love life matters, but for the record, I know exactly what to do with a 'real' woman."

Cassie laughed. "Hit a nerve, didn't I? Poor Alex, relying on all those little college girls to—"

He moved so fast, she didn't even finish her sentence before his mouth closed over hers.

His warm body felt lean and hard against hers, strong and vital.

His mouth fit hers perfectly, the firm pressure just right, just the way that made her want to open her mouth and let him inside.

"Don't hold back," he murmured. "I'm counting on you to show me how a real woman kisses. Don't disappoint me."

Low and seductive, it was a blatant challenge— and Cassie *never* refused a challenge.

She kissed him back, putting all her years of experience into it. His hands moved to her hips, drawing her closer against him. Those hands were so strong and capable, the kind of hands that made her want to surrender, to give in to his strength and let him take up the fighting and struggling . . .

The thought snapped Cassie back to her senses, and she upped the ante by pressing against him and opening her mouth. Martinelli went still, then he flicked his tongue playfully against hers.

The hard length of his body against her, the clean soap-smell of him, the rough feel of his denim jeans beneath her fingers, and the taste of him in her mouth . . . it was like a drug spreading sweet languor throughout her body, coaxing her to sink against him, to let desire sweep her away.

She'd always wondered if he'd taste as darkly sexual as he looked.

Rotten bastard. Magnificent, rotten, seductive bastard.

Her pride demanded she give back as good as she got. As the seconds turned to minutes, she gradually realized that what had started out as one-upmanship would rapidly go somewhere she couldn't allow if she didn't put a stop to it now.

With no small amount of regret, she pulled back. "Okay, I give. You've obviously had lots of practice at this and know your stuff. I'm impressed."

To her relief, she sounded calmer and more in control than her racing heartbeat should permit.

Martinelli didn't move back. "And you kiss like it's been too long. A little slow to warm up, and then . . . you're sizzling."

"I'm not sure if that's an insult or not," she said suspiciously.

"No insult. I like a partner who knows what she wants and takes it." He smiled slowly. "I pegged you as that type a long time ago."

It surprised her that he'd been thinking about *her* in *that* way for a long time, too.

"Don't think I'm flattered." She hoped the sarcasm disguised her discomfort at their mutual lust. "I can't believe we just kissed—we don't even like each other."

"I don't have to like you to want to have sex with you."

Cassie smiled, though his blunt honesty flustered her. "Fortunately, I'm more discriminating than you are. I have to like who I'm with, or the sizzle fizzles. Um . . . could you let me go? I believe we have work to do."

In silence, she and Martinelli settled into their work routines. Amy returned, casting nosy looks their way, and soon the rest of her crew straggled in. A low buzz of conversation, machinery, and computer equipment filled the room, covering the charged silence between her and Martinelli.

It didn't sit well with Cassie that she kept dwelling on that kiss. She didn't want to be one of those women too easily waylaid by their hormones, or who let a hot kiss erase years of arguments, humiliation, and bad blood.

Martinelli didn't seem to be dwelling on it, but maybe he was more willing to let bygones be bygones. She'd never been like that; once she sank her teeth into something, she rarely let go.

"Didn't get much sleep last night?"

As if her mood wasn't already bad enough, his question put her on the defensive. "Are you saying I look like crap?"

"No, I'm saying you look tired." He frowned. "Pull in the claws, Ashton. I'm only making conversation."

"I went to bed late, then couldn't sleep." She wasn't sure why she answered, except maybe the dream still troubled her. "And I had a bad dream."

"What was it about?"

"The usual nightmare stuff. I'm running, being chased, and can't escape. Things are clawing at me and dragging me down, smothering me."

"I could psychoanalyze that."

"Please don't bother." She leaned back, stretching. "I know myself well enough to understand what it means. That's the way it goes when you're the show runner."

"So why insist on working on this if it's causing you so much stress? You're so tense I can feel it coming off you in waves."

"Stress is a relative thing; you should know that. Some days are better than others."

"That's still not an answer to my question."

Cassie made a dismissive gesture. "Never mind. You wouldn't understand, anyway."

"Try me."

He looked serious, but she still hesitated, not certain she could explain it to him any better than when she'd tried to explain it to Wyatt. And why should she bother? He didn't really care.

To her surprise, she answered anyway. "This little animal is important to me for reasons other than advancing the greatness of science, or even earning me a lot of money."

When he didn't make a smart-ass remark, but waited patiently for her to continue, Cassie looked away, feeling oddly self-conscious.

"I've been hunting dinosaurs for a long time, but it's stopped being fun. I can't say when something I loved so much became such a struggle, or even why. I don't want it to be like that, and when I look at Trixie, I see a chance to rediscover that old feeling, a road back to the heart of why I fell in love with these long-dead creatures to begin with."

He sat still, with an intensity that made her pause, but she detected no scorn or mocking amusement.

"When I was little, I followed my father whenever he went rock and fossil hunting. It was our special time together, and after he died, I guess I wanted to keep that part of him alive. So in memory of those good times, I created Hell Creek Fossil Company."

She let out her breath. "But I don't enjoy that work like I used to, either. And sometimes I resent it because it kept me from going back to school and becoming a paleontologist. Which is really stupid, considering I'm exactly what I wanted to be, in all the ways that really count."

Why had she told him that? Why was she telling him any of this? Allowing a look inside her deepest fears wasn't a smart thing to do with a guy who'd spent years tearing down everything she'd accomplished.

Martinelli surprised her by putting down his tools and leaning forward, his chin propped on his hand, looking almost like a wistful little boy.

A low, deep pang of desire pulled at her again, and it was all she could do not to reach out and touch his face, smooth away the lines of care and weariness.

"I understand better than you'd think. But my problem was getting so caught up in funding and publishing and other bureaucratic bullshit that sometimes I can't remember *why* I'm doing this. Like you said, it's good to be reminded of why I love the work, to try to remember that awe and curiosity I had when I was a kid and dinosaurs were . . . Hell, they were magic, like monsters from some fantasy book. When everything gets reduced to numbers and money and statistics, the magic dies away."

"Magic," Cassie repeated, surprised at his unexpected understanding. "Magic *is* the right word for **it**."

He nodded. "And like you, I don't want to lose that magic. Somebody told me recently that I'd stopped caring, that I'm going through the motions. And as much as I hate to admit it, I think she's right. Maybe I'm hoping little Trixie here is all magic-coated and it'll rub off on me."

She stared at him for so long that he sat back, his expression uneasy. "What? Why are you looking at me like that?"

"Why are you being so nice to me?" she demanded.

He frowned, then picked up a delicate dental pick with his long, work-roughened fingers. "You know why."

"You want this fossil, and you're trying to be extra special friendly."

"You got it. And now that I've seen her, I want her more than ever."

"Well, if you're a good little boy, you just might get a shot at her."

He grinned. "One way or another."

Maybe even by kissing a woman he shouldn't be kissing. "Is that so?"

It was a relief, going back to the challenging banter; this was familiar territory.

"Yup," he said, his grin widening. "You strike me as the charge-in-and-attack type. I'm more the clever and patient type."

"How come you're being so honest with me?"

"It's not complicated, Ashton. It's just fair warning, from one respected adversary to the other."

He wanted to play fair, not dirty, and she respected him in her own way. It was good to know he respected her, too—in his own way.

But the whole adversary thing wasn't nearly as fun anymore. "It can't last, you know," she said quietly.

"What?"

"Being nice. Being teammates. Your world and mine don't mix. In the past you've tried to discredit me and put me out of business, and you will again. I don't trust you and I never will."

To her surprise, she saw regret in his eyes. "I know."

# Twelve

✦

CASSIE SPENT ANOTHER LATE NIGHT WORKING IN THE lab by herself. Nocturnal by nature, she found that the quiet, the low light, and solitude made everything fit in a way that it didn't during the day.

Tonight, the silence also allowed her to think about Alex. It still appalled her that she'd kissed him like a starving woman who'd gone too long without sex. And now that she knew he was a wickedly wonderful kisser, her thoughts kept straying to what he'd be like in bed.

Probably very entertaining and thorough. Lots of energy there, with patience and an attention to detail. The thought made her warm, and she shifted uncomfortably on the hard work stool.

The last time she'd had sex was over two years ago, with that temporary digger she'd hired. He'd been powerfully built and hadn't said much, but she'd caught him watching her, flirted back, and ended up sleeping with him once. The whole experience had been . . . lacking.

While she wasn't in any rush to get married again, she missed the companionship, along with the sex and knowing someone would be there for her at the end the day.

She'd been only twenty-two when she and Josh divorced, and now she could see the mistakes on both sides. Josh had been controlling, resentful of her need for independence, but she'd been selfish and demanding, too.

The thought thoroughly depressed her, since she probably hadn't changed as much as she liked to think. God, what kind of masochistic fool would put up with her for a few weeks, much less the rest of his life?

At this rate, she'd die an old lady surrounded only by cats.

Pushing the thought away before her mood worsened, she worked on Trixie until she couldn't keep her eyelids from drooping. Alex would be here bright and early, and she'd need a decent night's sleep to be able to match wits with him.

She covered the fossil with its sheet, shut off the table light, double-checked the lab's back door, and then headed out through the shop. As she walked around the cash register, catching the gleam of the moon through the window, a shadow moved fast from behind her.

She spun, and pain exploded white-hot as a blow slammed her back. She landed on a display box, knocking it to the floor. The intensity of the pain left her gasping; she couldn't even scream.

Then the black blur rushed toward her again, and instinct kicked in. She darted to the side, but not before her attacker landed a glancing blow on her shoulder. Pain burned down her arm, wetly warm.

"Sonofabitch," she yelped, more in shock than pain.

The silent shadow lunged forward and she quickly rolled to the other side of the counter, groping for the bat.

Where the hell was it? It was *always* by the register!

Cassie reached inside the display case, searching desperately for the allosaurus claw, and as her hand closed over it, she swung it toward her attacker.

The claw still worked as nature intended, and it ripped through flesh and jarred against bone. The man hissed in pain and staggered back with a low curse.

Cassie swiftly kicked open the door to the lab, and the alarm clanged shrilly. She groped for the light switch, but by the time she found it, her attacker was running out the front of the shop.

"Dammit!"

She dashed around the counter after him, still clutching the claw, but he disappeared into the darkness as the lights in the house winked on. The sound of a powerful engine reached her, but she saw no headlights. The yard lights weren't bright enough to pick up a license plate, yet she could tell that it was a dark-colored pickup truck, and she went cold with fear.

"Cassie! What's going on?" Ellen ran toward her in her nightgown. She took in the open lab door, clanging alarm, and merchandise and display racks scattered or broken over the floor. "Did somebody break into the shop?"

"Yes," Cassie said, as a sudden, violent trembling gripped her. "I was checking to make sure everything was locked before I headed back to the house, and he came out of nowhere."

"What's that in your hand?" Ellen demanded.

"My twelve-hundred-dollar allosaurus claw. I cut him, too."

"What do you mean—Oh, God, you're bleeding!"

"Not much, it's not deep." But it hurt like all holy hell.

"We have to call the police. Let me see your arm so—"

"No!"

All at once, memories coalesced into a smothering sense of dread: the dark truck on the highway, the swift leaking of Trixie's discovery, Cleary's hostility, Alex warning her he'd take anything he could get.

With more calmness than she felt, Cassie repeated, "No police."

"But you were *attacked!* And the shop was broken into, we can't—"

"I don't want that kind of attention." She headed back to the shop as that heavy foreboding hardened into a sudden resolve and motioned to one of the ranch hands who'd just arrived on the run. "Nick, shut that alarm off. Please."

"Let me see your arm." Ellen fussed over her as Nick silenced the alarm and started picking up the shop. "You're lucky it's not deep, but you should have a doctor look at it, and you really should call the police. For God's sake, Cassie, you were attacked . . . you can't act like it's nothing!"

Turning, Ellen snapped, "Nick, don't touch anything until the police arrive. I swear, boy, you don't have the good sense God gave a goose!"

"Don't be angry at him," Cassie said tiredly. "It's okay, Nick. You can let it be."

She looked down at the floor, fighting off light-headedness. She forced herself to stare at one spot, hoping it would keep her on her feet, then realized her mother was touching her hand.

Slowly, Cassie looked up. "Did you say something?"

"I said, why don't you put that claw down before

you cut yourself? You're holding it so tightly your knuckles are white."

Slowly, Cassie relaxed her hand, but she didn't let go of the claw. "I'll call the police tomorrow, okay? It's late, and I really just want to sleep." She paused, finally asking the question nagging at her. "Where's Wyatt?"

"Out with that Missy girl, probably," Ellen said, thin-lipped. "You know how he is."

Wyatt couldn't be behind this or the highway incident. He was capable of calling reporters or potential customers about Trixie, even if he'd denied it, but not this. Not this.

After a moment, she said, "Where's the bat?"

Ellen looked baffled. "What?"

"The bat by the register. It's gone."

"Somebody must have moved it. Cassie, that's not important right now."

It *was* important, but because she didn't want to have to explain why, Cassie let it go.

"And you're not thinking this through," Ellen continued impatiently. "If you wait until tomorrow, that man will be long gone. If you call now, there's still a chance to catch him."

"It'll take the county sheriff an hour to get here, and to see what? Tire tracks and a few broken shelves? He was dressed in black, he was wearing gloves and a mask, and I didn't see anything that would help identify him. He drove away in a dark-colored truck, which fits the description of most pickups in Wyoming."

She had to do something, but she needed time to sort through all the possibilities first. Everything that had happened recently might be explained separately, but taken together, it couldn't be coincidence or bad luck.

Somebody was targeting her and it had to be someone she knew. Maybe even someone she trusted.

Cassie shied away from the thought. "I'll call and report it tomorrow, for what good it will do. This isn't the first time someone's broken into the shop or looted our sites, and nothing's ever come of it. So it won't make any difference if I get enough sleep so I can function tomorrow."

"Was he after the fossil?" Ellen asked, frowning.

"Probably. What else?"

Her mother and Nick exchanged glances. "Then we'll put an armed guard out here for the rest of the night."

"Oh, for—What happens if Mae decides to come in to work early? I don't want my employees getting shot."

"Either we post a guard or you call the police." Ellen had that stubborn look on her face that told Cassie further protests would be pointless.

"Okay. Fine. Just make damn sure they don't shoot

Martinelli if he shows up at the crack of dawn. I *need* that man."

She put the claw down on the counter and headed for the house. All at once, every ache in her body throbbed with a vengeance. She hurt most where she'd been thrown against the counter, and where the knife had left a long, thin gash that was still bleeding.

Though she hadn't actually seen a knife; she could've cut herself on a piece of broken glass or Plexiglas.

Her mother followed, fussing and scolding even as she bandaged Cassie's arm in the bathroom.

Finally, Cassie escaped. Alone in her dark bedroom, she threw the bloodstained clothes into the waste-basket, then flopped back on the bed. Exhausted as she was, sleep didn't come.

Tonight's attack didn't make sense. If a thief had wanted to avoid her, it would've been easy enough to do so. Instead he'd blundered out of hiding and ended up with a nasty gash—and if she'd had that bat, she'd have bashed his head in. Why had he jumped out at her like that?

She must've spooked him, and he'd panicked. Her mother was probably right and someone had simply misplaced the bat.

Cassie rolled to her back, trying to ignore her throbbing arm—and the unwanted suspicions tap-ping at her wall of denial.

The sky was already growing lighter when she finally dozed off.

The alarm sounded at six-thirty, and every muscle protested as Cassie rolled out of bed to shut it off. A hot shower didn't help her multitude of aches, but the sting of soap on her cut jolted her wide awake.

One of the ranch hands was still in the shop, rifle in hand, sipping coffee and eating toast, when she arrived. He nodded at her and left only when she insisted on it.

"What the hell happened here last night?" Alex's voice demanded.

Cassie picked up the allosaurus claw, which was still on the counter where she'd left it. "Somebody broke into the shop. I surprised them, and we had a tussle." She held up the claw. "I think I won."

"Jesus! Are you all right?"

"Pretty much. He knocked me around a bit, but I did a lot more damage to him. I got him with this."

Then she saw the fresh, raw gash on Alex's hand. Eyes widening, she jerked her head up to meet his gaze.

He didn't pretend not to understand. "It wasn't me, Cassie. This happened earlier when I was loading gear. I was in a hurry and not paying attention, and cut my hand on a pickax. I didn't try to turn you into mincemeat last night."

"I don't suppose your little blond girlfriend can give you an alibi for where you were at about one this morning?"

"No, since I don't have a little blond girlfriend anymore. You'll have to believe me when I say I was home in bed, sleeping. Alone."

"What happened to the blonde?"

"She dumped me the other night at the bar. She decided you and I were two of a kind, and she didn't want anything to do with either of us."

"Oh."

She wanted to believe him—on both counts—and instinct told her he wasn't lying. It wasn't his style. Besides, he wasn't stupid enough to risk his career and reputation by suddenly resorting to thievery.

"Where's your brother?"

That coldness washed over her again, seeming to freeze her joints, until hot anger broke the moment. "It wasn't Wyatt." That she was even entertaining the tiniest of doubts infuriated her.

"He didn't come home last night, but that's nothing out of the ordinary for a thirty-year-old guy who's living in an apartment over his mother's garage. Thinking that your mother might hear you having sex when she's taking out the garbage puts a damper on the mood."

Alex grinned, and it struck her that he had a really beautiful smile; she liked the way his teeth contrasted against the darkness of his skin. Two parallel lines deeply grooved his cheeks, and his eyes crinkled at the corners, taking away the hardness of his looks. It made him look . . . comfortable, and she had a sudden, crazy urge to ask him to hold her.

"I can relate to that. Is that why you don't bring men home?"

"Why is this suddenly about me? We were discussing Wyatt's whereabouts. I know where I was when it happened: right here getting thrown over the counter like a rag doll."

The counter by which she could see, plain as day, the red baseball bat in its usual place.

Suddenly, she became aware of Alex's impatient voice: "Cassie? Are you listening to me? I asked if you're sure you're okay?"

She turned to face him. "Physically, yeah, aside from some soreness. Hey, was anybody in the lab when you got here?"

If her abrupt change of subject surprised him, he didn't let it show. "Amy and Mae were here. And the guy with the gun, which, I have to say, isn't the best way to start off the day. I thought maybe you'd changed your mind about having me around." Then, more seriously, he asked, "Are you scared?"

"A little."

"Good. If you're scared, you'll be more careful."

Her irritation over his high-handed attitude faded,

replaced by amazement. "Is that concern for me, Martinelli?"

"You're my favorite adversary. Life would be boring as hell if you weren't here to give me a hard time."

Cassie smirked a little. "Aww . . . that's so sweet."

"Stop being such a smart-ass. Call the cops. They might be able to salvage something out of all this."

Cassie moved closer to him and lowered her voice. "I think it's somebody who knows me. Something else happened the other night."

Alex leaned down, his frown fierce. "Tell me."

She hesitated, not sure where to begin. "The night I came home from meeting you at Dip's, a pickup tried to run me off the road. At first I thought it was some drunk, until he rammed the back of my truck. Not hard enough to wreck me, but hard enough to scare me. The truck on the highway and the truck the man escaped in last night were both big and dark-colored. Like the one you drive."

"So do most of the people on my dig. It's the standard University of Wyoming service vehicle."

"I know. Does Cleary drive one of the university trucks, too?"

"Cassie, I don't—"

She held up her hand, gesturing for him to hear her out. "The dinosaur hunting community is a small one. Even an innocent comment at a bar by one of my diggers could've made it to the ears of the wrong people. And maybe this isn't about me. Maybe somebody doesn't want *you* anywhere near Trixie. After all, everybody knows we don't get along. If there's trouble, how long would it be before I kicked you out of my lab?"

The possibility hadn't occurred to him; she could tell by how his eyes widened and his mouth thinned.

"So maybe we shouldn't be wondering only who hates my guts—which, admittedly, could be a lot of people—but who hates yours. You really piss off anybody lately, Alex? Besides me, that is?"

# Thirteen

❖

ALEX STARED DOWN AT CASSIE. "YEAH . . . I'VE PISSED off a lot of people lately, and over the years."

"And is there anyone who'd have cause to be jealous of you? Want to see you fail, even if it means they lose, too?"

Don Cleary's craggy, weary face came to mind, and he hated himself for even entertaining doubts about the man he considered both friend and trusted colleague. "It's not Cleary. As sure as you are that it's not your brother, I'm sure it's not Don."

But was he? He'd left Cleary at the bar that night and didn't know where he'd gone after that. The older man had said he'd needed to think things over, and Alex hadn't given any thought to what that could mean—until now.

Cassie's focus on him didn't waver, and finally Alex looked away, angry at his doubts. "I'm ninety-nine percent certain, anyway. The one percent is that I'm human and, it seems, a shitty friend."

"So who else would enjoy messing with you? An ex-girlfriend?"

"It's possible." He let out a sigh. "I have a few of those."

"Do any of them hate you?"

"Most don't have much reason to think fondly of me."

"Which reminds me—you said you're not seeing anybody. Is that true?"

At the question, all his instincts went on high alert—and he couldn't deny a hopeful expectation as well. "Why are you asking?"

"Not for that reason." She gave him a glare that would've reduced a less thick-skinned man to jelly. "It occurred to me that you have no business kissing me if you're involved with somebody else. And I had no business kissing you back."

Alex rubbed at his jaw, trying to hide a smile. "I told you the truth. We weren't a serious item, and she decided to go with somebody else. Nothing to feel guilty about."

"Glad to have that cleared up. Now if we could only clear up this other problem." With a sigh, she leaned back on the counter. "Do you think she'd try to get even with you?"

"No, Melissa doesn't have that kind of mean streak in her."

"Anybody else you can think of?"

"There's a few colleagues who'd love to see me fall flat on my face, but I doubt they'd go this far. It's a lot easier to bad-mouth a rival than to get off your ass and do anything about it, and I can't see any of them coming all the way out here to toss you around the room and then run away. And while Cleary's a strong old man, he's still old. He wouldn't have the physical stamina to go one-on-one with you."

"It's most likely somebody on my end," she said softly.

A twinge of sympathy tugged at him. They might be rivals, but he still didn't like seeing her this discouraged. "Probably."

"But why?"

"I don't know. If we figure out who it is, we can ask. Are you going to call the police now?"

She sighed, every line of her body infused with reluctance. "It's the smart thing to do, even if I don't want the hassle . . . and I'm half-afraid where it will lead."

"Call," he said. "I'll wait for you by Trixie. With coffee."

"No donuts today?" She sounded wistful, and for a second or two, he considered pulling her against him for a quick, comforting hug.

It had to be the cuteness factor. Cute little things in distress—even cute little things with fangs and claws—brought out the need to nurture and protect.

He smiled. "There might be some donuts, come to think of it."

He headed back to the lab, which was unusually quiet. He nodded at Amy and Mae—and then he noticed a man sitting beside Trixie's table. Alex quickly moved forward, alarmed.

The man turned at the sound of his footsteps, and Alex recognized Russ Noble. Although relieved, he still demanded, "What're you doing?"

"Since I was the guy in charge when this little lady was found, I figure I have a right to check on her now and again." Noble's amiable tone clashed with the harder lines of his face. Then, he smiled slowly. "So. You're the guy with the p thing she needed."

Alex stared. "Excuse me?"

"Inside joke. I've been hearing a lot about you, most of it not too complimentary, but I understand what you lack in human decency you make up for in dino smarts."

Alex sensed a pissing contest, "So I've been told."

"Cassie's pretty shook up about what happened last night."

"Wasn't me," Alex said. "I want this fossil way too much to be that stupid."

"Good to hear."

"Are you feeling proprietary over the little lady?" Alex asked, closely watching the other man.

"Which little lady?"

"The one on this table. Not the one in the other room trying to explain to the county sheriff why she didn't bother calling hours ago about such an inconsequential matter as being attacked."

"Then my answer would be no."

Something deep inside snapped to attention at the blatant challenge in Noble's dark eyes—and the instant Alex realized it, he frowned.

It was none of his business who came sniffing after Cassie Ashton. At least this guy looked like he stood a fighting chance of surviving an encounter with the woman.

Before Alex could respond, voices raised in anger brought every head in the lab whipping around.

"Ah." Noble grinned broadly. "Brother Wyatt has arrived."

"Is it always like this around here?"

"This is my first summer with Hell Creek, but so far I'd say sibling warfare is the norm rather than the exception."

"I don't have to answer to you about where I've been!" Wyatt, his hair damp, looked as if he hadn't had much sleep. Alex felt a twinge of solidarity as one beleaguered male toward another.

"I'm not asking for sexual details, dammit," Cassie snapped back. "We're talking about how the shop was broken into last night. The cops are on the way, and I can guarantee I'm not the only one who'll be asking where you were."

"You think I'm responsible?"

In the dead silence of the lab, Wyatt's incredulous, angry voice rang clear as a bell. Alex glanced away and noticed the others were doing their best to pretend they weren't listening.

Which was impossible, since Cassie had stalked into the lab, her color high, her brother hot on her heels.

"What I'm beginning to think," Cassie said, her tone darkly bitter, "is that I can't trust anybody but myself."

"I can't believe this!" Wyatt's voice was even louder than usual. "I can't believe you'd—"

"Don't take it so personally. Everybody in this room right now has a reason to upset the status quo." Cassie glanced around the lab before turning back to her brother. "Even me. A staged publicity stunt would earn me lots of attention. Maybe even enough to help fatten the wallet, right?"

For a long moment, nobody spoke. Tension wrapped around the room, cold and brittle, and even Alex had to admit she had a point. If he were in her shoes right now, he wouldn't trust anybody, either.

For the first time, it occurred to him that her discovery was turning out to be a mixed blessing, and Cassie was taking the brunt of the downside of it.

Probably the same way she took the brunt of everything else that went wrong.

Cassie broke the silence first. "The last few days have been tense, and a lot of unfortunate things have happened." She glanced at Alex. "And been said. We're all on edge, which isn't the optimum condition for keeping a cool head. Especially when some of us, namely me, aren't noteworthy for our cool heads even in the best of times."

Alex grinned. The woman was maddening as hell, but he had to give her credit for admitting her shortcomings. He admired that about her.

After a moment, the tension faded visibly from Wyatt's body, and he ran a hand through his hair again. "I didn't know. I walk in here, and the shop's all busted up and one of the hands is standing around with a rifle... I was worried, and I just started yelling. Sorry."

If Alex had come home to find his place trashed and his sister attacked, he wouldn't have been calm, either. Shit, he'd been furious and stunned just at the mess in the shop.

"Ah, don't sweat it," said Amy, smiling. "It's not like we haven't seen it all before. Gotta say, it's never dull around here."

Her comment broke the tension, and they all drifted back to their regular routines. As Cassie made her way toward Alex, he didn't miss the tired lines of her face, or the waves of tension still vibrating off her.

"Hey, Russ," Cassie said. "What're you doing here? I thought Betty had you scheduled to take a group of kids out to the Frankel ranch to poke around." She glanced at Alex. "An old floodplain. We usually have lots of fragmentary fossils there for the kids to find, and the Frankels don't mind."

"You don't need to give me explanations. I've toured my fair share of schoolkids around digs." He grinned at her surprised expression. "Seriously. The kids ask lots of questions, rarely stand still, and grab things they shouldn't, but it's still one of my favorite parts of my job."

Cassie nodded, amusement sparkling in her dark eyes. "Nothing like a group of curious kids to remind you why you fell in love with fossils to begin with."

"So I suppose I should be going then," Noble said, clearing his throat.

Cassie turned to face him. "Yes. Betty's in the shop now, so get the details from her."

Noble motioned at the table. "I wanted to stop by and see how things were going with Trixie."

"Trixie herself is fantastic." Cassie pulled back the tarp. "But I sure could do without all the other shit that's been happening."

"So what's going on?" Noble asked and smoothly inserted himself between Cassie and Alex.

Alex wavered between wanting to laugh and wanting to shove the man away. He couldn't say why Noble's interest in Cassie didn't sit well with him; he had no cause for going all territorial.

"Ask me later; I don't want to talk about it anymore. The sheriff's deputy is on the way, and he's already less than happy with me." She sighed. "But if you're worried, don't be. The ranch hands will be on guard duty, so a break-in shouldn't be an issue again. And Mother told me I'm not to work alone in the lab anymore."

Alex chuckled at her disgruntled tone. "And you have to listen to your mom, even at your age."

"Oh, shush, you," she said irritably.

Noble grinned. "Nice talking with you, Martinelli."

After the other man departed, Alex sidled up to Cassie. "So, what p thing do I have that you need?"

When a blush tinged her cheeks pink, he had a good idea of what the inside joke was. Cassie Ashton blushing, about him? How interesting.

She glared at him. "Your Ph.D. You don't have anything else that I could remotely need."

That color in her cheeks said otherwise, but he just smiled and held up the bakery bag. "Then I guess you won't be needing any of these freshly baked donuts."

She sighed in defeat. "I hate you."

"I know." Taking pity, he tossed her the bag. "But that's half the fun, isn't it?"

She pulled out a donut, sat down at the table, and started working.

When the sheriff's deputy arrived, Cassie stood, not hiding her frustration at the interruption. "This shouldn't take too long. You stay and keep working."

"Nope. I'll wait until you get back. She's yours, and I can wait."

Surprise flashed in her eyes, then a look of very real gratitude. She had an incredibly expressive face, one that advertised her every emotion—and she had quite the wide range.

Since he'd only ever pissed her off before, he'd never noticed that . . . and he thought now that it was too bad he hadn't been a little nicer to her over the years. Granted, he hadn't been as rude or dismissive as many of his colleagues, but he hadn't been particularly helpful.

He didn't like admitting he'd let ignorance and prejudice color his judgment. A Ph.D. didn't keep you from being a complete idiot.

While Cassie answered questions for the stocky, gray-haired deputy, Alex simply observed the infant rex.

The average person wouldn't understand his obsession with the fossils, and it was those messed-up priorities that had deep-sixed his marriage. He hadn't blamed his ex-wife for giving up on him; what woman wanted to play second fiddle to ancient bones?

Not Melissa or most of his past lovers. Probably not even the mercenary-minded Cassie Parker Ashton.

"Excuse me, sir. I'd like to ask you a few questions."

Absorbed in his thoughts, Alex hadn't heard the deputy's approach.

"After talking with Ms. Ashton, it's looking like whoever broke into her shop last night was after this thing." The deputy looked down, his expression telling Alex he saw only a jumble of bones and rock. "What is it, exactly?"

"It's an infant *Tyrannosaurus rex.*" When the deputy only raised a grizzled brow, Alex asked, "Did you ever see *Jurassic Park?*"

"Yeah . . . and the *T. rex* was that big bitch that ate the goat, right?"

Alex laughed. "Yup. That big bitch."

"And this is a baby one?"

"The only one in existence."

"So it's worth stealing."

"I'd say so."

"Can you tell me where you were between midnight and three A.M.?"

"Home in bed sleeping. Alone." He sighed. "I have a major professional interest in this fossil, and what I want more than anything is to study it. Which is what I'm doing right now, thanks to Ms. Ashton's generosity. I'm not about to screw that up."

The deputy grinned. "That's what she said. If we

need you to come into the station to make a statement or answer more questions, where can we reach you?"

Alex dug out a dog-eared business card. He rarely used them, but now and again they came in handy. "Either here or my cell number, or you can call my department and leave a message. I check messages at the office a few times a week."

The deputy nodded, then went off to question the others in the lab. Cassie sat down beside Alex, and he asked, "How'd it go?"

"He gave me hell for not calling right away, but I expected as much." She sighed, then rubbed at her brows. "Dammit. I have a headache."

"Have more coffee. It might help."

"Getting back to a normal routine would help, too. How about it? You feel like working?"

Nothing about the question should've made him pause—except that for the first time in a long, long time, he really *did* feel something.

Anticipation, excitement. Wonder.

Magic.

"Hell, yeah," he said quietly. "I feel like working."

# Fourteen

ALEX HARDLY NOTICED THE PASSING HOURS, AND when he straightened, massaging the ache from his cramped neck and shoulder muscles, he couldn't believe the time. "Shit, it's after dinnertime. We should take a break."

Cassie looked up, her focus gradually shifting as if she were returning from a distant time and place. Damn, she was cute when totally immersed in thought. Who knew a look of concentration could be so sexy?

"Did you say something?" she asked blankly.

"You. Me. Break. Dinner. How about it?"

A puzzled look crossed her face. "Are you asking me out for dinner?"

"Something like that."

Her brows shot up. "That was highly noncommittal."

He grinned. "Man-slut, remember? Noncommittal goes with the territory."

She laughed and pushed to her feet, her own movements a little stiff. "Right, I forgot. A change of scenery might help clear my brain."

"And that wasn't the most committal yes I've ever heard, either."

"I'm an expert in the art of playing both sides, remember?"

"Right. I forgot." He grinned. "How does Lenny's sound?"

"Perfect. Let's go."

The lab had almost emptied, but Amy, Mae, and Wyatt were still around, talking. Or Amy was talking to Wyatt while Mae stared at him with an adoration so plain that Cassie couldn't figure out how her brother could fail to notice.

"Where are you going?" Wyatt demanded, eyeing them as they walked past.

"Dinner. We're hungry and I need a break. Is that all right with you?" Cassie asked, her arch tone matching his.

"You're having dinner with him?" His look said that she was too easy for words. "I thought you'd hold out longer than that."

Irritated, Alex opened his mouth to tell the man to mind his own damn business, but Cassie's sharp elbow in his side kept him from doing so.

Ignoring her brother, she turned to Mae and Amy. "Either of you staying late tonight?"

"Not me," Amy said. "This girl's got a hot date."

"I have to get home early today. Mom stuff," Mae said, her tone embarrassed.

"Whoever is the last to leave, make sure you lock up and turn on the alarm. Even with guys on guard duty, I don't want to take any chances with Trixie."

"Will do," Amy said. "Enjoy dinner. Be nice to Alex."

"Don't worry, I'm too hungry and tired to do him any damage," Cassie said with a wink. Then to Wyatt, "Are you going to be home tonight, or are you spending the night elsewhere?"

"I'm staying. If just to make sure you don't accuse me of trying to steal your precious fossil."

Cassie said nothing, but Alex could tell she was embarrassed that he was seeing the Parker clan at less than its best. It made him glad he'd never had brothers or sisters.

Once they were outside, he said, "Your lab manager has a thing for your brother. And he's got an eye for your analyst."

"You noticed."

"Hard not to." He stopped in front of his truck. "We'll take my truck."

She eyed the battered vehicle, its university logo barely visible beneath the dirt. "Mine's prettier."

"Mine has shocks that work."

"Good point." Cassie climbed into the passenger's seat.

There was an awkward silence as he sped toward the highway. "How's things going at your dig?" she asked after several minutes had passed. "Igor have everything under control?"

He looked faintly irritated. "His name is Don, and yes, everything is fine. We've started picking up a few interesting skull fragments, so it looks like there's something inside the bluff. What it is, and in what kind of shape, I can't say, but it would be nice to pull out something besides pieces of another hadrosaur or other herd animals."

"The good stuff is few and far between," she agreed, understanding the frustration lacing his voice. She'd felt that way enough times herself. "Fortunately, I can sell teeth and bits of bone that have no real value, and our tour groups are happy even when finding just fish bones. Believe me, finding an infant rex wasn't something we were prepared for."

"You seem to have everything under control."

"Thanks." She glanced at him. "It's good to hear a compliment. I don't get them very much."

"Especially from me." After another long silence, he added, "I meant what I said. You and your people do good work."

"Thanks." She couldn't look him in the eye; it was just too . . . intimate.

"What's wrong? You look upset or something."

"Not upset, it's . . . I don't know. Talking with you is so much easier when we're arguing or insulting each other. I'm not sure how to talk to you outside work or an argument."

He smiled as he turned off the highway to a rougher county road. "Danger awaits when you venture into unknown territory."

"Mmmm." It was as noncommittal as she could manage. "I feel like I should be in mourning. After this, nothing will be the same."

"Change is good for the soul."

"God, you sound like my mother."

"Never tell a man he sounds like a mother."

Cassie laughed, and as the initial awkwardness eased, a new tension rose to take its place. Alex Martinelli was a very attractive man and she'd always had a thing for tall, dark, and arrogant men. Something in the arrogance was a challenge she couldn't resist. She didn't understand why she wanted a challenge; it wasn't a recipe for happily-ever-after. Normal couples didn't need a challenge or—

What on earth was wrong with her that she was thinking of couples and happily-ever-after with this man? A few days of civil behavior, a stolen kiss, and a truce for mutual benefit didn't erase the past.

"Now what's wrong? You're glaring at me."

He didn't sound particularly worried.

"You've been a real bastard to me over the years, you know that?"

His surprise soon sharpened into a look of irritated defensiveness. "Because, naturally, you've always been so nice to me."

"Don't dodge, Martinelli. It's beneath you." She shifted in the seat to face him. "All those awful things you've done and said—remember that time in Banner? You actually called me a *thief*. You said I was no better than a looter."

He was silent for a long moment. "I'd had a few beers, and you'd really pissed me off. The only time you'd come to me was to rub one of your successes in my face. That stegosaurus you found was on contested land, and I wasn't the only one calling you a thief."

"Your words carried more weight than those of the idiot who owned that land, or *said* he did. Everybody knew he was a lying little worm. But you were the University of Wyoming's golden boy. You had credentials. You had respect. Your accusation ended up costing me a lot of money and time when the cops decided to investigate me."

Alex kept his attention on the road. "I never filed charges against you, Cassie; you know that. It was somebody else with a grudge who went after you."

"But you never backed down from your stance. It was a big, black mark I had to work against for a long time, and you went merrily on your way like it was nothing to you. I had to let go some longtime employees because money was so tight, and for a few months, it was touch and go whether I could even keep the shop running."

"I didn't know that. I'm sorry."

"And if you had known, would you have cared? You wanted me out of business, out of competition with you."

"I believed then, and still do, that a lot of commercial fossil hunters are not ethical. Some *are* no better than looters."

To his credit, he wasn't yelling. His voice was tight and he was frowning, but he wasn't yelling.

"Not all of us, Alex."

"Look, I realize that. I already admitted I was wrong about you, but you're not representative of everybody who's bone-hunting to turn a quick buck. If every dino freak went off hacking and chopping at fossils whenever and wherever he wanted, it would do a lot of damage. You can't deny that."

"I don't. On the other hand, there are far more fossils out there than there are paleontologists to dig them up. You people don't have the resources to handle the demand, and half the time you're tied up in red tape."

"And you're never at the mercy of bureaucrats?"

"Of course I am; that's why I have a lawyer. I'm

just saying there's nothing wrong in making a profit. I don't think people should be selling rare specimens on eBay, but a few hadrosaur bones out of a multitude of hadrosaur bones isn't going to make or break the scientific community."

"But where do you draw the line, Cassie? And who's making those decisions?"

That was the heart of the problem.

"Everybody wants to be the one making those decisions, and we all have our reasons. I just want to support my family and feed my kid."

"Don't go the guilt trip route."

"Why? You don't like hearing the truth? You were so entrenched in your righteous credentials that you never stopped to consider if anything you said against me might cost me a dig, or meant I had to let workers go because I couldn't keep them on the payroll when legal fees were adding up faster than income was rolling in. And what did I ever really do to you, except hurt your almighty pride?"

He didn't answer, and Cassie looked out her window at the flat, mostly grassy land flashing by in a blur.

"Professional pride isn't anything to make light of," he said abruptly, drawing her attention back to him. "Just because the guys holding my purse strings wear lab coats or suits doesn't mean they're not going to rip me to shreds if they can. My own colleagues can be pretty damn cutthroat, and constantly losing out to a brash, mouthy, commercial fossil hunter made me look like a fool. I don't like being the fool, Cassie, and you took every opportunity to make me feel like one. Maybe you couldn't see it, but it mattered to me and it mattered to my peers. More than once, I've had to defend myself against accusations of incompetence."

He put on a snooty tone of voice. "No luck again? Why is that? I heard that Ashton woman found a couple of prize specimens, and all you ever come back with are herd animals we've already seen dozens of times. If she can find the good ones, why can't you? Why should we give you any more money or other resources? I hear there's a new guy in the department with a lot of fire. Maybe we'll give him a chance."

"They really said those things to you?"

"Not in so many words, but the implication was there, in the snide comments and the jokes that were supposed to be 'just' jokes but weren't. I've spent the past five years trying to prove I was as good as, or better than, a woman *they* didn't even want to admit was as smart and competent as any of them."

Hearing him say his cronies acknowledged her competence should've left her with a warm glow of satisfaction . . . but it didn't. "You never acted like anything I said or did was more than a minor annoyance."

"What can I say? I'm a hell of an actor." He sighed. "It's time to change the subject."

They talked about the weather, cattle, politics, music, and movies until they reached the diner. Even then, he didn't mention work again, and she didn't feel like bringing up the subject, either.

They had caused each other so much trouble and pain, when cooperating would've made much more sense. She was thirty-six years old, had raised a child by herself, and had built a lucrative business from practically nothing, but right now she felt as childish and selfish as any two-year-old—and it wasn't something she liked feeling.

The only thing that made it easier to bear was knowing Alex Martinelli felt the same way.

# Fifteen

❖

As far as dinner dates went, it wasn't one of the better ones, Alex thought as he paid the bill. After the "bare our souls" moment in the truck, Cassie had been unnaturally subdued. God, he'd never considered her side of things, or how his frequent dismissive comments would've affected her. He'd figured he was in the right, she was in the wrong, and only the strong survived.

Now he couldn't stop wondering about the workers she'd had to lay off, or if maybe her kid had had to go without something because she was out of money and it had been his fault.

For so long, he'd thought he had a grasp on what was right and wrong, what he was good at and what he wasn't good at, what he wanted and what he didn't want—now, none of it seemed as certain as when he'd started out.

Shit. He was too damn young for a midlife crisis.

Especially since spending time with Cassie was making him feel more like an oversexed seventeen-year-old than a mature thirty-seven-year-old.

All through dinner he'd watched her, trying to figure out what exactly made her so utterly sexy. Maybe he was simply attracted to cute, mouthy man-eaters, but it was more than that. She radiated a vitality and energy that he couldn't ignore. He'd simply refused to let himself acknowledge it before now.

Maybe when this mess with Trixie the Wonder Baby was settled, he'd ask her out. Could be disastrous, could be fun . . . but he wanted to find out if all of her tasted as good as that first kiss.

He didn't think any woman had ever fit his hands as well as she did, or roused such anticipation . . . God, the hunger and passion in that one little kiss had short-circuited all his rational thoughts. He couldn't stop thinking about her or looking at her, although he tried not to be too obvious.

He'd also caught her looking at him throughout the day and during dinner, sometimes faintly puzzled, other times speculative. What was going through her mind right now when she cast him that quick, sideways glance as he pulled into the drive by her lab?

"Are you thinking of getting more work in?" he asked, half hoping she'd say yes because he wouldn't mind spending a little more time alone with her, but also half hoping she'd say no so he had something to look forward to the next morning.

Amazing . . . when was the last time he'd really anticipated being with a woman? He couldn't even remember—not something to be proud of, considering the number he'd slept with over the past few years.

Cassie hopped down from the truck, and he got out as well, walking around to meet her. He intended to stick around until he could be certain she was safe.

"No. I have to call my kid before he starts wondering if I've forgotten his existence."

"Ah," Alex said, feeling a twinge of disappointment. "Kids can be a real pain in the ass."

"Hmph. You should try actually raising one. A more humbling experience, I can't imagine."

He looked down before she could see the hurt in his eyes, pretty sure she wouldn't approve of his parenting skills if she found out he did have a kid. "I have a hard time imagining you as a mother. You look like a kid yourself."

"Thanks. I think."

Maybe he'd best stay quiet while he was ahead. Every time he opened his mouth, he ate his own foot. "I should get back to my camp and check in with Don. I don't want anybody thinking I've deserted them and joined the enemy forces."

She actually smiled, a wide, bright, and pretty smile that crinkled her eyes at the corners, making her look as warm and friendly as someone he'd known all his life.

"God forbid. Can't have that. Thank you for dinner, though you didn't have to pay for my half."

"It wasn't a bribe."

She laughed. "Never crossed my mind. I can't be bought that easily, and neither can Trixie. So I guess I'll see you early tomorrow?"

"I might be late, depending on how things go with Don."

"Oh."

Was it his imagination, or did she sound disappointed? And what was taking her so long to walk away from him and the truck? It was almost as if she didn't want to leave.

Hmm. All day he'd wanted to kiss her again, so what did he have to lose except his pride? That had taken such a beating lately it couldn't possibly get any more deflated.

She was watching him with an unnerving intensity, and a small smile tipped the corners of her lips. "Don't even think it, Martinelli."

Those five provocative little words made up his mind.

Alex moved closer, effectively pinning her between his body and the side of the truck. The scant inch between left him wanting more of that hint of softness, of welcoming warmth. "Thinking? I'm done with thinking."

Unlike a younger, less self-confident woman, Cassie didn't giggle or protest, squirm or blush—and that confidence turned him on more than words could describe.

She wouldn't make the next move; he'd have to take it all the way. "I haven't forgotten what you told me the other day," he murmured.

She arched a brow. "How about you be more specific?"

Alex let his smile widen—then he leaned forward, hands braced on either side of her. This time, he could've sworn her breath caught.

"You said that men held no more mysteries for you. No surprises."

"Oh, that." Both brows arched now, giving her a dangerously innocent look. "It happens to be true."

"Except you don't want mystery. Or surprises."

"Really? So enlighten me as to what I want."

"Someone who, when you push, pushes back." She had an incredible mouth; and he was already imagining it under his, and everywhere else on his body. "You want someone like me."

"You don't push, you bulldoze—"

Alex kissed her.

When she pressed against him ever so slightly he responded with more urgency, moving his hands to her shoulders, then along the gentle dip of her waist.

Small, soft, and yet so strong; he skimmed her

curves, wanting to fill his hands with the feel of her. With a sigh, her lips parted, and he touched his tongue to hers, pulling her closer with one hand while cupping the firm roundness of her bottom with the other.

He made a low sound of desire and need, appreciation and frustration. "Touch me," he whispered.

For a moment Alex didn't think she would. Finally, she touched his chest: feather-light and hesitant, yet he could feel the heat of her skin through his shirt, each pressure point of her fingers.

Cassie smiled. "I lied, you know. You have a very nice chest."

With a soft laugh, Alex lowered his mouth over hers again, and this time she met him with a matching hunger.

Closing his eyes, he gave in to the sensations, tasting her, feeling her breasts press against his chest, hearing her sigh of satisfaction, soaking in the smell of her hair and skin—and he wanted her so bad, he couldn't even think straight.

He brushed his fingers along her breast and when she melted against him, he palmed the round softness teasingly, then rubbed his thumb over her nipple.

With a small gasp, she arched, pressing her breast into his hand as she pulled his T-shirt free from his jeans and slid her hands beneath, clutching at his back.

Skin on skin, heat to heat. Alex wanted more of

it, and now. He wanted to feel *her*. Still kissing her hungrily, their tongues caressing, he pushed her bra aside and covered her bare breast with his palm, rubbing and massaging its roundness before teasing the tip with his fingers.

Cassie gasped again, tremors rippling through her body, and her reaction sharpened his need. He wanted to see her bared and beneath him, and with the way she was moving against him, so close that she had to feel his erection, he knew she wanted him, too.

Without giving any thought to the fact somebody might be watching, he pulled back just enough to shove her shirt and bra up and take her nipple into his mouth, licking and sucking it into a taut peak as she made soft, needful sounds. God, what kinds of sounds would she make if he kissed her and played between her legs?

As he debated between moving either to the lab or his truck, he didn't immediately notice that her hands were now pushing him away instead of pulling him closer.

When his lust-fogged brain registered her insistent pushes, he broke the kiss and murmured harshly, "Why?"

She was still leaning intimately against him, her eyes wide and dark but not angry.

"We can't do this, Alex."

"Why?" he repeated.

She looked away and pulled her bra and shirt back into place. "You know why."

A sudden, unpleasant thought came to him. "I didn't kiss you to get that fossil, if that's what you think."

She sighed. "I can't be sure of that, can I?"

"Look, Cassie, I may not be a nice guy, but that's something I'd never do." He took a few steps back, tucking his T-shirt into his pants. There wasn't anything he could do about his erection, still straining against his jeans. He caught Cassie's quick look down south and could've sworn she let out a soft sigh.

"It's not just that. There's a dozen other reasons why you and I can't do this again."

"Such as?"

"Alex, it's getting late and I'm tired. Couldn't we just let this drop?"

She tried to move past him, and before Alex could think twice, he blocked her, bringing his hand down hard against his truck. She jumped, startled.

"You don't strike me as the running type, Cassie."

A spark of anger lit her eyes. "You know nothing about me. Don't presume otherwise."

"Maybe I want to know more about you."

"Why? Sex is out of the question. I'm a single

mother; I have responsibilities that don't allow me to knock boots with whatever hot guy happens to cross my path. And more than that, you and I don't even operate in the same world."

"Yes, we do."

"No, we don't," she said carefully, as if she were speaking to a very small child. "There's a lot of people in *your* world who don't like what I do. I'm the interloper, the threat to their tidily academic lives. If you cozy up with the likes of me, those jabs your colleagues take at you are going to get a lot worse."

"Why the hell should I care?"

"Don't be obtuse." She stared at him. "They're the ones who keep you in the money."

He knew she spoke the truth, but he didn't like it because what he wanted was *her*. Like a bolt of lightning, he realized that he'd always wanted her, from the very start. "I can handle the heat."

"There's always been an attraction between us," she said, echoing his thoughts, "but I'm being realistic. I have no intention of giving up my business or the way I live my life. Neither do you, and differences this big . . . they're what tear people apart, despite good intentions."

She laid her hand on his arm, which still blocked her escape. "Now let me go."

He did so, reluctantly. As she walked away, he watched the sway of her hips, the way her curling hair swung from side to side, brushing against the small of her back, and how she moved with such pride and determination. It filled him with a confusing onslaught of desire, admiration, and intense need to protect her from harm.

"I don't give up easily," Alex called after her. "And I still think you're running."

Her stride faltered for a moment, but she didn't stop.

Alex watched until he saw a light come on in the second story, where her room must be, then climbed into his truck to begin the long drive back to his camp.

# Sixteen

WHEN HER ALARM WENT OFF THE NEXT MORNING, Cassie threw her pillow at it, knocking it off the dresser with a satisfying clatter. It couldn't already be time to get up; it felt like she'd just fallen asleep.

It hadn't helped that a mind-numbing kiss and a few moments of hot and heavy action by the lab's back door had left her nerve ends alive and snapping with nervous energy—and a restless, unsatisfied desire. Letting him kiss her had been stupid; she'd known it, even while happily reciprocating. His sure touch, his hungry kisses, the powerful feel of him against her . . . it had been so damn good she'd temporarily forgotten who he was, who she was, and what was at stake.

With a heartfelt groan, she rolled out of bed and stumbled to the bathroom, grabbing a pair of khaki cargo shorts and a baggy black T-shirt. Yawning, she stared at her reflection in the mirror and didn't like the dark circles under eyes, the lines of tiredness etched beside her mouth. Even the shower didn't ease her taut sense of unease.

How could she face Alex after what they'd done? And what if someone had seen that kiss? It wasn't as if they'd been discreet.

She had to get her libido back under control, starting today. And she was going to have to do something about the nagging feeling that someone in her employ was causing all this recent trouble. She had no idea where to start, but maybe after a cup or two of coffee, her brain would start firing.

The hazy light of dawn was just beginning to brighten the sky when she walked into the shop. The youngest of their three part-time ranch hands was on guard duty, looking overly alert and stern.

"Morning, Fenny," she said, smiling at him.

He blushed to the roots of his coppery curls. "Mornin', Miss Ashton."

"Any excitement last night?"

"Nope. It was quiet."

"Just what I like to hear." She walked past him, turning on the lights back by the register, and retrieved a dozen or so phone messages from the day before.

Lots of calls on Trixie, including one from a respected paleontologist who'd always treated her decently. She'd give him a call back and ask him if he wanted to come play with the new baby, too. The more Ph.D.'s she had in her pocket, the better.

Ah, and the Japanese gentleman had called again, and a German—and some reporters. She recognized a few names and would return those calls; the others she'd ignore.

As she stuffed the phone slips into her back pocket, she swung open the door leading to the lab and quickly snapped on the lights. That tussle with the intruder still made her feel jumpy. She hoped she'd get back to her usual self soon; the constant upheavals were beginning to wear her down.

Cassie stepped inside, then stopped short, staring at Trixie's empty table.

Had somebody moved her and not let her know? No, no one would dare move Trixie without her permission. *Never.*

"Oh, God," she whispered, as a cold rush of fury and panic raised goosebumps over her skin.

Trixie was gone.

She whirled and ran back to the shop, yelling for Fenny.

He turned, eyes widening, fingers tightening on the rifle. "Miz Ashton? What's wrong?"

"You tell me! She's *gone!*"

"Who's gone?"

"Trixie, dammit! . . . Who else are we guarding?"

He went white. "Can't be. Nobody came in here. I didn't hear any trucks or nothing, and nobody could've just walked off with her by themselves."

"Well, she's *gone!*"

"Who's gone?" came her mother's voice. "What is going on?"

"Trixie's been stolen," Cassie said sharply. Ellen's eyes popped wide, and for once, she was absolutely speechless. Cassie turned back to Fenny and asked, "Are you sure you didn't see or talk to anybody?"

He looked terrified. "Yes, ma'am. I didn't see any strangers."

A sudden, heavy dread filled her. "Did you see any non-strangers?"

"Just Mr. Martinelli. He came by looking for his cell phone. He said he left it in the lab and asked if he could get it. He said he didn't need to bother you because he knew the alarm code and could let himself in at the back."

"There you have it," Ellen said sharply. "Wyatt told you not to trust that man, and you did anyway. Now he's taken—"

"He didn't do it," Cassie snapped. "For God's sake, he'd have everything to lose and nothing to gain!"

"Then he can tell that to the police when they go talk to him," Ellen snapped back and picked up the phone.

Cassie didn't bother arguing. Turning, she pulled

her truck keys out of her pocket and headed for the door as her mother shouted after her, "Where are you going?"

"He was set up, don't you see that? Everybody is *supposed* to blame him, including me. But he didn't do it."

"You don't know that!"

"Yes, I do." Cassie yanked open the door. "I know because he's just like me."

Alex was halfway to Hell Creek when his cell phone rang. He groped for it in his shirt pocket—where he'd been sure to put it after he'd inexplicably misplaced it yesterday—and to his surprise heard Cassie's voice when he answered. "Cassie? Yeah, it's me. Why are—"

"Where are you?" she demanded.

"I'm almost at Platte Junction. Why?"

"Stay there! Pull aside and wait for me. Do *not* come here."

Damn strange. "What the hell is going on?"

"You were in the lab last night, after you dropped me off?"

What was this? "Yeah. I was about twenty minutes away from your place when I realized I didn't have my phone, so I turned around and went back. It was on the worktable."

"And you didn't notice anything out of place?"

The tone of her voice set off alarm bells. "No."

"Trixie was there?"

He went cold. "Yes."

"Then that means you were not only the last person in the lab but the last person to see her. She's gone."

"You're shitting me!" Stunned, he pulled hard to the side of the road, gravel flying.

"I wish. And my mother's called the cops and told them all about it, including the name of the last person in the lab. Considering our well-known feuding, you can bet they won't waste any time going after you. I don't suppose you have an alibi?"

He didn't even bother answering.

"That's what I thought. And that's why I want you stopped right where you are. We need to talk before the deputies find us."

He sat in silence, anger simmering as the reality sank in. "My cell phone was in my shirt pocket. I never take it out."

"But you always take the shirt off when you work."

"Yes." It was stuffy in the lab, and working with the lights made it warmer. He usually took his shirt off soon after arriving and draped it over one of the nearby benches or stools.

"Somebody took my phone," he said. "And figured I'd go back for it."

"It was a good chance you'd do so. Have you stopped?"

"Yes."

"Okay. I'll be at Platte Junction in about fifteen minutes. We'll talk more when I get there."

After she disconnected, Alex sat back and stared down at his cell phone. It was often the only way to get in touch with him. He'd never thought about how much he needed it, or how somebody could use it to manipulate him. Granted, he could've just picked it up the next day. But like most people, he'd behaved as predicted and walked right into a neat little setup.

*Somebody had taken Trixie.*

The first person who sprang to mind was Wyatt, but Alex quickly dismissed the thought. The guy was an asshole, but he wouldn't put his sister in danger or steal from her. Hell, the way Cassie had people coming and going all through the day, it'd be easy for anybody to set something up once they'd gained her trust.

Jesus. How could this have happened? The one thing he and Cassie had always dreamed of finding . . . It had been within their grasp, and now it was gone. Just like that. Suddenly the magnitude of the loss swept over him.

At the sound of an approaching vehicle, he looked up to see a familiar battered, dusty truck zipping his way at a speed that far exceeded the legal limit. She hit the brakes and pulled up in front of him.

Alex got out of the truck, meeting her halfway on the weedy shoulder of the road. "Who do you think did it?" he asked, before she even had a chance to say anything.

"I have no idea. Somebody who knew you and me well enough to pick up our habits, that's for sure. Somebody with access to the lab, and somebody who the ranch hands would recognize as a friendly face."

That didn't leave a lot of possibilities.

"God, Cassie, I am so sorry this happened." He pulled her into an embrace and she leaned into him, all soft and warm and shaking with fear or grief or anger. Or all of it.

"I keep hoping it's just a bad dream, but it's not."

"What do you want to do?" Alex asked. "Whatever you decide, I'm right beside you."

"Thanks," she said quietly, her dark eyes sparkling with tears, and he had an irrational urge to punch whoever had made her cry.

"Whoever took Trixie has a good head start on us. I was in such a rush to find you that I didn't do a head count, but it looked like everybody was there that I'd expect to be there. We need to sit down and compare notes, then come up with a likely scenario before we talk to the police."

"They'll bring me in for questioning." Alex jammed his fists into the pockets of his jeans so that he wouldn't give in to the urge to punch the side of the truck. "That's bound to stir up quite a commotion."

"And by the time that commotion settles down and we get you cleared, whoever took Trixie will be long gone. The standard operating procedure here is going to hurt us and help the thief."

As he mulled over her words, he couldn't help but feel a grudging admiration for whoever had set this up. Cassie was right; while there might not be enough evidence to land him in jail, there'd be enough to cause him trouble for a few days—and give the thief plenty of time to get away.

"We could try telling all this to the cops."

"Right, and then they'll do . . . what? Take our word on it because we look like nice people? Go chase after nothing?"

As Alex ran a hand through his hair, his frustration gathering steam, he saw an old pickup camper approach them, then slow down.

Cassie groaned. "Oh, great. They probably think we need help."

Alex waved them past, but the two men inside misunderstood.

"Car trouble?" called the driver as he hopped out. He was tall and lanky, and moved with a slight limp.

"No," Cassie answered tightly. "We're just having a talk." After a moment she added, "A *private* one."

Alex nodded. "Sorry to have troubled you both, but you can go."

"Nope. Can't do that."

For a split second Alex didn't think he'd heard right. Then, as his instincts kicked in, he pulled Cassie behind him while he reached for his truck door, intending to grab the tire iron.

But the second, shorter man lunged forward, preventing Alex from opening his door.

"Cassie, get out of here!" Alex shoved her out of harm's way just as the short man punched him in the gut, hard.

Gagging, Alex dropped to his knees.

"Hey!" Cassie rushed toward Alex. "What the hell is this?"

"Get in the truck," Alex yelled, rolling quickly to avoid a punch to his face. "Get in and go for help!"

"I'm not leaving you here!"

Trying to avoid being kicked, he was dimly aware that Cassie was grabbing up rocks and hurling them at the driver, who was cursing and ducking—and then Alex saw the gun.

He froze. "Cassie, he's got a gun . . . don't move!"

"Time for you to cooperate," said the short man as he yanked a billy club out of his back pocket.

Caught between needing to protect Cassie and watching his own ass, Alex didn't dodge fast enough. He felt a burst of red-hot pain in his head, followed by thick, deep darkness.

# Seventeen

W̲H̲E̲N̲ A̲L̲E̲X̲ ̲W̲A̲D̲E̲D̲ ̲B̲A̲C̲K̲ ̲T̲O̲ ̲C̲O̲N̲S̲C̲I̲O̲U̲S̲N̲E̲S̲S̲,̲ ̲P̲A̲I̲N̲
pounded in his head and his first groggy thought was
relief. If he hurt so bad that he wanted to puke, he
couldn't be dead.

Then he realized his head was resting on something warm and soft.

"Don't move," came an equally soft and warm
voice. "And stay quiet. You took a hard hit."

*Cassie. Thank God.*

The memory of what had happened came rushing
back. Despite the agony in his head, he tried to sit
up but his hands were tied and he was too dizzy to
make it.

"I said—oh, never mind. Men are so damn stubborn. Let me help."

He winced as she nudged and braced him with her
body. The instant he was upright, tingling pricks of

pain skittered up his numb arms and he sucked in his breath. The bastards who'd tied him up hadn't taken any chances with the tightness of the ropes. "If you're bitching me out, you must be okay."

"I'm alternating between terrified and furious, but physically, I'm fine. We're tied up," she added.

"I noticed."

He'd turned so he could see for certain that she was okay. Her pale, wide-eyed face was dirt-smudged and she had a cut across her cheek that had clotted into a thin, dark line, but beyond that she looked unharmed.

Alex groaned in relief as much as pain. "My arms are numb. Or were. Now the blood's rushing back and it hurts like hell. So does my head."

He took stock of his surroundings. Small, dark, cramped . . . and unmistakably the interior of a truck camper. He'd lived in enough of them over the years to know. Probably the one the men had been driving. "Why are we in a camper?"

"I have no idea. I'd have expected basements, abandoned houses, torture chambers . . . Keeping us in the camper's got me puzzled, too."

"We're alone?"

"For now. The guys who bashed in your head and tied us up are outside talking, so keep it quiet. I have a feeling that once they know you're awake, they'll separate us."

"Have they tried to do anything to you?" he demanded in a low, terse tone.

"No. My butt is sore from sitting on this floor, but they've left me alone."

"What happened? I remember them pulling up, and then that little bastard hit me with a club . . . "

"Turns out they weren't Good Samaritans." Cassie sounded more annoyed than frightened. "After you were knocked out, they told me they'd kill you if I didn't cooperate, so I stopped fighting."

He remembered her fighting, and he couldn't hold back soft laughter, even though it made his head pound more intensely and heightened the feeling that he was about to heave his guts out all over the floor.

"So glad you find this entertaining."

"No, I remember . . . you were throwing rocks. Jesus, Cass. *Rocks.*"

"Would you have preferred I just stand there screaming?" she retorted.

"Not at all, I just . . . You're a hell of a woman, that's all. You never give up."

"Hmph." Despite her grumpy tone, her mouth turned up in a small smile. "They made me climb in here, tossed you in, then tied us up and took us on a road trip."

"We're not moving now."

"We stopped a few minutes ago. I think that's what woke you up."

Narrowing his eyes, his vision still a little blurred,

Alex looked out the window. "We're somewhere with lots of trees."

Which would explain why it was so dim inside the camper. That was a lot better than learning he'd been out cold all day.

"We went east, judging from what I could see of the sun and the terrain, but we didn't go very far. I think we're close to Laramie." She leaned into him, her expression anxious. "How are you feeling? You were out for a long time, and that's quite a nasty bump on your head. I was getting worried."

"How nasty is nasty?"

"Blood, bruising, and swelling."

No wonder it felt as if his skull would split in two. "Head wounds always bleed a lot, but aside from the headache pounding so bad I feel like throwing up, I'm okay."

She let out her breath in a long, shaky sigh. "For a few seconds there, I thought they'd killed you. I was so scared, Alex."

He wished he could pull her into a comforting embrace, or just touch her in reassurance. First chance he got, he was going to beat the shit out of those who'd hurt her.

"You said our keepers are outside?"

"The tall one said he had to pee, and they both went out."

"What the hell do they want?" Now that his head

and stomach had settled somewhat, he could try to figure out what was going on—but it didn't make much sense even with a clearer head.

"I wish I knew, but I have a few ideas. Except for tying us up, and making sure you were still breathing, they haven't paid much attention to us."

"Want to share those ideas?"

"In a moment. Scoot back and rest your head against the wall. When our friends get back, I'll ask if they have some Tylenol for you."

"You think they give a shit if I have a headache?"

"This is going to sound really strange, but yes, I do. They acted nervous until they were sure you were okay, and the tall one reamed out the short one for hitting you so hard. It makes me think they don't intend to harm us."

"Their definition of 'harm' is a lot different than mine. You have a cut on your cheek."

"Because I tried to kick the big one in the balls and he hit me. That's when he threatened to kill you. At the time, I thought he meant it. Now, I wish I'd kept fighting. Maybe they would've run away."

"Or maybe they'd have shot us both. The driver had a gun, Cass."

"They both do. Handguns, rifles, *and* hunting knives."

Alex stared at her. "And what about all that makes you believe they don't intend any shooting or stabbing?"

"Because when I asked what they were going to do

with us, they laughed and said they were keeping us out of trouble for a few days and after that, they were letting us go."

"And you believed them?"

"Yes. From what I could pick up from their conversation, somebody is paying them to keep us out of sight for a couple days. That's it."

"A kinder, gentler breed of kidnappers. I'm touched."

That made her smile, which improved his rotten mood. It was bad enough he was tied up, but he'd also failed to protect Cassie.

"Somebody just wants Trixie and is making sure no dead bodies complicate matters," she said, sounding tired. "Murder has a way of stirring up a lot of attention."

"Except a whole lot of people right now are probably worrying that we're already dead."

"Yes, and that's one more way to keep the police looking everywhere but where they *need* to be looking, which is finding my baby rex."

"Ah," Alex said quietly.

"Whoever organized this knows exactly what they're doing. The more I think about it—and I've had a lot of time to think while you were out cold—the more I believe somebody outside of Hell Creek put this together but used one of my employees as an inside helper."

"Which means our mystery person has lots of money."

"Or plans to have a lot of money, once they sell Trixie to the highest black-market bidder," Cassie said bitterly.

"Too bad we can't call the lab. I bet somebody's missing from work today."

Cassie glowered. "They took our wallets and cell phones, and they even took your belt and the pens in your pocket."

Anything he could even remotely use as a weapon.

"We'll figure something out," Alex said, soothing the fear she was trying so hard to hide. "We'll get Trixie back. Don't worry."

"I'm more worried about my family. And what happens when my son calls and finds out about this?"

"You said he's with his dad?"

"Yes. Josh is a good guy and I trust him to take care of Travis, but Trav will assume the worst. It's bad enough they bashed in your face and stole Trixie, but now they've worried my family and my son, who probably think we're *dead* somewhere!"

The tone of her voice warned him she was reaching critical overload. If she burst into tears, he didn't know what he was going to do. Weepy women usually made him want to turn tail and run in the opposite direction, but he realized with some surprise he didn't really feel that way now.

Just then, the two men returned to the camper. They wore large, wraparound sunglasses, and their ball caps were pulled low to obscure their faces. They were white, dark-haired, dressed in jeans and T-shirts, and were somewhere in their late twenties to mid-thirties . . . which described half the male population of Wyoming.

"Hey," said the shorter of the two, the one who'd clubbed him. "Looks like Sleeping Beauty here finally woke up. Have a nice nap, buddy?"

"Fuck you."

"Loosen his ropes," Cassie ordered coldly. "He can't feel his fingers."

"Sure." The big man hauled out a high-caliber, showy automatic equipped with a silencer. "With you right here as assurance he won't do anything stupid."

Alex watched in rising anger as the man hauled Cassie to her feet, holding the gun casually near her head.

"I'm not going to do anything to put her in danger."

"Good to hear," said the short man. "We're not asking for much, see. You don't give us any trouble, and in two days we leave and tip off the locals where to find you; then you're free. But give us trouble, and we'll get rough."

They were keeping to a schedule and a plan, one that meant the little fossil would be beyond their reach in only two days.

Dammit, by the time the police figured out what was going on, it would be far too late.

As the short man loosened his ropes, sending more sharp spikes of pain lancing through his arms, Alex asked through tight lips, "Who are you working for?"

"Someone who's paying us very well to keep our mouths shut and make sure you two are out of the picture for the next few days. Actually, we were just supposed to keep her out of the way." The man grinned down at Alex. "You were a bonus prize, but since you're here, we'll use her to make sure you cooperate."

If looks could kill, the glare Cassie gave the man would've obliterated him on the spot.

"The hands feel better?" the man asked politely.

"Yes, thank you, but they'd feel even better breaking your nose," Alex answered, his tone equally polite.

"I hate smart-asses," the tall man rumbled, frowning. "Cuff him to the table. Right wrist and ankle. Then do the same for the cutie here, but over by the bench. We can't have the two of you getting too friendly."

"What will you do when I have to pee?" Cassie asked, her tone sharp. "Follow me and watch me?"

"We'll do what we're doing now," the man answered evenly. "Hold a gun to your boyfriend's head to make sure you don't try anything. And only one of you will eat at a time, while the other one is under guard. We'll watch you twenty-four-seven until we get our call. You might as well sit back and enjoy a little quiet time. Think of it as an unscheduled vacation."

An overwhelming urge to kick the man's teeth

down his throat gripped Alex, but he kept quiet as he was handcuffed to a table bolted to the frame of the camper. It was marginally better than being trussed up.

After Cassie was cuffed to a built-in bench a short distance away, he asked, "Where are we?"

Along with the trees, he now glimpsed mountains that looked faintly familiar.

"Like I said, you're vacationing." Short grinned, and Tall gave a hoot of laughter, sharing a private joke.

Alex figured they were probably in a public park in the Laramie Mountains. Gowdy Park was his best bet.

And something else was clear: while Short and Tall were crafty, they weren't the sharpest tools in the box. If he and Cassie asked the right kinds of questions, the two might reveal more information while trying to be funny and clever.

"Hey," Alex said. "You got any Tylenol? My head hurts."

Short said nothing, but his scramble to find a bottle of pain reliever told Alex Cassie had been correct: whoever was paying these men didn't want Cassie or Alex harmed. He didn't like where that realization led, because it implied the culprit was somebody Cassie trusted. Like a friend, or even worse, family.

And now he and Cassie had only two days to find Trixie. Despite his pain and brain-fogging anger, Alex felt a spark of excitement. Nothing like impossible odds to force a man to rise to the occasion.

# Eighteen

✦

THEIR CAPTORS DELIBERATELY KEPT THEM JUST FAR enough away from each other to make collaborating on any plan of attack impossible, which added to Cassie's black mood. She let her temper have full rein: anger kept the spark going, kept the cold fear away. She tried not to think what her family was going through right now. And if that wasn't bad enough, somewhere out there, getting farther away by the second, was her priceless baby rex.

She knew frustration was eating away at Alex, too. The situation seemed hopeless, but she'd never given up on anything in her life. She'd negotiated, bargained, threatened, bullied, compromised, and sometimes bent the rules to the snapping point, and no way in hell was she going to give up now. Not with so much at stake.

But . . . what *could* she do?

As the hours passed it looked as if Alex's pain was worsening, and she began to worry that he'd been seriously hurt.

As if he'd read her mind, he called out to the two men, "Hey, I need more pills. My head feels like it's going to split open."

"I just gave you some." The tall man, who'd stripped off his shirt to reveal a black T-shirt and shoulder holster, turned around. His smaller friend appeared to be catnapping, sitting up.

"I need more. It's not working and I feel like I'm gonna puke all over the floor."

The man's lip curled in distaste. "Do that and I'll make you clean it up, Professor Boy."

"My goddamn head's exploding!" Alex squeezed his eyes shut, swallowing hard, as their other captor came awake with a gurgling snort.

"Alex, is something wrong?" Alarmed, Cassie straightened. "Maybe something broke or he's bleeding inside. He might need a doctor."

"If he can holler like that, he's not gonna die on me anytime soon," the big man said flatly. But all the same he walked toward Alex, throwing an order over his shoulder to his companion: "Watch the woman."

Even in the dim light, Cassie could see the sheen of perspiration on Alex's face. Unless he was a spectacular actor, he was in extreme pain and something was definitely wrong.

The big man stopped just out of Alex's reach and said, "I'll give you a couple more, but that's it. You'll get sick if you take too many, so you're just gonna have to be a man and deal with the pain."

Then Alex's eyes rolled back as he slumped back against the wall.

It happened so suddenly that Cassie could only stare in shock, cold fear tightening her chest until it seemed she couldn't breathe. For a moment, nobody moved, then Cassie shrieked, "Do something! He needs a doctor!"

"Jesus." The big man sounded unnerved. "You better not be faking. If this is a trick, I'll make damn sure you regret it."

As Cassie watched in horror, the man kicked Alex—but Alex only flopped limply to the floor.

"Oh, God," Cassie whispered. He wasn't faking. "He's unconscious! Stop kicking him, you'll just make it worse!"

"Is he having some kind of seizure or something?" the smaller man asked from behind Cassie, his voice taut with tension.

"How the hell should I know? Christ, you didn't hit him *that* hard."

"If he has a head injury, every minute you waste talking about it puts his life in danger." A tremor of fear slipped into her voice. "Look, I swear I won't say anything about either of you. Just call somebody to help him, please!"

"What should I do?" The big man turned toward his companion with a look of indecision. This was plainly something he hadn't counted on. Perspiration dotted his upper lip. "Shit. Maybe we should just get the hell out of here."

"We can't take off now; she's supposed to call in less than an hour. We *need* that money."

"And we don't get it if Professor Boy here dies on us!"

She? The person responsible for all this was a *woman?*

"Try to sit him up," the short man advised. "If he doesn't get better in a few minutes, we'll think of something."

"I dunno, he looks pretty bad. I don't want anybody dyin' on me, goddammit."

"Please." Cassie was desperate. "One of you can get him help, and I'll stay behind if that's what you need. Anything . . . I'll do anything, just get him to a hospital now!"

"I think we'd better do that," the tall man said grimly.

Alex was so terribly still; all that vitality, spark, and snap, just . . . gone.

*Please, please let him be okay.*

"Better make it quick. We were told to keep them out of the way until Friday, so this messes things up a lot."

"And we were also told not to harm anybody," the

bigger man grumbled. "At this point, we better just cover our asses and hope for the best."

He pulled out the keys and began unlocking Alex's handcuffs. "Watch the woman," he ordered, voice tight. "Just in case he's faking it after all."

As Alex exploded upward from the floor, Cassie stared in shock. He body-slammed the big man, who crashed backward into Cassie, knocking her against the man behind her, and all three of them sprawled in a heap of legs and arms and loaded guns.

She was sure someone was going to get shot—most likely her, in the middle of things—then she felt the two men go stiff.

Alex had a gun pointed at the big man's chest.

"Move, and I *will* blow a hole through your lungs," Alex said, his voice soft. "Because nobody's paying *me* to keep *you* alive. Cassie, push those guns toward me with your foot. And you there . . . don't even think of trying to stop her."

"What are you doing?" the big man demanded. "You can't—"

Alex fired the gun, drilling a hole in the floor right between the man's legs, dangerously close to his groin. "Then again, maybe I'll blow a hole in something else. You're not worth killing, but I'm okay with making you hurt."

"Jesus fuckin' Christ!" the big man yelped, his face pale.

Shaking, Cassie quickly shoved the rifles and guns toward Alex, then scooted next to him. Without looking down, he reached for a second handgun, handling both as if he knew what he was doing.

"Who hired you?" Alex asked.

"We don't know," Tall answered, licking his lips. "We only talk to her on the phone, and—"

Alex raised the gun, hand steady, gaze hard. "Name."

The big man hesitated, but preserving his manly bits was more important than getting rich. "Mae . . . her name is Mae!"

Cassie gasped. "You can't have heard right. It must've been something else."

"Look," the big man snarled, "this bastard has a gun aimed at my dick. I'm telling you the goddamn truth!"

But it couldn't be Mae. She was so quiet. So timid, so invisible, so . . . nice.

"Who hired Mae?" Alex asked, still holding the gun with unnerving steadiness. "Who's she working for?"

The big man shook his head, sweating. "She said his last name is von Lahr, and I swear that's all we know. She told us that when he got the cargo across the border, we'd get paid for keeping you two out of the way."

Alex's eyes narrowed. "Give the lady the keys to unlock her cuffs. Move slowly; I have a nervous trigger finger."

The smaller man immediately tossed Cassie the keys. Her hands were shaking so bad that it took several tries before she managed to insert the key and turn it. Alex asked, "Did one of you break into the Hell Creek shop the other night?"

"That was me," the short man said, his tone morose. "I was supposed to mess things up and make it look like someone was trying to rob the place. Mae swore there'd be no guns or anything, but chickie here had a knife. After that, I ran like hell."

White-hot anger rolled over Cassie. "I would've gutted you if my aim had been better. Were you the one who tried to run me off the road, too?"

The short man nodded, not meeting her gaze.

Once free from her cuffs, she retrieved the other set. "What should I do with these? Lock them up?"

"Look outside and tell me what you see," Alex ordered without moving the gun from the two men.

Cassie opened the door, checking over her shoulder. "Not much out here except for trees. I think there's a few other campers, but they're not in shouting distance."

"It'll do. Cuff them together, Cassie. And if they so much as twitch, you run."

She couldn't remember when she'd been so frightened. She did as he ordered, but every time one of the men drew a breath, she wanted to jump back. Finally she closed the cuffs around each of their wrists.

"Now we go outside," Alex said. "Cassie, open the door, then step back."

She had no idea what he was up to, but since he obviously had a plan, she did as ordered. Once the door was open and she'd stepped back, she picked up one of the rifles. She wasn't much of a shot, but she couldn't miss at such a short range.

"You two walk outside," Alex ordered, "very slowly and carefully. I'll be right behind you with guns aimed at your spines. So don't think about yelling or running."

Cassie followed, and a short distance away from the truck camper Alex said to the men, "See that pine tree straight ahead? I want you on opposite sides, faces to the bark."

Cassie got it; they'd use the other set of cuffs to secure the men around the tree.

"Cassie?"

"I'm on it."

She put her rifle down by Alex, then quickly cuffed the men around the tree. They didn't look comfortable, and she smiled in satisfaction. After retrieving the rifles, she edged closer to Alex, thinking he still looked a little pale. While she was glad he'd faked the entire fainting attack, part of her wanted to smack him for scaring her so much.

"Great. We've got their guns; now we just need the keys for the truck."

The big man grinned. "They're gone."

"What do you mean, 'gone'?" Alex demanded.

"We never planned on leaving in that truck. It was staying here with you two in it. I threw the keys out into the woods. I guess you could go looking for them, but pretty soon somebody's gonna notice two guys cuffed to a tree and start hollerin'."

The other man chuckled. "You're screwed. But if you unlock us, maybe we'll tell you where we parked our other truck. Deal?"

"Shut up," muttered Big. "God, you are so fuckin' stupid."

"I ain't the only one cuffed to a tree," Short retorted.

"Now what?" Cassie asked, glancing at Alex.

"We leave them here and get as far away as we can."

"Then we'll need our stuff." Cassie ran back to the camper and snatched up the bag that held their wallets and cell phones. As soon as she emerged, Alex grabbed her hand, and they took off at a run through the thick trees.

"What about the rifles?" Cassie asked, glancing back. "We can't just—"

"I pocketed the bullets and jammed the barrels in the ground to fill them with mud. We have the handguns; that's all we need."

Cassie blinked; she'd have never thought of disabling the rifles.

Within minutes, however, she didn't have time to think as they ran, dodging tree stumps, slippery leaves, fallen branches, gullies, and rabbit holes while avoiding nearby campers.

She'd recognized the distinctive skyline since she'd been here many times on family vacations. They were in Curt Gowdy State Park, whose abundant forests and steep mountains attracted a lot of hikers and campers. How crazy was this, trying to hide out in one of the most public places in the entire state?

They were in the densest part of the forest where it grew darker and cooler, smelling thickly of earth and pine sap and rotting leaves. Their progress alternated between short bursts of running in open areas and slow climbing over the more treacherous rocky areas. They didn't talk, and it seemed like forever, stumbling and sliding and occasionally falling, before Alex finally stopped.

"Now what?" Cassie asked, gasping for breath.

"Now we rest while I figure out where the hell we are. Those two back there are going to be concentrating on breaking free and hiding, but there's a chance they'll come after us. It wouldn't be hard to find us; we left a trail even my grandmother could follow and she's half blind."

"I'm assuming you have a plan, since you pulled that little stunt back in the camper—which scared the crap out of me." She smacked him in the arm. "Don't *ever* do that again!"

"Sorry. I would've told you if I'd had a chance." He shook his head, his expression a blend of amazement and contempt. "I can't believe they fell for that. It has to be one of the most clichéd tricks ever."

"You were exceedingly convincing. I thought you were having an aneurysm or something."

"Sorry, but it worked, and that's what matters. Cassie, we have only two days to find out where Mae took the fossil. Shit, I can't believe it was *Mae*." The confusion and shock in his eyes mirrored Cassie's feelings.

After a moment, she pulled out her cell phone. "I'm making a quick call to the lab. They need to know we're okay. And if something's strange with Mae, I'll find out about it."

"Keep the call short."

"I know." She figured Alex had reached the same conclusion as she had: heading back home wasn't an option.

She dialed, and after a few rings her mother picked up. The connection wasn't good, and she suspected her battery was about to give up the ghost—not good, since Alex's phone was broken, probably during the highway scuffle. "Mom, it's Cassie. Don't answer; nobody should know it's me on the phone, okay? Now say yes if you heard me."

Silence. Then, in a choked voice, her mother said, "Yes."

"Alex and I are fine. We were sort of . . . forcibly detained. I don't have time to go into details, but whoever stole Trixie and set up Alex to take the blame also wanted us out of the way. They probably hoped to make an easy escape during the confusion our disappearance would cause." She paused. "Mom, is anybody acting strange? Did anybody not show up for work? Answer only if you think it's safe to do so, and make it quick. My battery's running out."

"Oh, God, we were so worried! What's going on? Why can't you come home and—"

"Mom! Answer the question."

"Everybody's acting strange! What on earth do you expect?" her mother demanded. "And yes, everybody's here. Well, except Mae. Her mother is having surgery, remember?"

Cassie sat down on a tree trunk. "Mae's gone?"

"You forgot, didn't you? She said you would; you're always so busy with that fossil, and now look what's happened because of it—"

"What kind of surgery?"

Silence, then, "She didn't say anything to you?"

"No."

"Oh." Another brief silence. "She said her mother was having eye surgery."

"Eye surgery. Right." Cassie's heart was pounding,

and her head felt oddly light. "I have to go. I'll contact you again as soon as I can and try to explain what's happening in more detail. In the meantime, don't tell anyone about this call."

She disconnected in the midst of her mother's protest.

Alex moved close to her. "It was Mae?"

Cassie nodded. "If her mother was having eye surgery, she would've said something to me, but she never did. Come to think of it, all she said was that her mother was having knee trouble. Knees, eyes . . . why bother keeping the details straight?"

"She's been sloppy. Sounds to me like all she wanted was to keep you preoccupied until she made her move, then continue the same tactic until she was safely out of the state. Maybe even the country. What border do you think she's heading toward?"

"With only two days, my guess would be the closest, Canada. Which doesn't help much, since Canada is big."

He leaned forward, frowning. "Do you know where she lives?"

"She has a place outside Bosler. But that's a long way from *here*, and we have no transportation."

"I know. But since Mae's been careless, there's a chance she left something behind that'll help us figure out where she's headed. It's worth a shot. The police won't be looking for her, so we should be okay if we don't draw any attention."

He had a point. In fact, he was thinking a whole lot more clearly than she was . . . she was still struggling with the overwhelming urge to scream and punch something. "How do you propose we get there?"

"We can try to hitch a ride. I don't think we're far from the highway, and with all the traffic going in and out of the park, somebody's bound to take pity on a nice, safe-looking couple with car trouble."

"But won't the police be looking for us?"

He gave an impatient shrug. "Do you have any other suggestions?"

She didn't. "So what do we do now? Should we start walking?"

"Yeah, but I need a break first. I'm still not feeling too good."

"This is just awful." Cassie closed her eyes, swallowing a sudden lump of tears as she sat back against a tree, unmindful of the twigs and rocks and damp soil. "One minute, life couldn't get much sweeter, and the next, kaboom! It all goes to hell. And on top of everything, all that running made me sweaty and now I'm cold."

He laughed softly. "Come closer and we can share body heat."

She grinned. "First I need to make another call, before my battery dies."

"Your kid?"

"I don't want him worrying any longer than need be."

It took four rings before Travis picked up, and she heard a video game blaring in the background and the girls laughing. "Mom?" he asked, his voice pitched high. "Is that you?"

"Yeah, sweetie, it's me. I can't talk long, but I wanted to tell you I'm fine and everything is okay."

"But Uncle Wyatt said you were attacked and were missing and that somebody stole Trixie, and he said it was Dr. Martinelli!"

"Wyatt is wrong, as usual. Somebody did steal Trixie, but it wasn't Dr. Martinelli." She smiled over at him. "In fact, Alex is with me right now and we're going to try to get Trixie back."

"You're not coming home?"

"Not yet, but we'll only be gone for a few days."

"You should be home and let the police take care of everything. You don't know how scared I was when I heard . . . Why do those stupid dinosaurs always have to be more important to you than anybody else?"

Cassie was taken aback by the anger in his voice—and the tears she could hear beneath the surface. "Do you really believe that?"

"You're not *here*!"

*Safe where I can touch you and talk to you.*

"Trixie is important, but she is *not* more important than you or my family."

"Sure. You always say that."

"Because it's true, and you know it, honey. Calm down. Alex and I have a good chance of finding the fossil, but we only have two days. I know you're safer at your father's house with all this craziness going on. Your dad will take good care of you."

Silence.

"Travis?"

"What?" His voice was low, sulky.

"When I find the people who took Trixie, I'm going to punish them to the full extent of the law. But you know what?"

"What." Still low, still sulky.

"If they'd taken you, I'd kill them."

She could feel his surprise humming over the connection. After a moment, he asked, "Would you really?"

"Damn straight. Nobody messes with my kid. Ever."

"I want you to come home." He sounded tired, no longer angry.

"And I will. But nobody else stands a chance of getting this fossil back, and I just can't sit back and do nothing. "I'll call you again as soon as I can, okay?"

"What do I say if the police ask me where you are?"

"Tell them the truth. Your mom called and said she's gone to get back what was stolen from her."

"Where are you going?"

"I don't know, and that's the truth. I have to go now, Travis. I love you."

"Love you too. You be careful, and tell Dr. Martinelli he better take good care of you. Or else."

A single tear ran down her cheek. "I will."

After she disconnected, it took her a moment to gather her composure. "Well. That went about as badly as I expected."

"Doesn't sound like your son's too happy with you at the moment."

"No, I'd say he's not."

"He'll be okay. From what little I know about him, he's smart and tough. Like you."

Cassie smiled, grateful, and turned away to sniffle quietly.

"Hey."

At Alex's soft voice, she turned back to him. "What?"

"Were you serious that you'd kill anybody who hurt him?"

What a ridiculous question—she could hardly believe he'd asked it. "If someone ever harmed my child, I'd rip them to fucking pieces."

Alex nodded. "Mama lion. You're a good mom, Cassie."

She appreciated his comment, even if he was only trying to make her feel better. "Sometimes I think I am; then I worry that I spend too much time working and not enough time with my kid. I love him more than anything, but I can't always get him to understand that I have a life outside of being his mom. I don't know . . . Maybe I'm not as doting as I should be, but he seems to be okay, despite everything I probably did wrong."

"Don't let guilt get to you. He's what, fifteen? He doesn't need you around like he did when he was a toddler. You're doing fine with the parenting thing. I can tell."

There was something odd about his voice. "Thanks. I appreciate the compliment."

He hunched over, looking down as he worked a pebble out of a groove on his boot sole. "I have a daughter."

Cassie stared at him, stunned. "You have a *kid?*"

"I know what you're thinking. Guy like me, who sleeps around too much, it was bound to happen."

The thought had crossed her mind.

"I got married when I was in grad school, and we had a baby our first year. I thought everything was going fine, and I was publishing papers, working on getting tenure, busy with the fieldwork . . . Then one day my wife left me. I came home, and she was gone. With my daughter."

She could feel for his pain and loss, and said quietly, "I'm sorry."

"Yeah, it was a bit of a shock. I knew she was tired of being home so much with the baby, but I'd thought she understood it was just until I established my career. She never seemed angry or even all that unhappy. But I guess she was."

Not quite sure what to say, Cassie settled for something safe. "Where are they now?"

"My ex married an accountant and lives in Brooklyn. My daughter's a little younger than your son. She's fourteen."

"What's her name?"

"Jaelynn."

"It's a pretty name."

"It was what my ex wanted." Alex sighed, slumping back against the tree beside her. "I always went along with whatever she wanted, so it wouldn't cause any stress. I was too damn accommodating. I didn't want to jeopardize my relationship with my daughter, so I tried not to rock the boat during the divorce. I was so sure I was doing the right thing." He paused, then added quietly, "But all I did was bend over backward to let my own kid fade right out of my life. Now, it's too late to do anything about it."

"You've missed a lot of important years." Cassie hesitated, then reached over to take his hand. At first he didn't respond, then he gave her hand a quick, hard squeeze before letting her go. "But it's never too late to try to make things right."

"I've been wanting to start over with my daughter for a while now, and every time you talk about your son, I wonder what the hell I'm waiting for. I know I'll never be able to make up for the lost years and the long months between visits, but I want another chance, if she'll let me have one. She might tell me she doesn't need me in her life, and already has a father. You don't know how lucky you are, to be on such good terms with your ex."

Cassie scooted closer. If she'd been more certain of his reaction, she would've hugged him. "It wasn't always that civil, but we eventually settled into a pattern that worked out for the best. I always liked Josh; I just didn't love him enough to stay married to him. Truth is, I don't think I ever really loved him."

She pulled up her legs and hugged her bare, scraped knees. "I met Josh right after my father died, so there was that whole 'feeling needy' thing on my part, and then we were careless and I ended up pregnant. Getting married seemed the only option at the time. We were so young, and I resented everything that kept me from going back to college. You always have such big dreams when you're young—before life comes along and knocks you around a bit."

"Can't argue with that."

Cassie sighed, feeling weariness creeping up on her. "How's your head?"

"Better."

He still looked exhausted. "Do you want to rest a little longer?"

"A few more minutes would be good."

"And I'm still cold." It had more to do with fear than anything else, and she wanted him to hold her but didn't know how to ask.

Strange; he'd had his mouth and hands all over her just the day before, and she couldn't even ask him for something as simple as comfort.

"I told you to come over here and share body heat."

She hesitated. "Can I trust you to behave?"

"I'm thinking this isn't the best time for a seduction," he said wryly.

It made her laugh, and soon she was against his body, surrounded by his warmth and strength. Out in the middle of the dark wilderness, she felt small and far too vulnerable. "Now that you brought it up, I can't help thinking I could use a good kiss right about now. Though that's probably a bad idea."

Bad idea or not, his hands were already moving along her back in rhythmic strokes. It felt so good, and she needed the comfort, the closeness. She leaned further into him and closed her eyes, letting all her other senses take over: the soft feel of his knit shirt and hard muscles beneath, his scent, male and musky, with a hint of cologne and soap, the sound of his even breathing, and his heart beating steadily beneath her hand.

Opening her eyes, she met his gaze and held it for

only a moment before he leaned over and kissed her.

His firm lips fit hers so neatly, and before she could even think twice about it, she kissed him back, hesitantly at first, and then more passionately.

He grabbed her rear and pulled her close to straddle him, chest to chest, groin to groin, and in a split second she knew where this would end.

And she didn't care.

She wanted him; wanted to feel his hands all over her again, wanted to feel him hard inside her. She wanted the mindless, driving need to take her away, if only for a little while. More than anything, she wanted the sweet bliss of release, the breaking of the even sweeter tension already rapidly building within her.

"Make love to me," she whispered. She could feel he was ready and willing, and was only waiting for the green light.

He pulled away and reached for his back pocket.

She grinned. "Aren't you the prepared one?"

He returned her smile, then pulled her to him for another kiss, this time roughly, hungrily, and with a heat that fired her own needs. He had her pants unzipped within seconds and shoved them down along with her underwear. Cassie unzipped his pants as well, freeing his erection, and kissed him again as she ran her fingers over the hard length of him, loving the hot, smooth feel of his skin. Then, after halting long enough to take care of the condom, Alex grabbed her hips and pulled her down.

She felt the tip of his penis probing at her, seeking entrance, and then the sensation of him sliding inside, filling her deeply, stretching her with a pressure that was pure pleasure, and she gasped.

"God," he muttered, breathing tightly. "You feel so good."

She couldn't answer; all she could do was squeeze her eyes shut, focusing intently on the sensations where they joined, building with every movement. She didn't want to feel anything but that inner tightness, and willed it to swell, to break into waves upon waves of release.

Panting with the effort, she moved faster, and he helped, spreading her legs farther apart so that he could go deeper. She gasped again; a high, sharp sound as the first thrum of her orgasm rippled over her; then it completely took hold and she came hard, moaning as each tremor shook her, head to toe.

Sated, she melted against him, her hands clutching at his chest. Before her breathing and her heartbeat had a chance to settle down, he slipped his hand beneath her shirt and unfastened her bra.

"Now that we got that out of the way, let's have some fun." His low, breathless tone brought a fresh rush of desire.

Cassie yelped as he pushed her back against the ground and moved between her legs. He pushed her shirt aside, and the instant his hot mouth covered her breast, the sticks and little rocks beneath her ceased to matter. All she could feel was Alex's mouth, pulling and teasing her breasts, making her moan and arch against him, wordlessly urging him to slip inside her again.

His hand eased between her thighs, touching her where she ached most, stroking her with light, feathery touches until another orgasm rippled through her, this one short and sweet. The taut pull of pleasure had barely subsided before he was inside her again, and Cassie thought she would pass out because he felt so damn good.

Alex knew exactly where to touch her, how to touch her. He knew when to slow down, when to go faster. And when that sharp, intense pang began building from deep within her again, he rocked back, taking her knees over his shoulders, and thrust into her more quickly, each stroke going deeper until she went spinning into a pleasure haze, vaguely aware that he, too, had found his release.

Cassie lay gasping, unable to move, Alex heavy over her. She was completely spent, every muscle relaxed and liquidly warm. When the last eddy of desire faded, she was still trembling.

Good God, did the man know how to screw or what? She couldn't remember sex *ever* being this good.

Finally Alex recovered himself enough to move off

her, and she instantly regretted the loss. She wanted his closeness, his heat, his rock-solid comfort.

Instead, he reached for his pants, then tossed hers to her without saying a word.

Uneasily, Cassie sat up and quickly put her clothes back in order, wondering what was going through his mind right then. And wondering if she'd just made one of the biggest mistakes of her life.

# Nineteen

THEY WALKED FOR HOURS BEFORE FINDING THE HIGH-
way, then walked even more before hitching a ride
with a taciturn truck driver who took them to a truck
stop outside Laramie. They didn't talk about what had
happened, but Cassie could tell Alex was more tense
than a man should be right after having great sex.

Maybe he was regretting having taken things so
far, too. When life finally returned to normal, the
undeniable shift in the balance of power was bound
to lead to problems.

But she couldn't worry about that now. It was
done, and there were more pressing concerns.

When they reached the truck stop, Alex talked an
old cowboy into driving them the rest of the way to
Mae's for the hundred-odd dollars left in his wallet.

Mae lived on the outskirts of Bosler, in a little
unincorporated village called Branston, which didn't

claim more than a hundred residents. The old cowboy dropped them off on Main Street, and by the time Cassie and Alex walked up to Mae's house, it was late in the day.

Mae's house was a tiny prefab, well-kept and pretty, with the nearest neighbor a quarter mile away. Standing by the back door, Cassie tried to figure out how to get inside—then watched, gape-jawed, as Alex smashed the door's window with a rock and reached inside to unlock it.

"That wasn't very . . . covert."

He shrugged. "I'd pick the lock, but I don't know how."

Still stunned, she said faintly, "I know someone who picks locks."

He pushed the door wide. "Sounds like you have some interesting friends."

"You don't know the half of it." Cassie wished Diana were here; she'd would know exactly what to do.

A few seconds later, they were inside. Mae, like most rural people, had no security system. But then, she didn't have much worth stealing.

"So what are we looking for?" Cassie asked.

"I have no idea. Let's poke around and see what we find."

In silence they began searching the small house, finding food in the refrigerator, clothes and shoes in the closet, toiletries in the bathroom.

"She just left everything behind," Cassie said. Mae's betrayal finally felt real, and sadness and anger dragged at her, making her want to flop down on the floor and cry.

"I have a feeling she's not coming back." Alex was now searching her computer. "Hey . . . I think I've got something here. Come take a look at this."

She came up behind him. "What?"

"Gotta love browser history files and caches—these are the most recent websites she visited." He started clicking on links. "Lots of Vermont pages . . . maps, general information."

"She's going to *Vermont?*" Cassie stared at the changing screen images, dumbfounded. "Why all the way across the country, when she can just cross the border in Montana?"

"Don't know, but there must be a reason . . . and look what we have here, the U-Haul site. Betcha she made a reservation online."

"Can you find out?"

"Depends if she's auto-logged in." He clicked on the log-in link, but the form came up with only Mae's e-mail filled in. "We need a password."

Cassie frowned. "Try Trixie."

Alex's brows shot up, but he did so. The first time it didn't work. On the next try, using all caps, he got in. "Looks like she's dropping off an eight-foot trailer in Newport. Christ, that was easy."

"I figured since this was all about Trixie, maybe Mae would do the obvious."

"If I weren't so pissed off, I'd almost be embarrassed for her."

"She wasn't expecting us to get away from her hired goons, much less end up here. I think you're right about her not coming back, so she probably didn't care what she left behind. I have a friend who's a private investigator, and she says most crooks aren't terribly bright. Though I don't think Mae's a professional."

"I agree. I think this von Lahr made her an offer she couldn't refuse." Alex looked up, frowning. "You know PIs *and* lock pickers?"

"The PI and the lock picker are getting married. It's their wedding I'm going to."

Alex stared at her, surprise plain in his dark eyes. "Okay."

"And now that I'm thinking about it, Diana specializes in black-market and antiquities thefts, so she might know about this von Lahr." Cassie eyed the phone on the desk. "Well, hell. We may as well give the local law enforcement folks a clue about where to start looking. I'm calling Diana."

"I guess it can't hurt."

"And then I'm going to make a few other calls, because I just had a brainstorm."

Diana was in her office. "Hey, there. What's up?

You calling about wedding stuff? You're not backing out on me at the last minute, are you?"

Just like Diana—charmingly blunt. "I'm fine. I'll be there to see you shackle yourself to Mr. Wonderful, providing I'm not in jail."

Silence. "Is there something you want to tell me?"

"Long story, and I don't have time to go into details. Remember that little treasure I found? The one I told you about a few weeks ago?"

"Yes."

"Somebody stole it, then kidnapped me and Alex, but we got away and—"

"Alex who?"

Oh, boy. This could be embarrassing. "The man otherwise known as that arrogant ass from Laramie."

As Alex started laughing, Diana said, "Oh, *that* guy. This sounds complicated. Are you okay?"

"I'm mostly pissed off. One of my own employees set it all up."

"Oh, Cassie . . . I'm sorry."

"Thanks." The concern in her friend's voice helped soothe some of the sting of betrayal—and reminded her the world was full of decent people, too. "But I have a question for you. It looks like somebody recruited my employee, and I think his name is von Lahr. I was wondering if you'd ever heard of such a person. Someone who'd be able to fence something as valuable as an infant *Tyrannosaurus rex*?"

"Did you say von Lahr? Urk!"

"Yes, and what," Cassie demanded, exchanging looks with Alex, "does 'urk!' mean?"

"It means you don't mess with this guy." Diana's voice was serious. "The U.S., French, British, Italian, and Turkish governments have been after Rainert von Lahr for years but have never managed to catch him. He's something of a black-market mercenary."

Cassie's mouth suddenly felt dry. "Guys like that exist?"

"Oh, yeah. Never underestimate what rich, powerful people will do to get something they want, and von Lahr is one of the ways they acquire little trinkets they have no business acquiring. He's dangerous. It's rumored he has no qualms about killing."

"He didn't kill me or Alex," Cassie pointed out.

"But he didn't directly deal with you, did he?" Diana countered. "It was one of his flunkies."

True. "So how do we catch this guy?"

"You go to the authorities and let them do it."

"No can do. Alex was set up to look like the main suspect, and we don't have enough time to get through to the right people and convince them that he's not guilty and we're not crazy. If she's taken that fossil across state lines, the FBI would have to be involved, and then you've got all these law enforcement types getting in each other's way. By the time they cross all their T's and dot all their I's and argue over who gets to be top dog, it'll be too late. If that fossil leaves this country, we'll never see her again."

After a moment, Diana said, "Besides, it's personal."

Cassie smiled. "There is that. You know me."

"Yes, which is why I know it's futile to tell you to leave this to the professionals. I see your point, I just don't like it. Let me make some calls to try to dig up more dirt on this guy. Is there a way I can get hold of you?"

"No, but I can call you if you give me a date and a time."

"Will do. Do you know where your ex-employee is going?"

"Newport, Vermont, by the looks of it."

"And you know this, how?"

Cassie quickly explained, and there was a surprised silence before Diana said, "I'm impressed. Good job. Okay, I'll see if anybody can help narrow down points of departure von Lahr might use. He's probably heading into Canada by a private airfield, and since Vermont's not exactly a hotbed of crime, knowing even that much should help. How quickly can you get to Newport?"

Cassie chewed on her lip, frowning. "A guy who freelances for me also works for a wilderness expedition outfit and has his own plane. He'll fly us out there if I ask. He might also know about airfields."

"Do that. Get there as soon as you can, and once you're there, call me if you still need my help."

"Will do."

"I really can't talk you out of this?"

"I'm not taking any chances, Diana, even if it gets me into trouble with the authorities. That kind of trouble can be sorted out with enough time, but losing that fossil can't be fixed—ever. She's a one-in-a-million find. I'm not giving the feds or a bunch of interstate lawmen a chance to bungle this."

She hung up, then turned to Alex. "Did you get the gist of all that?"

"This von Lahr guy is seriously bad shit, and your friend thinks we're idiots for not turning this over to the cops."

"Wow. Very good."

"And your brainstorm is to call Russ Noble and ask him for a lift to Vermont."

"Exactly. I suspect Russ likes excitement and would get involved just because he's bored."

She dialed again, and her mother answered. There was another short, tense conversation before Cassie interrupted and said, "Is Russ there?"

"Um . . . yes, I think he's with Wyatt. We've canceled everything until this mess with you is straightened out. The police—"

"Put Russ on the phone. I need to talk to him."

"Cassie, I wish you would rethink all this! Let the police handle it, that's their job."

This refrain was getting old. "I can't. Put Russ on, please. The clock's ticking, Mom, and I don't have time to explain everything. You're just going to have to trust me. For once, can you do that?"

Her mother was silent for a long moment, then she sighed. "Hold on. I'll get him."

A few moments later, Russ said, "Cassie? It's Russ. Are you okay?"

"I'm fine. A little pressed for time, though, so I'm going to be brief. I need a favor. Can you fly me and Martinelli to Vermont?"

"Uh, I guess. Where to?"

"I'm not exactly sure, but around Newport would be good. I'm hoping you can help us pin down private airfields in that area." She quickly summed up the situation, including the details about Mae and von Lahr, and waited for Russ's response.

"This is definitely one of the stranger requests I've ever had. I can narrow things down for you, since there's not a whole lot of options if they're taking a private plane, which would be my guess. If they're using a truck or a boat, though, you're screwed."

"It's a risk we have to take."

"Where are you now?"

After Cassie gave him the general directions, Russ

said, "Okay. I know where that is. I can leave right now, and it'll take me about thirty or forty minutes to get there. Then we can drive to where I keep my plane. It's just outside of Laramie."

Cassie exchanged looks with Alex and signaled him with a thumbs-up. "Thanks, Russ. I appreciate this."

"No problem. I was getting tired of sitting around and watching your family detonate. And Wyatt's here; he wants to talk to you."

"Tell him I said hello and I'll be home soon." Cassie hung up. Cowardly, yes, but she wasn't up to dealing with Wyatt. "Russ will be here in about a half an hour, then he'll take us to his plane."

"This is good." Alex stood up from the computer desk and stretched, smiling. "If Russ can help us find the right airfield, and if Mae and von Lahr are taking Trixie out by plane, we have a chance of intercepting them. Either way we'll get to Newport before Mae, even though she has nearly a day's head start on us. Then we'll keep an eye out for a U-Haul driven by a nerdy brunette who's turned out to be a real pain in the ass. Why do you think she did this?"

"I just don't know. You think you know someone, and trust them, and then they go do something like this. I don't know what to think anymore. Let's just focus on finding our baby and bringing her safely back home."

# Twenty

❖

IN THE BRIEF TIME THEY HAD TO WAIT, ALEX DECIDED they should take advantage of the shower and kitchen. Cassie showered first, and he would've joined her if he hadn't been so sure where it would lead—there wasn't time for that. He showered after her, then joined her in the kitchen to get something to eat.

Alex was still eating when the sound of tires crunching on gravel caught his attention. "Looks like Russ is early," he said, walking toward the door. "He must've broken a few speed limits to get here this fast."

He cautiously separated the aluminum blinds to look outside.

"Shit!"

Cassie froze, alarm flashing in her eyes. "What's wrong?"

"It's not Russ."

Alex reached for the gun he'd shoved in the back of his jeans. The big black pickup outside—with a dented front fender—wasn't familiar, but the two men inside were. "It's our friends from the truck camper."

"What?" Cassie came up beside him and peered through the blinds. "How the hell did they get away from the tree, much less find us *here?*"

"Somebody probably cut them loose. And if they're trackers, it wouldn't have been hard to follow us to the highway." Another thought came to him, and he glanced at Cassie. "They were waiting for Mae to call. If they talked with her and told her what happened, she'd know we'd head for her place. And now she knows we're coming after her."

Cassie briefly closed her eyes. "So what do we do? Russ is going to be here any minute! He's going to drive right into a very bad situation."

"We're not in such a great position, either. We have guns but not much ammo. So if we start shooting, we risk running out of bullets before they do. They also have a truck, and we don't. And I'm not sure if I can take either of them out."

Her eyes widened. "You mean kill them?"

"I'm not seeing a lot of options if it comes to them or us. Or Russ."

Cassie nodded, understanding. She took the other

gun in a firm grip, although he could see her shaking slightly.

It made him oddly proud; God, she had guts. He had no idea what he would've done if she'd burst into hysterics.

She said, "I'd say our choices are either to wait for them to come in here and jump them, or to blow out their tires and then take our chances and call the cops." She met his gaze. "What do you think?"

Alex hesitated, knowing now was the time to call the police in. Trixie was important but not worth dying for—and in Cassie's eyes he saw quiet acceptance.

"The cops," she said quietly. "It's our only choice now."

Then Alex saw a rooster tail of dust approaching fast. The men in the truck, seeing it as well, leaped out, rifles in hand.

"Sonofabitch," Alex muttered. "It's too late. Russ is coming, but they're going to think it's us." He glanced over his shoulder at her, and a sudden, absolute calm took hold of him. "Get down. Now."

Eyes wide, she dropped to the floor just as he opened fire through the window. He had the gun with the silencer, so Tall and Short didn't notice until the truck's windshield shattered.

Alex ducked down just before the boom of a high-powered rifle answered, taking out the window above him in an explosion of glass. Cassie screamed as Alex covered her with his body.

"Call the cops," he ordered. "Keep low to the floor and watch out for the glass. I'll hold them off as long as I can."

He hoped that Russ Noble, hearing the gunfire, had slammed on the brakes and was hightailing it back the way he'd come.

Scrambling a short distance away, he popped up to fire off a few more rounds, praying it would force them to take cover—or decide to cut their losses, hop back in their truck, and drive away.

Another volley of rifle fire ended that hope. Cassie flinched and dove under the desk, grabbing for the cordless phone.

Before Alex raised his head to risk another look and locate his targets, the chilling sound of a rapid-fire assault rifle cut across the silence. He froze, waiting in an agony of frustrated helplessness for the rain of bullets that would kill them both.

But the bullets didn't come.

A split second later, he realized the assault rifle was firing *away* from the house.

Cassie, stopped in midcrawl, was staring at him. "What the hell is that?"

"An M16," he answered grimly.

The shooting stopped. Silence followed, a silence

so absolute that Alex could hear the ticking of the wall clock from the kitchen.

Then Russ's voice shouted: "Cassie? Alex? Are you in there? Are you okay?"

Alex met Cassie's gaze, her shock equal to his, and then he yelled back, "We're here! We're okay. We're coming out."

Alex slowly opened the front door, which had a hole blown through it, Cassie right behind him, and took in the scene outside. Russ, standing in front of a beat-up old Jeep, casually held the M16 pointed toward the two men lying facedown in the dirt, hands behind their heads, fingers laced.

Alex glanced at Cassie and said, "And you let this guy tour schoolkids around?"

"Hey," Russ called before she could respond. "The cavalry's arrived."

He was grinning. The crazy bastard was actually enjoying this.

Alex pulled Cassie close to him. "Thanks for the rescue."

"No problem. There's a roll of duct tape in the back of my Jeep. Wrap them up good and tight, and let's get out of here. Even from half a mile away, the neighbors will have heard the guns, and the cops won't be far behind."

Ignoring the dozen questions crowding his mind,

Alex motioned for Cassie to follow him. They quickly duct-taped Tall and Short, and before slapping tape over the big man's mouth, Alex got him to admit that Mae had ordered them to the house.

Then Russ hopped into the Jeep, stashed the rifle, and regarded them calmly. "You still want that ride to Vermont?"

Alex turned to Cassie. "I do, but this isn't a decision I can make. What do you want?"

"If we stay and wait for the police, what happened here will just make everything worse." She squared her shoulders and got into the Jeep. "Let's go."

Alex jumped in and wasn't even in his seat when Russ hit the gas.

They took back roads and dirt tracks that barely qualified as roads. As the minutes passed and no flashing lights or sirens followed, Alex relaxed a fraction, though he still felt the adrenaline rush in his pounding heart, his shaking hands. Christ, that had been a little too close for comfort.

"Hey, Russ," he called. "What the hell are you doing with an M16?"

"I decided to come prepared for trouble," Russ answered, glancing back at them with his usual amiable expression. "I also do big game hunting outside the States, and some of the countries I travel in aren't the safest places in the world. This little baby has come in handy a few times."

Alex wasn't sure he believed Russ's answer, reasonable as it sounded. "Ex-military?" he asked shortly.

"Yup. So are you."

Cassie finally spoke. "You were in the military?"

Alex nodded. "A two-year stint in the Army, so I could cash in on the G.I. Bill and go to college. My family didn't have a lot of money."

She laughed. "You're G.I. Dino Joe!"

Relief washed over him to see her already bouncing back. She had a few small cuts from the window glass, as he did, but nothing serious.

Russ picked up the main highway to Laramie, and as he accelerated to the on-ramp, he said, "In all the excitement back there, I forgot to tell you I found a few airfields in Vermont that might work for what you're after. I'll tell you more about it when we get to my plane."

He soon turned off the highway onto a narrow dirt road that led to an airfield with only one runway and two hangars.

A small, beat-up red plane was parked outside, the very epitome of a bush pilot's plane.

"Is that it?" Cassie asked, sounding doubtful.

"Yeah. It doesn't look like much, but it'll get the job done. Trust me." Russ brought the Jeep to a halt by the plane, then climbed out. "She's ready to go, so hop in and get comfortable. I'll grab something to eat and a few supplies."

Russ trotted off, and Alex exchanged looks with Cassie. "I guess for him this is business as usual."

She smiled a little ruefully. "I think I can't possibly be surprised anymore, yet it keeps happening. Even you keep surprising me. I suppose we should get in that thing. We've come this far, we may as well finish it—though I'm sure there'll be hell to pay when we get home."

He agreed, grateful to have her alone for a few calm minutes. Ever since they'd made love, she'd avoided getting close to him, avoided talking about what happened between them. He didn't get it; sex wasn't exactly something you forgot, not like forgetting where you left the car keys or your wallet.

Not that there'd been many chances to talk. And he hadn't been real smooth in the follow-up department, either, but he'd had the distinct impression she'd only wanted him for comfort. After the initial buzz of pleasure had faded, the realization had bothered him.

Now wasn't the time to tackle the issue, but he pulled her close for a quick, possessive kiss. She kissed him back, but he didn't push it any further.

"You okay?" he asked, quietly.

"Feeling a little out of my element, but I'm all right."

Alex opened the main door and helped her inside the plane. The interior was small and worn-looking, and smelled like fuel, but it was tidy and well-maintained. Russ joined them a few minutes later, and after he'd gotten the engine started, he tossed a well-stuffed backpack at their feet and settled into the pilot's seat, pulling on the radio headset and dark aviator sunglasses.

"Uncle Sam teach you how to fly?" Alex asked, as he and Cassie buckled their seat belts.

"I was a Navy transport pilot, but I've been flying since I was a kid. Both my parents were pilots, and we'd make lots of trips to northern Minnesota during the summers. You ready back there?"

Cassie nodded.

"Once I get to cruising altitude, we'll talk. Hang on. Planes like this are bumpier than passenger jets."

Russ looked at ease at the controls, and within minutes he had them airborne.

Alex had flown in small planes before but had forgotten the steady, droning noise of the engine, the roughness of the ride along the air currents. Good thing he wasn't prone to airsickness. He looked at Cassie and didn't see any greenish tinge to her skin, which was a relief. The long trip to Vermont would be much worse if she were throwing up the entire way.

From the small windows, he watched buildings and roads shrink, and as the plane began to level out, Cassie called to Russ, "How long until we get to Vermont?"

"It's pretty much a straight shot, but we'll need to make a few stops for fuel. A Cessna 180 isn't exactly a jet," Russ answered, looking back. "Factoring in the stops, it'll take between twelve and fourteen hours." Seeing her dismay, he added, "Sorry. That's the best I can do."

"No, it's okay." She smiled. "There's no way Mae can make the trip in less than two days. She has to sleep. We'll get there in time."

"What can you tell us about those Vermont airfields?" Alex asked.

Having reached cruising altitude, Russ set the plane on autopilot and turned toward them. "I have a couple leads on airfields where someone might try to sneak Trixie out."

"You came by that information pretty damn fast," Alex said.

"In my line of work I live in small airports, and I run into all kinds of people," Russ explained. "And if my own observations don't give me what I need, a few phone calls usually do the trick. There are four private airfields along the Vermont-Canada border that shady folks might use. All of them have had incidents with the law and were under scrutiny after the terrorist mayhem. They're lax about following proper procedures and are known to have been involved in drug trafficking."

Russ dug in the pockets of his cargo pants, then

pulled out a map and spread it open in the cramped space between them. He took a pen out of his shirt pocket and circled three spots on the map near the Canadian border.

"These are my best guesses." He made an X over a fourth location. "This is another possibility but a remote one. I'll be dropping you off as close as I can to this place, Accord Airfield. It's the shadiest of them all, and I figure the most likely. However, McMullen over here, and Weinstein and Heller over here, are also likely candidates. You should check them out if possible."

Russ pulled a wad of bills out of another pocket and handed it to Cassie. "This is from your mother. She said you'd probably need cash."

At the look of amazement on Cassie's face, Alex smiled. She had a rocky relationship with her mother, but when push came to shove, Ellen had come through.

"Thanks." Cassie quickly stashed away the cash. "I'm sure it'll come in handy."

"What do you plan on doing if you find Mae and this German guy?" Russ asked. "If he's as dangerous as your friend says, it's not a good idea to take him on yourselves."

"I haven't thought that far ahead," Alex admitted.

"And here I thought digging for old bones was going to be boring." Russ grinned. "I'd like to stick around and help you out, but I can't. And if my boss gets wind of what I'm up to, he'll have my head."

"We don't want to get you into trouble—"

"Nah, it's okay. I was exaggerating. Ben's okay with shit like this, providing I cover my ass, but he's not the kind of guy you want to piss off. By the way, there's food in the bag, towelettes, and some Band-Aids. Help yourselves."

"Thanks. I appreciate what you're doing for us," Alex said.

"Hey, I was the guy in charge when Trixie was found, and I want her back as much as you guys do."

Alex doubted that. *Our baby*, Cassie had called it, half jokingly, and the description felt oddly right.

Trixie wasn't a living person who'd never forgive him if he let her down, but somewhere along the line, his connection to that infant rex had struck a deeper emotional chord. He knew what lay behind his guilt and the need to get the fossil back. A baby dinosaur wasn't the same as the daughter who'd become a stranger to him, but it was close enough that he didn't want to fail.

Second chances, chasing after dreams—whatever he wanted to call it, it was important to hold on to the hope that, as Cassie had said, it wasn't too late to start over.

The flight was long and uncomfortable, punctuated by frequent stops to refuel, each one adding to Alex's impatience to reach their destination.

At the next to last fueling stop, Russ told them he needed a short break—which translated into sleeping in the plane itself. Alex didn't think either he or Cassie could possibly sleep in their seats, but he'd underestimated how tiring the day had been. They fell soundly asleep, and Alex woke to Russ shaking his shoulder.

The long flight finally ended with the sun rising just as Russ landed at a little airfield a short distance from their main target.

"This is the best I can do for you. I don't want to raise suspicions by landing at Accord." Russ slid the map toward Alex. "The airfield is about a forty-minute drive from here, and you're going to need transportation."

"Don't worry. We'll figure something out."

His expression hardening, Russ said, "If the stakes get too high, you bail. And if that happens, contact me. I'll find you." The warmth returned to his dark eyes. "I'm Indian, and I can track anything."

Cassie grinned and patted his arm. "Give it up, Russ. I read your résumé and interviewed you, remember? You're only half Cheyenne, and you were born and raised in Minneapolis."

"Ah, but it's genetic." He winked. "That's why I'm so good at my job."

Exactly what that job entailed, Alex wasn't sure, but he suspected it was more than escorting rich businessmen around the globe to play Big White Hunter.

"Thanks for everything, Russ," Cassie said. "We couldn't have done it without you. I owe you one."

"Technically you owe my boss, but we'll talk about that when you get back home." Russ glanced at Alex. "You take good care of her."

The warning in his voice was clear, and Alex nodded. "Will do. And like the lady said, thank you."

Alex and Cassie stood out of the way as Russ turned the small plane around and taxied down the runway for a smooth takeoff.

They watched until the Cessna was just a dark speck in the sky, then Cassie said, "Well. Here we are in Vermont. Now what do we do?"

"We find transportation."

"If this was a typical airport, I'd say we grab a taxi or rent a car. But I don't see anything that qualifies as a terminal, much less a taxi line."

"We can call one. We have time on our side."

"Providing Russ's guess about Accord Airfield is the right one," Cassie said. "I trust his instincts, though. A taxi will cost us a small fortune, but the sooner we get to this little town here"—she pointed to the map—"the better."

# Twenty-one

❖

As it turned out, a friendly mechanic getting off work and looking to make a little extra cash offered to drive them to town. The man talked the entire way about his new wife, his new baby, his job, engines, and planes, which meant they didn't have to answer any inconvenient questions.

"Eventually, our luck is going to run out," Alex said, as they stood by a gas station in the quaint little town of Bushman's Corner and watched their chauffeur drive away in his puttering old truck. "Then the shit's really gonna hit the fan."

"I think I'm getting used to it, actually. It's almost like, 'Ho-hum; I've been kidnapped and shot at. How mundane.'" She traded grins with him. "This isn't much of a town, is it? No chance of escaping notice around here. Then again, the same goes for any shifty

Germans and geeky girls toting huge, heavy crates. What do we do now?"

"Find a place to stay."

"Where? I don't exactly see any Holiday Inns or Marriotts around."

Alex jabbed his finger at a point on the map. "The Merry Woods Campground. It looks as if there are a lot of campgrounds in this area . . . but I guess there's not much else to do when your main resources are trees, big hills, and tourists."

"Alex, we don't have a camper or a tent. Somebody will notice if we're just lurking around a campground."

"We can get a tent. Or we might get lucky and find visitor cabins, or a camper we can rent. And if I'm reading this map right, the campground is only about a thirty-minute walk from here."

"Well, we look like hiker types, so let's get these boots a-walking."

They set out down the road that cut through the downtown area lined with turn-of-the-century storefronts. Traffic was light, and most of the people they passed smiled politely at them. As they neared a small diner, the smell of fried hamburgers and coffee wafted out and they exchanged looks, then turned on their heels and headed inside.

"Food," Cassie said with a sigh. "I've almost forgotten what real food tastes like." She planted herself in front of the diner. "Must. Stop. Must. Eat."

Alex grinned. He liked that she could make even simple things, like ordering a hamburger, fun. "Sounds good. I was getting tired of Russ's protein bars, trail mix, and bottled water. He eats like a damn herd animal."

Inside the diner, they found a booth off to the side. The overstuffed vinyl bench felt like heaven. After everything they'd been through in the last twenty-four hours, it was good just to sit in normal surroundings.

After ordering, Alex lounged back and watched Cassie. She looked tired, stress adding careworn lines to her face. Still, she was one of the most beautiful women he'd ever met. Everything about her pushed all his buttons: the right buttons, the wrong buttons . . . and especially the hot buttons.

With so much crazy stuff going on, he'd hardly had time to reflect on the fact that, not long ago, he'd made love to her; had been deeply, blissfully inside her. Just thinking about it made him hard, which was damn inconvenient, considering their situation.

What did *she* think about the sex? She hadn't said anything, although he sometimes caught her watching him, an almost puzzled expression in her eyes. If it had been only about comfort to her, he wasn't sure he wanted to hear it.

"You're awfully quiet." Cassie's soft voice broke through his thoughts, and he met her gaze across the table. Her dark eyes were unreadable, and he had an overwhelming urge to reach over and brush those wild curls away from her face so he could feel the soft, smooth skin of her cheek.

Christ. He was mooning after her like a kid again.

"Just thinking," he said. "My brain's still trying to catch up with everything that's happened with us."

Her cheeks flushed, and he knew she understood what he meant.

"That was probably one of the stupider things we've done. Probably best not to think much about it."

"I figured you'd say that."

She shifted, looking down as she played with her napkin. "You're saying it wasn't one of the dumber things we've done?"

"I'm saying I wouldn't be too quick to jump to conclusions, since this is hardly the best moment for—" For what? "For that." Then he added, "Though you acted like you didn't mind too much."

A small smile curved her mouth, but she still didn't look at him. "If you're fishing for compliments on your studliness, have no fear. You rocked the Casbah."

That startled a laugh out of him. He sensed she wasn't exactly comfortable with the emotional stuff. Most women were all touchy-feely when it came to things like this, and he'd gotten pretty good at dealing with it. It was just his luck he'd get seriously involved with a woman who threw everything he knew as normal right out the window.

Then again, he should've expected as much from her.

"I just wanted to make sure you were okay with it."

She laughed. "Martinelli, I'm thirty-six years old. I knew what I was doing. No regrets. It was nice."

*Nice?*

Their food arrived, but he still couldn't get her out of his mind, since being with her felt so . . . right.

What a lousy time to lose his head over a woman.

"What are you smirking about?" Cassie asked, eyeing him with humor.

"Three guesses."

"Pervert."

"Did I tell you I really like smart women?"

She grinned, opened her mouth and bit down on a fry, then slowly sucked it into her mouth.

*Goddamn.*

What on earth was wrong with her? The last thing she should be thinking about right now was getting naked with a man, no matter how hot he was.

Like she'd ever had any doubts Alex Martinelli would be great in bed. Everything about him was physical, sensual, and vital. Just being near him made her nerve endings tingle.

She still wanted him. It was that simple.

Sex with him had been incredible, but she didn't think it would be wise to repeat it.

Too bad, really, because it had been so long since she'd felt like a desirable, sexy woman.

"Why do you sleep with so many women?" she asked. Alex choked and nearly spat his soft drink all over the table.

"Where the hell did that come from?" He quickly glanced around as if embarrassed. Who'd have thought the notorious Alex Martinelli could be embarrassed over a question about sex?

Okay, so it *was* a bit personal. And rather abrupt. "I'm just wondering. Since you've added me to the scoreboard, I'd like to know."

He frowned, then slumped back in his seat. "I don't know. You're not the first person to ask. I guess I just don't want to be alone, and sometimes that's the only way I'm not."

His simple honesty touched her. "We should try trading places. I'm *never* alone. My family, my friends, the people who work for me, the customers . . . Sometimes I desperately wish for a little me time."

"Is it really all that bad?"

She hesitated, then said, "No, but even when I'm surrounded by all those people, I still feel alone, because they don't really understand me. The only people I could really talk to, besides my father, were my best friends from college."

"So you boss people around to keep yourself a part of everything."

"I do not boss people around! I—"

"I sleep with warm bodies," Alex interrupted, raising a brow. "You act like a dictator. We all have our coping mechanisms."

She couldn't help smiling. "Okay, I'll grant you that one."

A few moments passed as they ate, then Alex said, "I know what you mean about feeling alone; I was always living in my own world, too. I got along well with other kids and was popular, but there was always this feeling like I couldn't . . . connect. I guess that's what you mean."

Cassie nodded. "I don't make close friends very easily. I've never been much for socializing, and I have trouble relating with other women—they don't relate to me well, either. My college friends were the only people I could be myself with . . . and you, for some reason. Really, you're the nicest guy I've ever hated."

He smiled. It made her go all warm in places best not warmed in public, and she reminded herself that she didn't want to get involved with a serial heart-breaker.

"We should go find that campground. Then I suppose we should start asking questions," she said.

Alex nodded. "Yeah, the making-it-up-as-we-go-along thing has been working out pretty well so far, but it'd be damn embarrassing if these guys flew in and out with Trixie while we were eating lunch."

"I'm glad you're here," Cassie said quietly. "I couldn't have done this alone."

"We make a good team."

"When we're working toward the same end, sure. But that's not usually the case. You know that, Alex."

He didn't answer, and they finished eating and set off for the Merry Woods Campground in silence.

# Twenty-two

❖

"THE GODS ARE ON OUR SIDE. I KNEW IT," ALEX SAID, staring. "Would you look at that?"

The Merry Woods Campground had a quaint, worn charm, with its retro log cabins and signs that had been on the cutting edge of advertising in the 1950s, but now looked hopelessly naïve.

But what had really grabbed his attention was a Winnebago RV parked outside the campground's office. At least twenty years old, it had a sun-faded FOR SALE OR RENT sign propped crookedly on the windshield.

"Alex, you can't be serious."

"It's worth a shot. We can park it at the airfield and tell people we're waiting for a friend to fly in, or something."

"That could work—providing it even runs."

"All it has to do is get us to the airfield. If it dies

while we're there, that'll give us even more of a reason to stay."

"And what if we have the wrong airfield?"

"Then we'll check out the others."

Cassie laughed. "You really know how to show a girl a good time, Martinelli. Okay; let's go for it."

The elderly woman who shuffled forward to meet them in the campground office looked as original to the place as the general decor. She wore stretch shorts, a cat T-shirt, and fuzzy pink slippers.

"Hello," she said brightly, her smile showing a fine set of dentures. "Welcome to Merry Woods Campground. I'm Mrs. Merry."

Alex grinned back, liking the woman on the spot. There was something to be said for being comfortable with your eccentricities. "Hi. My girlfriend and I want to ask about that Winnebago out front. Is it still for rent?"

"Certainly! But," she added sternly, "only on an as-is basis."

"I understand. Does it run?"

"Yes, yes. My great-grandson works on it and sometimes takes it out for a drive. He's seventeen and learning about cars and engines. He's quite good," she added quickly.

"We're in need of a camper since our reservations got messed up," Alex said. "How much?"

"For renting, we were asking two hundred a day, but I'm thinking fifty dollars is more reasonable."

"Deal," Alex said, then turned to Cassie. "We'll rent it for three days."

She blinked. "Why are you looking at me?"

"Because you're the one with all the money."

"Oh. Sorry, I forgot."

He waited as she dug out the wad of cash her mother had provided, peeled off three fifty-dollar bills, then handed them to the woman.

"I'll get the keys and the paperwork, and then you can be on your way," Mrs. Merry said. "Nothing too formal, I'll just need to see your driver's licenses."

*That shouldn't be a problem,* Alex decided. Nobody in Vermont would be looking for them. Not yet, anyway. "Sure. Does it have a full tank of gas?"

"Probably not, but the nearest gas station is just down the road a bit. Wait here. I'll be right back."

The old woman shuffled away, leaving them in silence except for the game show blaring on a nearby TV.

"I can't believe I just threw away a hundred fifty dollars on such a worthless piece of junk," Cassie said, wrinkling her nose.

"Didn't your mother ever tell you not to look a gift horse in the mouth? Adapt or fail."

She laughed. "Only a paleontologist would use Darwinism to justify renting an ancient Winnebago. But I get your point."

The old woman returned with papers and a key

chain. "Here's the rental form. I'll go photocopy your licenses while you fill it out. By the way, I forgot to ask your names. How rude of me!"

"I'm Alex, and this is Cassie," Alex said, as they handed over their licenses.

"It's very nice to meet you, Alex and Cassie." She walked over to a small copier. "Are you visiting Vermont? New to the area?"

"First time in the state," Alex said, filling out the very basic form, then signing it. "We're meeting up with some friends to go hiking, but they're running late."

"So you plan on doing some sightseeing as well?"

"Yes," Cassie answered, signing the form as well "Though we didn't actually do much planning. We're just taking things as they come."

"Sometimes, my dear, that's the best way to live life. Enjoy your stay in Vermont!"

"Okay, this is your brainchild," Cassie said once they were outside. "So you're driving this sorry excuse for an RV."

"I've driven worse." He unlocked the passenger door and opened it for her, and she slowly climbed in. The RV smelled old and musty, the seats were split and patched in places, and a fine film of dust covered everything, but it looked serviceable.

"I'm not feeling the love here," Cassie said, looking around gingerly.

Alex went around to the other side and climbed in. "It's not much different from what we sleep in while we're living in the field. It might even be better," he added after checking out the back. "It has a real bed."

She shot him a quick look. "Yuck. God knows who slept in it before us, and if we have to sleep there, I want a blanket over it first."

Women could be so fastidious at the strangest times. They'd had sex out in the woods, and she made a living crawling around dirt and rocks, but an old mattress gave her the willies. "Okay," he said with a grin. "Later we can head back into town and pick up a few things."

"You don't even know if this thing is going to go two feet down the driveway, much less to town."

Alex put the key into the ignition and turned it, and a grinding sound answered as the engine worked to turn over. After a few seconds, he stopped, not wanting to flood the engine. He waited, then tried again, carefully pumping the accelerator. The engine continued to whir and whine; then, with a teeth-rattling grind, it rumbled to life and the whole RV started shaking.

Cassie grabbed at her seat. "Whoa, it'll rattle apart!"

"It'll hold together, but it won't be the smoothest ride." Still grinning, Alex put the clumsy vehicle into gear. Over the years, he'd driven—and had to repair—semitrucks, ancient pickups, and even heavy equipment; this wasn't any different. "Hey. This is gonna be fun."

She glared at him, grabbing her seat as the RV rocked toward the road. "You have a strange definition of fun."

"I'd be lying if I said I wasn't enjoying this."

It was true; for some reason, he felt a sizzling, alive kind of spark he hadn't felt for such a long time. The situation sucked, they were probably getting themselves into serious trouble, everybody thought they were crazy, the chances of ultimately succeeding were next to zero—and he couldn't remember the last time he'd felt so right with his life.

He glanced at Cassie, and she laughed. "You know what? You're right. I'm not cozy and comfortable, but I'm . . . feeling good about things."

"Two of a kind, you and me," he said, pointing the RV toward the road. "Natural-born fighters."

At the gas station, while Alex fed gallon upon gallon of gasoline to the hungry beast they were driving, Cassie stocked up on convenience food and a few toiletries. The old gas station also served as a general store, a small diner, a bait and tackle shop, and a very modest wilderness outfitter. The selections were slim and prices thievishly high, but beggars couldn't be choosy.

Cassie gave a hefty portion of her money to the

congenial man at the cash register, then joined Alex in the Beast. He took in all the bags she deposited in the back, brow raised.

"Nesting?"

"No," she retorted, "I'm establishing some semblance of civilized living. Are we ready to go?"

He patted the guns he had stashed in the back of his jeans, hidden by his shirt. "Ready as we'll ever be."

"Then let's get Beast on the road."

Alex grinned and set the Beast rumbling toward their destination. "Where do you suppose Mae is about now?"

"Half the country lies between Wyoming and Vermont. Even if she's driving straight through, which I doubt, it'll take a few days. Why do you think they didn't fly Trixie out of Wyoming? Why go through all this trouble?"

"To slow down any pursuit," he said. "All the diversions and movement complicate the situation. They're counting on that. Also, carting around a big chunk of rock isn't exactly inconspicuous, so regular air travel is out of the question. Between the distance and distractions and flying the cargo over the border from a private airfield half the country away, I'd say it's a damn good plan."

"Maybe. But von Lahr didn't factor in that we're the most stubborn people on the planet." Cassie folded her arms across her chest. "I can't wait to see the look on Mae's face."

"About that—when we do confront these people, you take Mae and let me handle the German. If what your friend says is true, the guy is dangerous. He'd probably kill you *and* Mae, given half a chance."

"And you're immune to death because you have a Y chromosome?"

"I'm the one with the guns, and I know how to use them. I'm not exactly commando material, but I can get the job done."

"There's so much about you I don't know."

The RV picked up speed, and Alex glanced at the map on the floor between their seats. "Goes both ways. It's not like we ever tried to get to know each other before. We spent a lot of years assuming things."

She couldn't argue with that. "How long until we're there?"

"About forty minutes. This thing doesn't have speed on its side."

"What are you going to say when we get there?"

"That we're waiting to pick up some friends who are flying in, but we're not exactly sure when they'll arrive."

"Except they probably know who's coming in and when, and they'll have no record of our mythical friends."

"Somebody must've forgot to file the flight plan."

"They'll be suspicious. Shady people are suspicious by nature."

"Is that right?" He gave her that wide, infectious smile that made her want to crawl onto his lap and nibble his lips. He was totally nibblicious.

They exchanged casual talk for the rest of the ride, and even though Cassie's nerves were strung tight, she appreciated the view as they drove along. Vermont was calendar-pretty, with its rolling, tree-covered hills and little burgs tucked into gentle valleys. It seemed almost blasphemous to use such a pretty place for such ugly purposes.

"The airfield should be right up this way," Alex said, and as they turned off the main road, they saw a weather-worn sign: ACCORD AIR — PRIVATE.

"Uh-oh. It has a locked gate."

"So we ask to be let in."

There was a battered courtesy phone at the gate, and Alex motioned for her to make the call.

"Why me?"

"Women aren't as threatening. Whoever answers is more likely to be helpful with you than with me."

Cassie shrugged. "Well, here goes." The instructions were long since faded, so she took a guess and hit 0. After a few rings, a man answered.

"Accord. How may I help you?"

He sounded professional enough, and she did her

best to morph into Susie Hiker: "Um, hi? Is this Accord Airfield?"

A short silence. "Yes."

"Okay. Just making sure, because the gate out here is locked."

"Who is this?"

"My name is Ashley. I'm here with my boyfriend, Martin, and we have a friend flying in? We're supposed to meet with them here, but I'm not sure if it's today or tomorrow."

"What is your friend's name?"

Uhhhh . . . "Russ. Russ Noble. He's with Sheridan Expeditions, a wilderness tour outfit."

She hoped Russ wouldn't mind, and she really hoped these people hadn't a clue who Russ really was. Or Sheridan Expeditions, for that matter.

"I don't recall any scheduled flights by this pilot or company. Are you sure you have the right airfield?"

"Are there any other Accord Airfields in Vermont?"

The man on the other end sighed. "No, but we're a private airfield. Our customers are usually businessmen, not tourists."

"Well, our friend said he was coming in today or tomorrow and gave us this name and address. Could somebody open the gate and let us in? Maybe we could talk to your manager?"

"I *am* the manager. Wait for the buzzer. After it

sounds the gate will open. Drive through to the main office. You can't miss it, since it's yellow and there's a sign that says 'Main Office' out front."

"Okay. Thanks." After Cassie hung up she told Alex, "Well, they don't sound too shady, just unfriendly. 'We don't do tourists,'" she said, imitating the man's voice.

"I don't care, just as long as they open this gate. I wasn't expecting locked gates," he said, a little irritably. "But that makes picking up the RV even better. If you have to ram a gate, you need something big."

"No gate ramming!" Cassie leveled her fiercest frown on him. "We need to keep a low profile. Remember, we're just a couple of confused, harmless hikers."

The gate made a squawking sound and then opened, its hinges protesting.

"God, it's like the creaky sound of doom from a horror movie," Cassie said, as Alex put the RV in gear and moved forward. "If I were the superstitious type, I'd be peeing my pants right now."

He glanced down, grinning. "Good thing you're the ballsy type." Then he leaned forward, narrowing his eyes. "Okay, here we go. Pay attention to the layout; remember where everything is."

Obediently, Cassie looked around. It was a small airfield; nothing much to see beyond a dozen aluminum hangars, rusted from years of harsh weather, and a modest runway with side roads for maneuvering and taxiing. "There's the main office—what a hideous shade of yellow. Why on earth would anybody paint a building that color?"

"Maybe it's a landmark from the air. Or maybe they painted it yellow so any airplanes sneaking around in the dark with illegal cargo won't run into it."

Cassie laughed. "I doubt airplanes sneak around. Hey, there's planes in the hangars. Do you think our German is already here?"

"There's a good chance he is."

"How are we going to find out without warning him off?"

"Powers of observation. We be patient, and listen and look."

"Somebody just came out of that ugly office. Must be the guy I talked to on the phone."

"Probably. Time to flex your acting skills."

*Keep it simple*, she reminded herself. The simpler the lie, the less likely they'd make mistakes.

The man who watched their approach was young, tall, fair-haired, and ordinary-looking.

Alex said, "Hi, I'm Martin. You talked to my girlfriend a couple of minutes ago. Sorry to be such a bother, but I appreciate your taking the time to help us clear up the confusion."

"Come on inside. I'm Van Hollander, the day manager." He motioned them into the concrete block building, which was plainly furnished and smelled like a mechanic's shop. "I checked the log again, and there's no flight plan registered for any Russ Noble or a Sheridan Expeditions."

"Is it possible somebody just forgot?" Alex asked.

"Yes, but not likely."

"I don't know what to tell you. This is the place where he said to meet him."

Hollander's pale gaze shifted beyond Alex to the Beast parked outside. "Are you part of a tourist group?"

"Oh, no," Cassie chimed in. "We're just a bunch of friends getting together to hike through parks."

"Do you have a number to call?"

"We didn't think to bring it. This was kind of a last-minute trip, and we didn't plan it too carefully," Alex said.

"I see. Perhaps you have a cell phone number where I can reach you should your friend show up?"

"I do." Cassie held up her cell phone, and did her best to look embarrassed. "Except I forgot the charger at home. Would you mind terribly much if we just parked our RV somewhere out of your way and waited?"

The man was shaking his head before she even finished the sentence. "I'm sorry. I can let you wait here for a short time, but you'll need to leave after regular office hours."

Alex shrugged. "Not a problem. We'll just come back later."

"Your choice," he said curtly. "But I'd appreciate it if you didn't cause any disturbances."

Turning up the cuteness factor, Cassie said earnestly, "We're just waiting for our friend to show up. We're not troublemakers."

Caving, Hollander smiled back. "Fine. If you'd like, I can do a search for Sheridan Expeditions and find their phone number."

*Yikes!* "Good idea. I should've thought of that."

"If you remember your friend's phone number and want to call him, you can use one of our phones."

"You've been a big help, thanks." Cassie smiled sweetly. "For now, we'll wait outside so we don't bother you."

# Twenty-three

❖

OUTSIDE, CASSIE GRABBED ALEX'S ARM. "WHAT'LL WE do if he calls Sheridan Expeditions?"

"At least Russ works for them. Good call, using his name."

"Not if it pisses off his boss and gets him fired," Cassie retorted. "Crap. I'm no good at this sneaky stuff. I just want to charge right in and have at it."

"Patience. I know you have it; I've seen it."

"Sure, for raising kids and digging up bones."

"While we have a chance, let's walk around. Remember, you're my girlfriend." He took her hand.

"I remember," she said tartly and didn't pull away.

"Good. Then you won't mind this, either." He pulled her close and kissed her.

Cassie kissed him back, molding her body against his, soaking in his heat, the feel of him. Mmmm, *so* nice . . .

"Okay, let's walk. Or else I'm going to throw you down right here, and to hell with whoever's watching."

She laughed, knowing he wasn't serious. At least, not completely serious. Holding hands, they strolled off.

"Over there looks like the maintenance hangar. I'm thinking most of the others are private," Alex said.

"It's not the busiest place," Cassie observed. "Somebody over there is working on a crappy looking plane. Somehow I don't think a notorious international thief would be buzzing about in something like that, but I could be wrong."

"He's more likely to pilot something like that." Alex nodded toward one of the open hangars, at an obviously later-model plane that was all white and silver and shiny. "It looks new and expensive."

"Is there something I can help you with?"

They turned at the sound of a voice behind them. It was the mechanic they'd just seen.

"We're here waiting for a friend's plane to arrive, but we're not sure exactly when he's flying in," Cassie answered. "Is it okay for us to stretch our legs? We've spent most of the day driving."

"This a private airfield. Did Hollander let you in?"

"Yes. He knows we're here."

The mechanic nodded, satisfied. "Okay."

"Hey, what kind of plane is that? I'm not much of a plane guy, but that's a beauty."

The mechanic perked up at the opportunity to talk shop and strut his stuff. "Ain't it, though? It's a Piper Meridian. Just a year old. Top of the line."

"Does it belong to this airfield?"

The mechanic laughed. "Hell, no. It belongs to some German businessman. He flies in and out of here a few times a year. A real quiet guy, keeps to himself. But he has fine taste in planes—and women."

The German guy had to be von Lahr; it simply couldn't be a coincidence.

"Must be nice to be rich," Alex said, a wistful note in his voice. "All I can afford is a piece of shit like that old camper. A plane's way out of my price range."

The mechanic grinned. "Mine, too, man—mine, too. Feel free to walk around, just don't go into the hangars. They're private property or else hazard areas."

"We'll look but not touch."

"Right." With a nod, the mechanic returned to his work.

After he was out of hearing range, Cassie leaned toward Alex. "I think we just scored the big one. How many rich Germans do you think are lurking in Vermont near the Canadian border at shady airfields?"

"Yep, Russ was right. Now we just wait for a U-Haul to pull up, and then we make our move."

"Which is?"

"We scare the shit out of Mae and grab Trixie, and then we run for it."

"Nice and simple. I like simple."

"Let's head back before anybody starts getting nervous."

They walked back to the ugly little yellow building but didn't go inside. Avoiding conversation where possible seemed the smartest thing to do. Unfortunately, the manager was a meticulous kind of guy and came out with a telephone number for Sheridan Expeditions.

"Here you go. It wasn't hard to find; it's a big-time tour agency. I called them on your behalf. They don't know exactly where your pilot friend is."

"Dammit," Alex said, his expression annoyed. "He's a hell of a pilot, but not too good with the details. If they don't know where he is, then he must be in the air."

"Probably," the manager agreed. To Cassie's relief, she couldn't detect any suspicion. "Somebody must've forgotten to file a flight plan after all. But don't worry, it won't be a problem for him to land even if he didn't get proper clearance ahead of time. We're never that busy."

They hung around for the rest of the day, watching a few planes buzz in for a landing or leave. They also kept an eye on the silvery Piper in the hangar, hoping for a glimpse of von Lahr. Finally, at a little before five, the manager came out and told them they had to leave.

Alex obliged without a protest and drove a short distance before pulling off onto a side road and parking the Beast. The RV sputtered into silence when he switched off the engine.

"We'll stay here," he said. "We're not close enough to the main road for anybody to notice us, including the guys in the airfield, but we are close enough that we can spot a U-Haul driving past. It's the only road to the airfield, so Mae has to come this way. When we see her, we'll go after her and get her before she reaches the gate. That way we avoid von Lahr. Once we have Trixie, we call the cops and get busy doing a little damage control."

"Sounds like a very good plan. So for now we just lie low?"

"Spending a few hours horizontal sounds real good to me."

"Sleeping?" she asked, archly.

"If that's what you really want. But I've been picking up different vibes."

Cassie had to admit the suggestion held a powerful allure. He made her feel so good, and it had been so long since she'd done anything just for herself. So why not? She was an adult. He was an adult. They had few illusions about each other or what this was all about.

"Okay." She smiled, then walked over to him. He was sitting on the bed, so all she had to do was wrap her arms around his neck for him to nestle his face in her breasts. He made a low, contented sound, then pulled her between his legs.

Since she knew what she wanted, and he wanted the same thing, there was no need for coyness, no little courtship rituals. It was sex at its purest, all about raw sensation and fulfilling the aching, inner demands.

Alex couldn't get enough of her. He loved her responsiveness, loved that she didn't need coaxing and babying. She wanted him the same way he wanted her, and he grinned as she pulled off his T-shirt and then started working on his jeans.

"This is much better than the last time," she said. "Having a bed is nice."

"Can't argue with that." He sucked in a quick breath as she pulled his jeans down, along with his underwear, and the ends of her hair brushed his oversensitive skin.

"You just lie there," she said, pushing him back. "I want to take my time and explore. We were in too much of a hurry before."

"Explore all you want. But I'd like it better if you explored naked."

She raised a brow. "I can do that."

Cassie undressed slowly, teasingly, pulling up her

shirt to reveal her smooth, sun-browned skin one inch at a time. Shaking back her hair, she threw the shirt aside, then slipped the straps of her bra off her shoulders, letting the lacy cups soften beneath the weight of her small breasts. She unsnapped the fasteners, then tossed her bra on the floor beside her shirt. Bare-breasted, her taut, pink nipples playing peekaboo with him through the unruly curls of her hair, she straightened, smiling. Alex didn't have to look down at himself to know he was as hard as he could ever get.

"You are so damn beautiful," he said.

"Mmm, so are you." She ran a finger down his belly, then lightly stroked him. For a second, he had to close his eyes and breathe steadily to keep from grabbing her, throwing her back on the bed, and screwing her mindless.

She did the same slow, teasing game with her pants, until finally she was as bare as he was.

"Can I move yet?" he asked, lazily watching her as she straddled him, admiring her small, muscled body, the dark curls between her legs, the breasts peeking through her hair.

"Not yet," she whispered, then bent and kissed him with soft, nibbling kisses along his lips, jaw, and earlobe.

Then she moved lower, along his neck, his chest, and down his belly. Knowing what was coming, he closed his eyes in anticipation. He couldn't hold back the groan of pure pleasure as her hot, wet mouth closed over him and her tongue began stroking the length of his penis as she lightly fondled his balls. She worked him with her mouth, licking and sucking, until he felt the pressure build to the breaking point.

"Cassie, I'm going to come," he said tightly.

She sat back, leaving him frustrated. "Not yet, you aren't."

He couldn't help laughing. "Does this mean I can move?"

"Please."

Alex hitched himself up on his elbows. "Is there something in particular you'd like to do?"

He could look at her like this all night, naked and so refreshingly open about it.

"I don't know. Is there something you'd like to do to me?"

What a question. "Cassie, you have no idea what's going through my mind right now."

"Show me. I'm sure I'll like it."

How could he say no to that? He swiftly put on a condom, then knelt and pulled her toward him. First he paid attention to those pretty breasts, and when he sensed his play had gotten her as hot as he was, he turned her around so that she was facing the bed.

"You have the prettiest ass. You know it, too."

Her muffled laugh made him smile as he admired her rear, running his hands along its taut, smooth curves. She had the kind of bottom that made a man just want to squeeze it and never let go.

And made him want to do something else, as well.

He moved her knees farther apart, and she rested her elbows on the mattress and raised her hips. He touched her between her legs and heard her moan.

"Alex, please . . . "

"Begging already and I haven't even done anything." To tease her a little longer, he slipped two fingers inside and felt her contract around him.

"Unless you want to miss the show, you better stop that."

Excellent.

He nudged her legs farther apart, pulling her hips up toward his, and then slowly pushed inside her, feeling her envelop him completely. She let out a high sound that made him smile, and when he pulled out and thrust again, she gasped. Already he could feel her orgasm begin, and he slowly withdrew, then thrust again, over and over, until she was gasping and grabbing at the blanket. She came fast and hard, and he slowed so that he didn't end things too quickly.

"Oh, God. That was incredible," she said, gulping air. "I think I saw stars."

He began moving inside her again. "You gotta remember to breathe."

"Mmmm, maybe . . . oh, that feels good. Just like that . . . right there."

She made it so easy to make love to her; she gave everything and held nothing back. Knowing what pleased her, he was more than willing to keep on giving. Pulling out, thrusting back in, harder and deeper each time, he just let the feelings take him, losing himself inside her until there was nothing but the need, the pressure, and finally the intense pleasure of release inside her sweet, hot body.

They collapsed on the bed, and Alex pulled her closer and held her tightly.

"You know, we should do this more often," he said, trailing a finger down the warm curve of her back.

"Alex, when this is all over and life gets back to normal, we go our separate ways. You know that."

"Maybe I don't want to let you walk away. Maybe I want to keep you."

"Huh. You can try."

"I was hoping you'd say that," he said with a soft laugh, then rolled her over, smothering her budding protest with a hard kiss, and then his hands and body put all thought of protest clear out of her mind.

# Twenty-four

❖

AFTER GETTING DRESSED, THEY FELL BACK INTO THE bed together, Alex holding Cassie close against him. He dozed, but fitfully. As much as he wanted to let a deep sleep pull him under, with Cassie warm and soft in his arms, he couldn't give in to his weariness. Mae could arrive at any time, and if either he or Cassie missed it because they were sound asleep, everything they'd risked would have been for nothing.

Still, it was Cassie who snapped alert at the sound of an approaching engine, just as dawn began to lighten the sky. He heard it a split second later, and they both sat up, listening intently, then slid off the bed and headed for the window.

Before long, headlights appeared. Out of a misty, early morning haze, the dark shadow took shape: a compact car with a U-Haul trailer attached.

"That's it," Cassie whispered, excitement sharpening her voice. "I recognize Mae's car."

Alex quickly made his way to his seat, Cassie right behind him, and buckled the seat belt with one hand as he cranked the ignition with the other. After grinding in protest for a couple of seconds, the engine turned over, and he let out his breath.

"Ready?"

Cassie squeezed her hands in her lap, jaw hardening. "Yes."

"We gotta catch her before she makes the gate." Alex put the Beast in gear and mashed the gas. The engine clacked and whined in protest, but the RV shot forward. "Keep that gun with you, just in case. She's come this far, she's going to be desperate not to get caught. Be careful."

Cassie nodded, then slipped the gun into the waistband of her shorts. "We should call the police now."

He spared her a glance as he wheeled the RV around the corner. Up ahead, he spotted the taillights of the U-Haul, moving away fast. "They won't get here in time."

"And they won't get here in time to stop us, either. I'm not taking any chances with Trixie, not after everything we've risked already, but von Lahr and Mae are their concern, not ours."

The U-Haul suddenly picked up speed.

"It's too late. Mae spotted us."

Alex stomped his boot down hard on the gas, and he and Cassie lurched forward as the RV accelerated. She braced both hands on her seat as he gunned the engine and ordered tersely, "Hold on. I'm going to try and force her off the road."

The Beast may have been beyond its prime, but it had enough juice to catch up to a puttering old compact hauling a heavy trailer. Drawing closer, Alex could hear the higher-pitched whine of the smaller engine as Mae tried to outrun them.

The trailer swerved dangerously, but with no way to turn off, and with grassy fields on either side, Mae had no choice but to keep driving for the airfield.

"Careful," Cassie hissed, her knuckles white. "Trixie is in there!"

"I know," Alex said grimly as he pulled up alongside Mae, close enough to see her wide eyes and slack-jawed fear and anger.

He turned the steering wheel and bumped the RV into the side of the trailer; even a glancing impact was enough to jar clear through his bones. He hit the U-Haul again, this time to the sound of crunching metal, and fought to keep the RV under control. Distantly, he was aware of Cassie's tight-lipped, white face and Mae's desperate attempts to keep the car and trailer on the road.

"We're almost to the gate," Cassie said quietly. "They're going to see us."

There wasn't anything he could do about that, and he concentrated on forcing Mae off the road. Another impact jarred the RV, and it slid and wobbled as Alex, swearing, steadied the wheel.

Cassie braced her hands on the dashboard. "She's not stopping!"

A split second later, Mae crashed through the metal and wire barrier, Alex right behind her. The head-on impact to the gate was too much, and Mae lost control. Her car swerved, swinging the trailer toward the RV.

Alex slammed on the brakes, but not in time to avoid smashing into the rear of the car and the front of the U-Haul. Even with the seat belt, he hit the steering wheel hard and saw Cassie snap forward and then as suddenly slam back into her seat as the RV abruptly stopped.

The tangle of RV, car, and trailer had skidded for a short distance, and the sound of crunching metal and squealing rubber had to have alerted everyone at the airfield.

"You okay?" Alex asked, reaching for the door handle as he looked over at Cassie.

She nodded, her face pale. "Go, go! We've got to get Trixie out of the trailer now. Or at least get the trailer free of the car!"

As Alex jumped down from the RV, several details registered at once: Mae was inside the car, dazed but otherwise unhurt, and a tall, fair-haired man in a dark suit had run out from the Piper's hangar.

*Von Lahr.*

With an effort, Alex resisted the white-hot urge to go after the bastard. His only priority had to be grabbing the fossil and getting all of them safely away.

But his fury must've been plain on his face, because when he yanked open the door of Mae's car and grabbed her by the front of her shirt, she looked so terrified that, for a split second, he felt sorry for her. "Give me the keys," he growled. "*Now.*"

Mae didn't argue. She pulled the key chain from the ignition and tossed it.

As he caught it against his chest, Alex glanced at Cassie. "Watch her. I'll check on the fossil."

Mae shrank back into her seat, eyes darting toward the far hangar. Alex followed the direction of her gaze and saw the nose of the Piper emerging from the dark interior.

Von Lahr was going to make a run for it, leaving Mae to face the consequences alone. What a great guy.

Cassie, her expression stony, blocked Mae's exit from her car. Alex, glancing at the airfield's main office, spotted two men running toward them.

At the most, he had thirty seconds before they reached him.

As he unlocked the trailer's back door and pulled it

open, he saw a large wooden crate inside, wedged at an awkward angle between the sides of the trailer. Alex kicked the top open, the wood splintering and cracking, and as the sound of angry shouting grew closer he shoved aside the protective padding to reveal rock and plaster and glimpses of fossilized bone.

*Trixie.*

A high-pitched scream whipped him around, and he leaped from the back of the U-Haul, grabbing for his gun.

"Let me go!" yelled Cassie, struggling to break free from the two men holding her against the car: the night manager and another man wearing a mechanic's jumpsuit.

Ahead of her, Mae was sprinting for all she was worth toward the hangar and von Lahr's plane, already taxiing to the runway.

Shit.

No way would von Lahr stop for Mae; he'd run her down. As angry as he was over what she'd done, Alex couldn't stand by and let her get herself hurt. Or worse.

Shoving the gun into the back of his jeans, he turned to the two men. "The pilot of that airplane and the woman who was driving this car are thieves. What's in the trailer belongs to the woman you're holding. I strongly suggest you let her go, and call the police."

He spun and raced after Mae. In better shape and with longer legs, he was sure he could catch her. But von Lahr already had the nose of the Piper pointed forward, preparing for takeoff, and as he opened the throttle, the engine roared with power.

"Wait!" Mae's scream was nearly lost in the sound of the engine, and she frantically waved her arms as the Piper shot forward. "Don't leave me behind! *Please!*"

If Alex could clearly see von Lahr in the cockpit, von Lahr had to see Mae, but he never slowed. Alex saw the second Mae realized that von Lahr didn't care if he ran her down.

She stopped abruptly, frozen in fear, watching the plane's rapid approach.

Alex pushed himself harder. Goddammit, he was so close! For a split second, he considered firing at the Piper, but realized he couldn't get off a shot in time, and the plane might veer into Mae anyway. The Piper was bearing down on her with lethal speed.

"Get down," he yelled, even though she couldn't hear him.

With a final burst of speed, he leaped and slammed her to the ground just as a hot wall of air flattened him over Mae's body. The sound of the engine filled his head until he could feel nothing but its vibrations rumbling through his muscle and bone and the trembling of the ground beneath him as the plane took off.

Once the sound of the ascending plane faded away, Alex rolled off Mae, then grabbed her and pulled her up. "Of all the stupid things you've done, that had to be the worst," he snapped. "He would've killed you."

From her expression, he wondered if she'd have preferred being mowed down by the Piper. Then a glimmer of fear suddenly lit Mae's eyes, and Alex turned to see Cassie running toward him. Behind her, the night manager and the mechanic stood by the tangled vehicles, and the manager was on the cell phone, making short, terse movements with his hands as he talked.

"Alex!" Cassie caught up to him and immediately pounded his back and shoulder with her fists. "You *idiot*! You could've been killed. Do you know how close you were to those wings?"

She was crying, the tears rolling down her cheeks. "My heart stopped—I swear to God it did!"

As he hugged her close, Alex realized that his hands were shaking. "I'm sorry. But I couldn't stand by and do nothing. It's okay," he said. "Nobody's hurt."

Cassie pulled away and turned on Mae. The other woman shrank back from the raw fury in Cassie's face. "You! You're damn lucky he's not hurt, or you'd be drawing your last breath right now. I don't care what happened to you or even that box of bones back there, but if he'd died—"

"Cassie," Alex murmured. "Take it easy." He'd never seen her this angry, and even through the adrenaline rush still pumping hotly through him, he couldn't believe she'd said what she had.

As he watched, she sucked in a long, slow breath, her eyes briefly closing as she struggled to rein in her temper.

After a moment, Mae whispered, "I'm sorry . . . I'm so very sorry."

"But not sorry enough not to have stolen my baby rex and put everyone I care about in danger," Cassie said bitterly. "How could you do this? After all I've— I thought we were friends. Why?"

Although she was sweating and gray-faced with fear, Mae's eyes sparked with malice and contempt. "Money, of course. He offered me five hundred thousand dollars for bringing the fossil to him, so why not? Where was I going at that job? I had nothing, and nobody even knew I existed."

Mae laughed, but it had a panicked, ugly edge to it. "It's true money can't buy beauty or fame, but I have noticed that it has a way of making up for the lack of both. With that kind of money, somebody would've finally noticed me. And even if it was only because of the money, it would have been better than what I had."

Cassie let out her breath. "Is this about Wyatt? I know you were—"

"Wyatt?" Again, Mae laughed. "If I had that kind of money, I wouldn't want anything to do with your loser brother. I'd aim for somebody who'd go a lot higher than he ever will."

A hurt look crossed Cassie's face before she turned away and said tightly, "I'm going back to sit with Trixie. If I stay here, I'll hurt her."

Alex heard the wail of sirens in the distance. Catching Cassie's gaze, he said quietly, "Now comes the hard part: explaining to the police what the hell just happened here." He glanced up at the fading dot that was von Lahr's plane. "I don't think they're going to be happy with us. The bad guy got away. Or one of them, anyway."

Cassie looked back at the U-Haul—and the crate with its precious bundle of magic and wonder. "We did what we had to. We'll deal with the consequences."

# Twenty-five

❖

EXPLAINING HAD BEEN THE HARD PART—AND THERE'D
been yelling involved, as well. After two days, a lot of
talking, and innumerable telephone calls, the local
police finally agreed to let them go back to
Wyoming. There'd been a bad moment when the FBI
stepped in, and Cassie feared they'd seize Trixie as
evidence against Mae, but in the end she and Alex
left with impending fines for property damage, tres-
passing, and a few other minor transgressions. It
could've been worse—but the airfield authorities, in
the awkward position of trying to explain the presence of a notorious international criminal on their
customer list, had prudently allowed Alex and Cassie
the roles of heroes and didn't file major charges
against them.

The FBI was happy to have Mae in custody, and to
have the chance to add her knowledge of von Lahr

to their files. Somebody, someday, would grab him, and then he'd be locked away for a very, very long time. With Mae cooling her heels in jail, the feds could afford to be generous with two people who hadn't done anything except act recklessly. As one of the agents dryly said, "If we arrested people every time they did something stupid, we'd never have time to catch the real criminals. But you're damn lucky nobody ended up hurt or dead."

It was true, and Cassie hadn't said a word. Neither had Alex.

The only casualty was the old Winnebago. It had given up the ghost after its moment of glory, so they'd rented another RV—one that was new, clean, and in perfect working order—to drive Trixie back to Wyoming.

It had been an agony, waiting to make certain Trixie had come through her adventures intact. When the authorities had finally let them have her crate back, Cassie and Alex had cracked it open immediately.

"How are you doing, little one?" Cassie murmured, poking aside a prodigious amount of packing material and thankful Mae had taken extra precautions. "All in one piece?"

"As much as she was to start with," Alex said, as they thoroughly examined the fossil.

Cassie sighed in relief. "Typical kid. Getting into

trouble the second the adults turn their backs." She smiled up at Alex. "Well, let's load her up. Time to take her home where she belongs."

After another exhaustive round of telephone calls to assure their anxious family, friends, and colleagues that all was well and they were on the way back, Alex got behind the RV's wheel while Cassie tucked herself into the seat beside him.

"I think the last few days have finally caught up with us," he said as he headed down the highway. "We'll have to break early. I was looking at the map. I think maybe we should pull aside here, at this wayside. We'll catch a few hours of sleep, then get back on the road again."

"Sounds good to me. It'd be pretty damn embarrassing if we survived all that, only to fall asleep, crash into a ditch, and smash Trixie into little pieces. Not to mention us."

By the time Alex pulled off the highway just over the Vermont border, Cassie could barely keep her eyes open, and she knew he was fighting off exhaustion as well. After a quick snack of sandwiches, soda, and chips, they practically fell into the bed.

Sex was the last thing on her mind, in all honesty, and she was so tired she expected they'd both fall asleep within seconds of hitting the mattress.

To her frustration, however, sleep didn't come. Perhaps the accumulated excitement from the past few days had made her too jittery to relax.

"Alex? Are you awake?"

A low sigh answered her. "Yes, dammit. I can't seem to wind down."

"Maybe we should lie here and talk for a while. Try not to force it."

"Do you want to talk about what happened with Mae?"

"No. For now, I'm in avoidance mode."

"We could talk about what we're going to do when we get back."

She sighed, letting her eyes drift shut. "Not much to talk about there. We plop Trixie back on the table and pick up where we left off."

Silence. "I was talking about you and me."

"That's something I'd prefer to avoid as well."

"Why?" He sounded tense.

She'd known this was coming but couldn't help wishing he'd waited until they were back home, where there was space, a place to retreat. "Alex, you're not thinking far enough ahead."

He sat up. "What the hell do you mean by that?"

Bracing for what was bound to be an unpleasant clash of wills, she pushed herself up and faced him squarely. "What we shared over the past few days was nice. Okay, it was beyond nice; it was incredible." Cassie touched his arm, feeling the tension in his muscles. "But let's not try to make it into something more. We helped each other out when it mattered, we don't hate each other's guts anymore, we found respect for each other, and we also had some great sex."

He frowned. "You're making it sound like we were bored and didn't have anything better to do. It wasn't like that."

She sighed. "Having great sex doesn't mean we love each other. But if that's what it took to make things right between us, then I'm glad it happened. I don't regret anything."

After a moment, he said, "I don't understand. If you like me, and I like you, why can't we—"

"Because all the *real* problems between us are still there. They never went away, the only difference is that we've made our peace about it. I'm still a single mother. I still can't have sex with whomever I want, whenever I want. The divorce was hard enough on Travis. I can't have him getting attached to men I like who'll be moving out of his life in a few months. It's not fair to him. And it's not fair to me."

"I think you're hiding behind your kid."

She looked away. "Believe what you want. It's the truth. And for God's sake, think for a minute. Just because you and I now respect each other doesn't mean your colleagues will feel the same. If we're together, what do you think that'll mean for your career? Are you going to pretend I don't exist whenever you're at university functions or conferences? Are you going to defend me to every asshole who feels like making jabs? And they'll punish you for taking up with someone they see as a threat to their entire way of life. These are the guys who review your papers and grant proposals, who decide if you get promoted or not, or even if you ever get into the field again."

"Maybe I don't give a shit."

"Alex, they would make your life miserable. And what about your students? What about everything you've accomplished so far? What about your own dreams?"

"I've never let anybody tell me what to do. Why should I start now?"

"Because I'm not going to let you trash your career just because we had sex a few times. You're letting your dick think for you. I'm trying to tell it like it is." Cassie looked away from the hurt in his eyes. The last thing she'd expected was that Alex would want a lasting relationship. "Why are you making this so hard? It's not like there weren't plenty of women before me, and there'll be plenty after me, too."

"What we had was more meaningful than casual sex." He moved closer. "Unless *you* really only wanted the sex."

She didn't miss the irony. Wasn't that supposed to be her line? Wasn't he supposed to be the player, walking away after breaking her heart?

"I'm being realistic. I have no intention of giving up

my business and I don't want to subject myself to the hostility of your fellow academics. After a while you'd resent it, I'd resent it, then the fights would begin, and in the end we'd be in divorce court, chalking up failure number two. I learned my lesson the first time. You should've, too."

"That was a low blow."

"You said yourself that relationships aren't your strong point and you don't like being alone. There's a hell of a difference between a warm body in bed and a lifetime commitment."

"I'm also a lot older and wiser. You are, too."

"And what about my work? Where does that fit into things?"

"What about it? You continue to do what you do, I continue to do what I do. I don't see where it has to make a difference. And by the way, can I just clarify one thing here? I'm not asking you to run off and marry me. I'm asking if we can see each other, and if it works out, why not take the chance?"

"And if it doesn't work out?"

"No hard feelings. These past few days have shown me I still make mistakes and can learn a thing or two. I was hoping you might feel the same way."

"I don't know. I need to think about this some more."

"Think about what? There's—"

"Alex. Please. After all the recent stress, I can't make these decisions or answer these questions. Let's give each other some time when we get back, a little distance. If we're meant to be more than co-workers, then it'll happen. If not, then it won't."

"What are you really afraid of?"

"Enough, Alex. Let's get some sleep." She rolled over, giving him her back. After a moment, he got up and walked to the front of the RV. She felt terribly alone in the bed, and it couldn't have been comfortable for him to sleep in the driver's seat.

Before long, her thoughts reluctantly drifted back to his question.

What *was* she afraid of? Losing? Leaving the comfort of the known behind, opening up to somebody only to be disappointed in the end?

*All of it.*

Her life was nice the way it was; she had her routines, the satisfaction of being in control. Everything worked out the way she wanted it, and she wasn't anybody's inferior. She liked that comfort.

But was that the way life should be? Always comfortable and safe?

She thought about what Alex had said—that he'd coped with loneliness by sleeping around and she'd done it by controlling everyone near her. She reflected on the tension between her and Wyatt, the sadness in her mother's eyes, the fact that Travis wasn't a little boy any longer.

Was it failure she was afraid of? Or changes in the

status quo of her little world? Maybe it really *was* all about her being a control freak, as Wyatt had claimed.

Dammit. Now she was confused as well as depressed. Sex was nothing but a nuisance, and men did nothing but complicate a woman's life.

Who needed them, anyway?

She sighed, hugging the pillow close to her— knowing the answer deep inside, but unsure if wanting Alex around was the same thing as needing him.

What the hell was Cassie's problem?

She had to know how good they were together, and how much they had in common. Alex couldn't say that about any other woman he'd ever known, not even the one he'd married.

How could she not see this?

Anger simmered. Over the past week he'd come into a better understanding of what made Cassie Ashton tick, and he suspected that her real problem had less to do with commitment and more to do with position and control, and most likely, a fear of the unknown.

Which irritated him all the more, because she so plainly didn't need to worry about any of that. She was his equal in every way that mattered, and to hell with whoever felt differently. Why should some stranger's opinion matter to her more than his? Mixing careers always took adjusting, but it wasn't as if there was any real place he belonged. He lived in an apartment when he was teaching, and the rest of the time he lived in tents, trailers, or the back of his truck.

That ranch house back at Hell Creek could accommodate one more person. It'd mean a longer commute during teaching semesters, but almost everybody commuted to work these days. They didn't have any small children to contend with, and since he liked kids and kids seemed to like him, he didn't anticipate any problems with her son. Even her family had warmed up to him a bit.

And it wasn't as if Cassie were a complete stranger to his field team. With less hostility on his part, he suspected most of them would get along with her or at least tolerate her. She had a point about his professional colleagues, but he could deal with that. He already had a reputation for being controversial, with a hide thicker than a pachycephalosaurus skull, and he didn't waste much time worrying over his peers' opinions of him. As long as he stayed true to his vision for why he did this work—a vision Cassie had helped refocus—that was what mattered.

But how the hell was he going to persuade this skittish, sexy, exasperating, volatile woman to his side?

He grinned, despite his frustration, and closed his eyes. How? Very carefully, and probably not without a few wounds to his ego.

# Twenty-six

Once they pulled into the drive at the Hell Creek shop, they were mobbed.

Alex could hear the shouts before he turned off the engine, and before he'd unbuckled his seat belt Cassie was out of the RV and lost in a swarm of tears and embracing arms. Awkward with all the familial emoting, he took his time getting out of the RV.

The outside-looking-in feeling was a sharp reminder that he didn't fit in with these people—and that maybe Cassie's fears were more reasonable than he'd thought.

He'd have his own well-wishers back at his site, but that was one more reminder that things between them were already heading in separate directions.

"Looks like you survived everything without too much damage," said a voice from behind, and Alex turned to see both Wyatt Parker and Russ Noble grinning at him.

"I've had better weeks." He answered carefully because he wasn't sure what Wyatt meant: that he'd survived his misadventures in dino baby snatching or that he'd survived spending time, alone and in close quarters, with his sister.

"Man, we've all had better weeks," Wyatt said, with feeling. "It's good to have you guys home again, but I'm still trying to wrap my head around the fact it was *Mae*, for Chrissake. It's like . . . Lassie turning into a werewolf. Too damn weird. And I can't help wondering if I'd just talked to her more, or paid more attention, if I could've stopped—"

"Don't blame yourself; it wasn't your fault or Cassie's. Mae succumbed to greed, that's all there is to it." Alex looked past Wyatt, smiling as Cassie hugged her son, who topped his mother by almost a foot.

Wyatt asked, "Is there something Russ and I can help you with?"

"You can help me unload Trixie and move her back to the lab, and then if one of you could give me a lift to my place, I'd appreciate it. Or tell me where my truck is."

"I think the police have your truck, but I can give you a ride back," Russ offered. "The way things look here, there'll be heavy-duty family time for a while, and like you, I'm not a part of that."

"Bullshit." Wyatt sounded irritated. "You're welcome to stay. Both of you."

"Thanks, but I have a lot to do myself, now that I'm back," Alex said. "And, Russ, I wanted to thank you again for flying us to Vermont. We couldn't have gotten the baby back without your help."

"You're welcome, but like I keep saying, I have a vested interest. I want my name in the history books, too." He grinned. "The boss man wasn't too happy, but everything worked out. Come on. Let's get her back inside the lab."

With one last look at Cassie, still hugging her son close as she tried to hold three conversations at once, Alex turned away. Then he, Wyatt, and Russ carefully moved Trixie back to her table.

He smiled at the familiar sight. "Here you go, little one. Back where you belong."

"I swear I won't bitch about all the trouble she's caused, not after this." Wyatt rubbed a hand over his unshaven jaw, and Alex finally noticed that Cassie's brother looked dead tired. "I got bits and pieces of the story, and it sounds like you two had a close call."

"I think of it as a kind of family vacation. Mom, Dad, and Baby on the road."

"Some family." Russ laughed, shaking his head. "You ready to go?"

"Yeah. Say good-bye to Cassie for me, would you, Wyatt? I'll try and see her tomorrow. The RV needs to go back, but—"

"Don't worry about it. I'll have somebody take

care of it," Wyatt said, and for once Alex didn't hear any hostility in his voice. "You head on home. Looks to me like you haven't gotten much sleep lately."

He hadn't, but not strictly because of stress, and the frank curiosity in Wyatt's gaze told Alex that Cassie's brother was a lot smarter than he'd given him credit for.

"I'd say the same about you."

"It's been rough around here," Wyatt admitted. "I'm just glad everybody's back in one piece."

"Me, too," Alex agreed. "And it'll be good to sleep in my own bed tonight."

*Just not so good to be doing it alone.*

As he and Russ drove away from the ranch, Alex looked back, but he couldn't see Cassie anywhere.

"You okay?" Russ asked, glancing his way. "Seriously?"

Alex only nodded.

"How'd things go with Cassie?"

"No problem. Why do you ask?"

"Because you're both acting strange. She won't look at you, and you can't stop looking at her."

Great. He so wasn't in the mood for this. "Try not to take this the wrong way, but it's none of your business."

Total chaos greeted Alex when he finally connected with Don Cleary and his crew, and he found his patience taxed with repeating the story of what had happened over and over.

By the time he got his own affairs in order, it was

too late to call Cassie, so he figured he'd give her a day to settle into her usual routines before he inserted himself back into her life.

But when he drove back to Hell Creek two days later, it was only to find that Cassie, with Travis, had left for New Orleans without so much as leaving him a note. Wyatt, standing by the coffeemaker in the lab, had delivered the news in a strangely flat tone.

As Alex stood in stunned silence, Wyatt put his coffee aside, then asked, "She didn't say anything to you, did she?"

Hot anger swept over Alex. "Tell me where I can find her."

Wyatt regarded him for a long moment, his expression unreadable. "Why do you want to know?"

"That's between your sister and me."

Wyatt nodded slowly. "I figured as much. Sit down. You and I need to have a talk."

# Twenty-seven

New Orleans in August was hot and hideously humid. Cassie always forgot about the humidity factor, which meant she always overdressed.

"It's hot," Travis complained from beside her, slowly plowing through a plate of beignets at the Café du Monde, powdered sugar dusting his face, fingers, and clothes. She'd warned him not to breathe while eating one, but he hadn't listened, so there'd been a coughing fit when he'd inhaled powdered sugar. She half suspected he'd done it on purpose; boys could be weird that way.

"That's why New Orleans is considered tropical."

"Why are you so grumpy?" he asked, glowering. "You keep yelling at me, and looking at me—"

"I do not."

"Just like that! See? You should see your face. What'd I do?" He slouched in his chair. "I should've stayed home."

His behavior was a little off today. Cassie put it down to too much excitement, too much heat, and way too much sugar. "I thought you wanted to see Diana."

"I do. She's hot."

"Oh, for God's sake, Travis!" Cassie laughed, even though she probably should've been appalled.

"Well, she *is* hot, even if she's old . . . for me," he quickly amended. "But I like hanging out with Fiona more. Diana just pats me on the head like I'm a dog or something."

"That's because Diana isn't kid-savvy and Fiona spoils you rotten. That woman really should have kids of her own."

"Yeah, she should get married again."

"She doesn't think it would be right until her husband is declared legally dead. He's been missing for years now, so it shouldn't be much longer. Then maybe she'll feel like she can start her life over again."

"Why not before? It's stupid to wait for some dead guy to come back, and it's not like she's getting any younger. Though she's still pretty hot, too."

"You're at the age where anything female under eighty is hot." And sometimes this child was amazingly astute for his age and gender. "But I agree with you. I always tell her it's dumb to wait, and she just stabs me with her elbow. I've learned to shut up about it. Adults can be stupid, too, you know."

"Yeah. I know." He chewed on a beignet for a while.

"How come you never got married again? Dad did."

Ordinarily she would've given him her usual response of not enough time and slim pickings, but today she didn't take the easy way out. "I don't know. I want to say it's just because I'm too busy, but that's not entirely true."

"Don't you want to get married?"

She realized he was asking her in an adult-to-adult way, and it struck her all over again that his voice had changed, his face was changing, he was taller than she was, filling out, mooning after girls, and had very much grown into his own person.

"I'd like to, yes. Eventually. In a few years you'll be living on your own, doing your own thing, and I've been thinking I'm not ready to be alone. It would be nice to have someone in my life, someone who's a friend and someone I can love, who'll be there for me. Other times, though, I think I'm fine the way I am. I'm not unhappy being unmarried, Travis. Most of the time I hardly give it a second thought."

Until lately, anyway. They'd been in New Orleans only a few days, and not only did she miss work, but she missed walking into her lab and finding Alex waiting for her, working with her, talking with her, teasing her, and simply . . . being there.

"You shouldn't be alone," Travis said matter-of-factly. "I don't like thinking of you that way."

"Honey, I'm never *really* alone; I practically live in

a zoo. Sometimes, I think I'd sell my soul for just thirty minutes of solitude in a bubble bath."

He stared at her. "Bubble bath?"

"We have two bathrooms in that house, but only one has a tub. I can't remember the last time I had a bubble bath. What's that look for? Do you think only little kids like bubble baths?"

He grinned. "I guess."

"Well, news flash. Big kids like them, too."

"Maybe you should be nicer to that Martinelli guy. He's okay. And you act as if you like him."

Where on earth had *that* come from?

"He's my mortal enemy, remember?" She put a light, joking tone into her voice, because the last thing she wanted was Travis cuing in to her miserable mood—and the reason behind it. "That's against the rules."

"But he's pretty decent. I like him, and you're both dinosaur freaks, so that's good."

"Did you just call me a freak?"

"In a loving way, Mom."

She laughed, even as she felt her face warm. Her son was frankly discussing how to hook her up with a guy—whom she'd already slept with, though Travis didn't know that—and now she was blushing as if *she* were the teenager who hadn't so much as scored a first kiss.

This was definitely one of those weird parenting moments the child care books failed to mention.

"Right now I'm busy playing tourist in New Orleans with you, and tomorrow I'm going to watch my best friend marry the man of her dreams, so I'm too busy to think about such serious stuff. Are you about done?" When he nodded, she gave a sigh of relief. "Thank God. I can't believe you ate all that. You'll be sick, especially with this heat."

"Nope. Stomach of steel." He suddenly straightened in his chair, eyes widening. "Oh. I've gotta go."

Startled, she asked, "What? Go where?"

"That mall down by the river. It has a music store. I need the new Godsmack, and I forgot my Nirvana at home."

What a tragedy. As she got to her feet, Travis darted to her side, slung an arm around her shoulder, and pushed her back down onto the chair. "I promise I'll turn the volume down when the screaming starts."

"You're such a kind child. Now let me up."

"Love me?" he asked, with a dramatic show of puppy dog eyes.

Cassie laughed, though puzzled by his odd behavior. "Love you."

"Always?"

"Yes! Always."

"Excellent. Then don't kill me when you see who's standing behind you."

"Who's standing . . . ?"

But she already knew, as if some ancient inner

sense had homed in on his presence even before her brain registered him standing before her.

"Oh, my God. Alex." Staring up at him, overwhelmed with confusion and shock, she couldn't even move. "What are you doing here? How did you—"

She turned back to Travis, now standing a few steps away, nervously chewing on his lip even as his eyes gleamed with excitement. "You knew he was coming here," she said to her son. "How?"

"Remember when Uncle Wyatt called last night? He asked me to call him back when I was alone, so I did while you were in the shower. He told me Dr. Martinelli needed to see you, but it had to be a surprise. Wyatt said it was a guy thing."

A guy thing. Wyatt and Travis and Alex, working together.

Cassie slowly stood to face Alex. "You ganged up on me."

He shrugged. "Isn't that what family is for?"

"I'm leaving now. I'm going to the music store, then walking back to the hotel. Slowly," Travis said. "You two talk. I've done my part, and you and Uncle Wyatt owe me. Big time."

Alex smiled. "Thanks."

Before Cassie could protest, Travis had disappeared in the crowd around Jackson Square. She wasn't worried about him getting around; their hotel was a few short blocks away from the Quarter, and he'd already made numerous forays in and around the area while she followed up with wedding-related appointments.

But she was annoyed—and dismayed—that he'd pulled a stunt like this, leaving her alone with Alex and without him to—

Hide behind. Use as an excuse. Oh, God. She just kept screwing up. And she wasn't prepared for this at all.

"I'm not very fond of surprises. Or ambushes."

"Let's go somewhere more private," Alex suggested, then hooked his hand around her arm and, not giving her a choice, pulled her along with him as he walked away from the café.

"This is the French Quarter. It's crammed with tourists," Cassie said, amazed at how calm she sounded. "There's no place to go that's private."

"I'm staying at the Prince Conti, a few blocks away. We'll talk there."

Cassie didn't protest, her pride not allowing her to have a public argument in the middle of a busy tourist hot spot. She practically had to run to keep up with Alex's long-legged strides, all the while peeking furtively at him, by turns alarmed at his hard-jawed anger—which she deserved for being so cowardly—and giddy at seeing him again.

Veering away from Jackson Square and St. Louis Cathedral, he pulled her along Chartres, then to Conti. He didn't say anything, and by the time they passed Bourbon, she was so tense she wanted to scream. Maybe she should just tell him to stop and talk to him later. She slowed her steps. Her own hotel was on Canal; it would be easy enough to—

"No. You're coming with me. And don't even think about arguing, because I'm not in the mood for games, Cassie," he said, in a warning tone.

It was too late to bolt anyway; she could already see the red awnings and wrought-iron balcony of his hotel, and the flags mounted above its entrance gently furling in the breeze.

The inside of the Prince Conti was airy and elegant and very Old World French, with its pale colors and rich, dark woods, brocades, and brass.

Once inside his room, he released her, and she sat down on the big four-poster bed, her knees suddenly a little shaky. "So why are you here? You had no right to—"

"Save it," he snapped. "*You* turned tail and ran away. Whatever you needed to say, you should've had the guts to say it to my face, especially after everything we went through together."

Why was she arguing with him at all? Even now, knowing she was in the wrong? How hard could it be simply to admit that much? She sighed. "I know. I shouldn't have done that, and I'm sorry. I guess I just . . . panicked."

Alex sat down on the bed beside her. "Why? Did I

give you a reason to feel afraid? What did I do that was so wrong?"

She didn't know what to say. The heat of his body and scent of his cologne wrapped her with a comforting familiarity. Despite the fine lines around his eyes that hinted at his tension and high temper, she wanted to fall into his arms.

Yet at the same time, she wanted to run as fast and as far away as she could. "You didn't do anything wrong. I needed time to think, that's all. You didn't have to come all the way down here."

It made her feel a thousand times more guilty knowing he'd gone to such trouble.

"Yeah, I did—because it's the only way you'll really listen to me and see I'm dead serious." He ran a hand through his hair, leaving part of it sticking up, and she wanted to reach up and smooth it away. Instead, she curled her hands tightly in her lap.

"Look, Cassie, I know that being together will be inconvenient at times. I know it won't be easy. But you have to stop selling yourself, and me, short. We can handle it."

Tears gathered, and she had to swallow them back before she trusted herself to speak. "You shouldn't have involved Travis. He seems to like you, and I don't want to see him hurt."

"Don't sell him short, either. He's not a baby. You can't control everybody's feelings and reactions, as much as you might want to. And it so happens that all I wanted was your hotel phone number. Wyatt and Travis cooked up this secret meeting thing. They were probably right; if you'd known I was coming, you'd have run off again."

Cassie couldn't meet his eyes; doing so would demand honesty, and it was simply more than she could give him right now. She'd left for New Orleans earlier than planned to avoid him, desperately hoping time away would convince her she didn't need or want him in her life.

The hiding hadn't worked. At the rehearsal dinner, Diana and Fiona had noticed right away that something was wrong, but because she didn't want to be the damper on everyone's festivities, she'd said nothing to her friends.

Anyway, they would've told her she was being stupid and stubborn, and she didn't need anybody to tell her what she already knew.

"Cassie, look at me," Alex ordered, his voice soft but firm.

Reluctantly, she did so.

"I understand better than you think. Ancient bones will never disappoint you, and that makes them a safe center in your life, but they can't give you what I can, if you'd just let me. We're a hell of a team, and I've always said that success is the best revenge. I don't see why we can't find that success together, and to hell with what other people think. What's important is you and me making a place together. If we get that right, everything else will sort itself out."

Again, tears stung her eyes, and she blinked them away. "You think so?"

"I wouldn't be here if I didn't."

"But what about our jobs? The conflicts of interest, the way you—"

"We can work it out. It's all about being equals, and you will never be anything but my equal. I believe in you; isn't that enough?"

*Equal.*

For how many years had she yearned to hear that from him? Cassie wanted to believe him, but old doubts and habits were hard to break. They'd come together because of Trixie. What would they do when the baby rex was gone?

Taking a deep, steadying breath, she said, "You've been a great help to me, Alex. I can't even begin to tell you how much I appreciate everything you've done for me."

He went very still, gaze narrowing on her. "What are you getting at?"

"I'm telling you that you're off the hook. You don't need to be nice to me to get Trixie. I've already decided that you've more than earned her. I'll sell her to your department for whatever she costs me in work hours and supplies."

"I appreciate the gesture, but that's not why I'm here. And it sure as hell is not why I slept with you." He sounded furious, even speaking so softly. More like the old Alex.

For a moment, she wished they could go back to their old selves, back to what she knew and understood—but there was no going back. Too much had happened. Too much had changed.

"So now what?" she asked and was surprised by how helpless she sounded, even to her own ears.

"That's up to you. I took the big step into your do-not-trespass zone, so either you chase me away or you let me inside your life."

"It would be . . . really messy."

"Probably—and I don't care. You've brought a spark back into my life, and that's too important to let go. *You're* too important. The immediate problem, as I see it, is that I know how I feel about you, but I haven't a clue how you feel about me. Except that you like the sex."

As if she needed the reminder, sitting alone with him in this beautiful room, on the big, soft bed. She fleetingly thought of distracting him with lovemaking until she felt more sure of herself, but that would be unfair to him. There was only one way out of this mess she'd made.

"It's been a long-standing habit, avoiding or explaining away my feelings for you," she said quietly.

"I hated that I felt anything at all for you, because of how you treated me. Even now I want to think nothing's changed between us, but I know that's not true. We've changed, even if the conflicts between us haven't. Right now I'm sure of two things. One is that I'm afraid of making another mistake." Cassie paused, briefly meeting his gaze. "And the other is that I think I'm in love with you."

There. She'd said it. When she dared a quick peek at him, she saw a small smile playing at the corners of his mouth.

Just that half a smile filled her with relief.

"I've been crazy over you for a long time, too." Alex eased back on the bed, and the tension that had radiated from him suddenly seemed to vanish. "I should've known the heat between us meant something more than hate, but I was too pigheaded and full of myself to see that. You weren't the only one dodging. But if it were easy, it'd be boring." He grinned and gave her a quick kiss on her forehead. "And as you like to say, it's never to late to start over again."

Cassie smiled and finally allowed herself to lean against him, to trust in his solid strength. "Actually, these past couple days I've been thinking of taking my own advice. What would you say if I told you I've been considering going back to school?"

"It would depend on why you want to."

"Not because I need to; I want to do it for myself.

I'd have to cut back on work at the lab. Wyatt would have to pick up some of the slack, but I don't think he'd mind."

"Something tells me you're right."

She still couldn't believe her brother had teamed up with Alex Martinelli, of all people. When she got home, she'd kill him. Then she'd hug him. She had a few fences there in sore need of mending, as well.

With a sigh, Cassie flopped back on the bed. "I can hardly remember the last time I did something just for me. To make me feel good."

"That's a good enough reason as any. And if you don't go back, that's all right, too." His smile widened. "But there's something I could do right now that would make you feel good, as well."

"I was wondering when you'd get to sex."

"I like making love with you." He shifted on the bed and kissed her deeply.

She marveled at how Alex had chased her down, called her on the carpet about her behavior, made the muddle in her head so clear with just a few words and a kiss, and she couldn't wait one more moment to get into bed with him.

Within seconds, Alex had her naked and he was inside her, and the feel of him did indeed make everything better. So, *so* much better.

He teased her breasts with his tongue as he moved his hips in a slow, steady rhythm that drove every thought but one out of her head. She grabbed his shoulders, hanging on to him, biting her lip and trying not to make too much noise as the bed rocked and creaked.

He brought her to release quickly, then held her for a long while. As the minutes stretched out, she became aware of a sense of completeness settling over her, and the contentment of knowing without a doubt that she belonged with this man. There'd be rough spots ahead—she had to make a few changes in her life, and he had a daughter he needed to fit back into his—but they'd make it through.

They were two of a kind, and no other man would ever fit into her life as rightly as Alex. "We should've done this a long time ago," she said.

Alex laughed softly. "That's what Don Cleary told me, that day we met at Dip's to negotiate over Trixie."

Startled, Cassie glanced at him. "Really?"

"Yup. He said if I'd just hauled you off to the nearest motel, it would've saved everybody a whole lot of trouble. Guess I should've tried sleeping with the enemy a long time ago. But"—he smiled lazily— "better late than never."

# Epilogue

❖

Diana and Jack's wedding was perfect.

It went off without a hitch, managed by the matron of honor, Fiona, who'd always been Detail Girl, even back in their college days.

Diana looked impossibly beautiful in a simple ivory sheath gown that bared her back and shoulders. Its softly tailored lines and the luminous sheen of the silk were lovely—as was the pearl necklace Jack had bought her for the occasion. She'd worn her blond hair pulled back in a simple French braid twined with pearls and lilies of the valley, and her bouquet was also simple: white roses, lilies of the valley and, inexplicably, a dash of brilliant orange tiger lilies.

When Cassie had asked about tiger lilies, Diana had winked and said it was a private joke.

Jack was Hollywood handsome in his tuxedo, and between the perfect couple and the perfect ceremony, and the perfect sex she'd had the day before with Alex, Cassie spent the entire wedding in a warm, fuzzy haze of satisfaction.

That delicious feeling lasted straight through to the reception at the ornate Pontchartrain Hotel. Soft lights, expensive champagne, the twinkle of jewels as women danced with their partners to the soft strains of violins . . . it was as magical a night as she could've hoped for Diana and Jack.

"You're unusually quiet," Alex said from beside her. They sat in a quiet corner of the room, champagne glasses in hand. "What's going on in that head of yours?"

Cassie smiled, thinking how handsome and urbane he looked in his black suit. She'd never seen him in anything but jeans and T-shirts, so she hadn't known how . . . civilized he could be.

Except for the gleam of desire in his eyes that he didn't bother hiding. Dating women with children sometimes required ingenuity—but it was amazing what one could get away with in a powder room.

"What am I thinking? That you look wonderful and smell delicious. I want to lick you all over. Later."

He laughed, but the flare of heat in his eyes made her go warm. In a lighter tone, she added, "And I'm thinking how much I love weddings. I even love my bridesmaid dress." Elegant satin in an icy blue, it had simple lines that matched those of the bride's gown.

"But I shouldn't be surprised. Diana has great taste in clothes."

"Still wishing you'd caught the bouquet?" Alex asked, watching her over the top of his glass as he sipped his champagne.

"Like that would ever happen. Bobby Halloran's girlfriend is an Amazon. She towered over the rest of us *and* she used to play basketball. Fiona and I never stood a chance of catching that bouquet." Cassie added, "Besides, I'm pretty sure Diana was aiming for Emma. It was probably her way of telling Bobby to get off his ass and ask Emma to marry him."

"Bobby was the groomsman with you, right? The cop?"

Cassie nodded. "Emma's also a detective."

"He doesn't look much like a cop."

"Well, you don't look much like a paleontologist right now, either."

"Touché," Alex said, laughing. Then, more seriously, "You have nice friends. I like the PI and her lock picker, with whom, by the way, I had a long talk about excavations. You didn't tell me he was an archaeologist."

"Slipped my mind. People were shooting at us at the time, as I recall."

"I like the freckled redhead, too. Fiona. Unless I'm mistaken, she's been keeping Travis out of our hair so that we have some time to ourselves?"

Fiona had introduced Travis to three girls his own age, and he'd spent the entire reception flirting and keeping an über-cool, macho distance from the mother ship. "That's Fiona. She likes to manage people and things, like me. She's just quiet about it."

"Hmm. Looks like we're about to have company," Alex said, and Cassie turned to see Jack Austin, the man of the hour, walking their way.

"And how's the new husband doing?" Cassie pulled out the empty chair beside her, and Jack sat with a grateful sigh.

"Taking a break from dancing. And the drinking. I want to remember my wedding night."

Cassie gave him a fond pat on the shoulder. "You're such a good guy. If I haven't said it already, congrats. It was a beautiful wedding."

"It was, wasn't it? I'm not sure what Diana sacrificed to the wedding gods, but it must've been something damn good." Jack leaned forward. "So are you two going to cozy up here all night, or are you going to come out and play with the rest of us? I know Diana is dying to know more about your arrogant ass from Laramie."

"Jack!" Cassie swatted him and then laughed when he gave her an exaggerated wink. "You're such a dork."

"So Diana says. And speaking of my lovely bride, I think her limited store of patience just ran out. She's

coming over here to drag you out onto the floor—
and she's brought reinforcements."

Regal and elegant, Diana seemed to glide to their
corner. Fiona was with her, and behind Fiona came
Bobby and his girlfriend, the bouquet-grabbing
Emma Frey, whom Cassie had last seen handcuffed to
one of Bobby's ex-girlfriends. She'd tried to explain
that bit to a baffled Alex but finally gave up.

"Well, well," Diana said cheerfully, swooping close
on a wisp of musky perfume. "Look who's still all
kissy-kissy in the corner."

"Diana," Cassie said with a sigh. "We're not all
kissy-kissy."

"Maybe not technically." Diana sat beside Jack,
the pale silk of her skirt pooling around her and over
the black fabric of his tuxedo. "But it still seems to
me that matchmaking is in the air. There are three
people in my life very dear to me, three people I've
worried about and wanted to see happy, and tonight
two out of those three have reassured me that life has
a way of working out the kinks if you give it enough
time."

"Or a nudge," Jack said, leaning over to kiss
Diana's cheek.

"Sometimes a two-by-four upside the head works,
too," Emma added, eyeing Bobby with amusement
before she grinned at Diana.

Fiona, her red hair coming loose from its braid to

frame her face in an ethereal, Pre-Raphaelite way, took Alex's hand. "I want to dance with this gorgeous creature you're hiding back here, so I'm stealing him. You don't mind sharing, do you?"

"Just as long as you remember he's mine," Cassie said, her smile blossoming into a wide grin. Alex looked delighted, but then he was probably used to women squabbling over him. "Just watch where your fingers stray, Fi, unless you want to lose them."

"And girls are supposed to be sugar and spice and everything nice," Bobby said wryly, his blue eyes sparkling with amusement.

"Hah." Alex stood, trailing his fingers along Cassie's bare arm, sending a delicious shiver through her from head to toe. "A smart man knows the female of the species is the deadliest of all."

"Rawr," Cassie playfully growled, then nipped his lip. "Smart man."

*Passionate about reading?*
*Don't miss any of these unforgettable*
*romances from Pocket Books.*

## RUN NO MORE
### Catherine Mulvany
How do you outrun your past
when your future's just as deadly?

## ALWAYS
### Jude Deveraux
An evil from the past...A hope from the future...
A love that will last forver.

## OUT OF THE STORM
### JoAnn Ross
There is no shelter from the storms of passion.

## OPEN SEASON
### Linda Howard
She's hunting for a mate—
but now someone is hunting her.

## CROWN JEWEL
### Fern Michaels
A true, passionate love is the greatest treasure of all.

## NO WAY OUT
### Andrea Kane
When a woman's deepest fears and strongest desires
clash, a child's life hangs in the balance.

Wherever books are sold.